PRAISE FOR THE RED HOT NOVELS

"*Red Hot Liberty* is Devin O'Branagan's masterpiece! Her characters live in a disturbing but hilarious world of political, social and spiritual turmoil. *Red Hot Liberty* reads like the adored lovechild of Janet Evanovich's Stephanie Plum Series, if Diesel was British and Grandma Mazur was a patriotic dog loving revolutionary." -*Pagan Culture*

"Sassy and simply hilarious!" -*Women Writers Worldwide*

"Captivating!" -*Boulder Women's Magazine*

"From the first scene to the last, O'Branagan keeps the reader hooked with a blend of suspense, heartbreak, and most prominently—humour." -*Literary Endeavors*

"A witty light read, loaded with vivid unforgettable characters who are sharply drawn and universally identifiable...hilarious." -*The Lyons Recorder*

ALSO BY DEVIN O'BRANAGAN

Red Hot Property

Show Dog Sings The Blues

The Twilight Bone

Glory

Pretty Sacrifices

Genesis

With Brave Wings She Flies

Threshold

Witch Hunt

Witch Hunt: Of The Blood

Of The Blood Of Witches

Resistance

DEVIN O'BRANAGAN

Cornucopia Creations Press

Cover by Sue Campbell Graphic Design

The poem "*Vitae Summa Brevis*" was written by Ernest Christopher Dowson (1867-1900)

This book is a work of fiction. Names, characters, places, and incidents are products of the author's imagination or are used fictitiously. Any resemblance to actual events or locales, or any person, living or dead, is entirely coincidental.

ISBN: 979-8-9910361-2-2

Published by:

Cornucopia Creations Press

To Sue Campbell.

Kindness is never forgotten.

"Courage is a choice." -Valentino DeMitri

PROLOGUE

Molly O'Malley decided to become a real estate agent because the Cuban psychic, Havana Santiago, told her she should. That was five months ago.

Havana had correctly predicted professional success for Molly, but she also gave ominous warnings involving the spilling of familiar blood. Tragically, familiar blood did flow. Despite the accuracy of Havana's vision—or perhaps because of it—Molly returned for another consultation.

Havana met with her clients in the parlor of an old Victorian home in the Capitol Hill area of Denver. Not much had changed since the last time Molly was here. The décor was still 1960s retro: a turquoise vinyl couch, plastic end tables, lava lamps, an electric Coca-Cola sign, and a jukebox playing early Beatles tunes. When Molly walked in, the iconic Fab Four asked, "Do You Want To Know A Secret?"

As before, Havana was a study in pink: sloppy pink sweats, big fat pink curlers in her hair, and a huge wad of pink bubblegum that periodically emerged from her mouth in gooey orbs of bursting thunder. However, her furry pink bedroom slippers had disappeared, and in their place thick bandages encased bare feet.

Havana noticed Molly's attention to her feet. "Marina Night, she try to kill slippers and send me to hospital. Berry bad." Havana's blood-red fingernails clawed the air. She bared her teeth and hissed for emphasis.

Marina Night was a Tonkinese cat perched on Havana's shoulder in place of the talkative myna bird who had been there on Molly's last visit. Marina Night emitted a blood-curdling whine, and Molly wondered if the cat had eaten the bird.

"Hokay, sit," Havana said.

Molly followed the trail of voodoo dolls and Virgin Mary statuary to a small round table in the center of the room. She sat down across from Havana and Marina Night.

"What you want to know?" Havana asked.

On the drive from her new home in the foothills west of Denver, Molly had thought about questions to ask but now had trouble putting them into words. "After my daughter's uncle and cousin were killed in a drive-by shooting, I moved her out of the *barrio* to a small college town. I wanted her to be safe. I became a real estate agent, bought us a nice home, built a new life. Then Val—the best friend I ever had—was murdered." She fought back tears as the recent horror of his death washed over her yet again. "I'm so frightened now. It seems nowhere is safe. I want my daughter to have a good life, and it all seems so hopeless." Molly struggled for the question that Havana wanted. "Are we going to be safe?"

Havana grunted. "Hear what spirits say."

Previously, Havana had divined using a disgusting pile of bird bones. Now she used a more politically correct crystal ball. As the psychic lost herself in the crystal, a chill seized the room. Molly wanted to slip back into her coat but was reluctant to move and risk being a distraction. While waiting for Havana to speak, she tried to avoid Marina Night's intense, smoky blue eyes.

"All around chew is dragon's breath and smell of sulfur," Havana said. "I see a devil woman, fear, and loss."

Molly resisted the urge to bolt from the room. What

had possessed her to come here again? She struggled to find her voice. "So, the spirits see only bad things for us?"

Havana's gaze sank even deeper into the future, and she shook her head. "I see a knight who slays dragons and an angel who sprouts wings. Jour family, it grow bigger."

Molly's hand flew to her belly. *A baby? Not good timing.*

Havana shuddered. "Spirits, dey say bad blood and a berry bad seed. Dere be crazy peoples and angry guns."

Despair claimed Molly. "But why? I'm just a real estate agent."

Havana's head snapped to attention, her eyes captured Molly's, and her words suddenly held no trace of an accent. "Oh, kitten, you're so much more than that."

Molly struggled to breathe. Havana's tone and inflection had morphed into Valentino's. "Val?"

"Oh, my very precious kitten, *promise* me that you won't let the demons win."

CHAPTER ONE

A week before Valentino DeMitri died he dressed up as Cher for the Café au Gay's annual New Year's Eve costume party. A gorgeous Italian, Val's role as the exotic woman was well cast.

Val arrived late to pick up Molly, as the party wasn't slated to begin until ten o'clock. When she opened the door to him, she was floored by how perfectly he resembled Cher. In the four months she had known and come to love him, she had never before seen him in celebrity drag. Tonight she was tickled to witness his genius in action. He chose Cher-the-Ice-Queen as his persona for the evening. Besides being a gorgeous choice, it was also a practical one since the Colorado night was especially frigid. His form-fitted, white velvet gown was split up one leg to reveal glittering silver nylons, and his white leather knee-high boots had stiletto heels. The fur-lined cape studded with blinking rhinestones dazzled, as did the impressive tiara perched atop his long, curly mass of black hair. Delicate white feathers and rhinestone icicles dangled from the tiara's crown. Val's nails and makeup were heavy on the glitter and glam, but the image was made complete by his distinctive nasal-toned voice, limp-wristed mannerisms, and confident, sexy swagger.

"Wow," Molly said in greeting.

"Wowee," Molly's eight-year-old daughter Angelina said.

"Whoa," Molly's boyfriend Steve said.

"Woof," Steve's yellow Labrador Retriever Blondie said, but her greeting wasn't meant for Val—it was for his dog, Talisman, who trotted in on his heels.

Talisman, a blue merle Australian Shepherd, was in costume as well. She was in her best Ellen DeGeneres get-up: a snappy little vest, a neck scarf that said CALL ME ELLEN, and a rainbow-colored leash. With her bright blue eyes, shaggy hair, and innate love of dancing, she made an excellent Ellen.

Molly ushered Val and Talisman into the house and shut the door.

"Is Tali going with you guys to the club tonight?" Angelina asked.

Val brushed the hair out of his face in a classic Cher gesture. "No, her Ellen crush just got the better of her today. Well, that, and she wants to ring in the New Year by performing our daily rousing celebratory tribal dance of success. I thought maybe we could all do it before Molly and I head out."

Molly laughed. She loved performing the daily rousing celebratory tribal dance of success with Val. They usually did it in the office every morning before beginning their workday—much to the chagrin of the other real estate agents at Broker's Best—but that day they missed their morning ritual. She held out her hand to him. "I'm guessing you brought some Cher?"

"But of course." He slapped a CD into her palm. "Play 'If I Could Turn Back Time.'"

Molly went to her stereo, entered his choice, and punched up the volume.

As music filled the air, Val threw himself into the performance of a lifetime. His voice morphed into Cher's husky style, and he sang his heart out while prancing, twirling, leaping, and gyrating with passion. The lights on his cape seemed to blink in tempo to the music.

Molly also danced with gusto—with his help she had been working hard to overcome her self-consciousness. Val created the dance ritual to build confidence and banish fear, and Molly needed the magic it invoked. They had been performing the dance together ever since their first day on the job as real estate rookies.

Angelina shimmied, and Talisman wiggled her tailless bottom, but Steve and Blondie weren't quite in the spirit. Steve seemed rather overwhelmed by the spectacle, and Blondie just sat down in the middle of the room and howled.

Molly stuck out her tongue at Steve and shouted, "You need to loosen up!" They had only been dating a short time, but in truth what she did love about him was his middle-class, all-American, down-to-earth normalcy. Dancing with a gay drag queen and a dog who thought she was Ellen DeGeneres wasn't especially normal.

He grinned and winked at her but remained firm in his resolve to perform strictly as audience.

After getting warmed up, Talisman really decided to put on a show. She crouched in a play bow, then leapt into the air where she spun around and landed facing the opposite direction. Falling to the floor, she rolled completely over and bounced back to her feet. She kicked each foot in turn, in sync with the music, then pranced about in a circle, a look of total ecstasy on her face. Val had taught her well.

The song ended, and the humans in the room exploded with applause while the dogs barked with joy.

Angelina threw her arms around Val. "I love you so much. You make us happy."

Val enfolded her in his cape and pulled her tight. "I hear you'll be nine next month. Why don't we have a big birthday party and both dress up as Jennifer Lopez? We can perform a duet."

Angelina squealed. "Omigod, I so totally love J.Lo.

That would be such an awesome birthday present."

He ruffled her hair, tossed his head, and said in his best Cher, "Well, she's not as fabulous as me, but—"

"How do you do that?" Angelina asked.

"What?"

"Sound so much like Cher?"

"I learned by holding an ice cube on the roof of my mouth."

Angelina giggled. "Really?"

"One of my professional secrets. Don't tell anyone."

Angelina's eyes grew wide, and she said with utmost sincerity, "Oh, Val, I would never betray your secrets."

"You truly are an angel, Angel." He glanced at Molly and whistled. "Damn, you look just like a holiday treat with your fabulous red hair, dreamy evergreen dress, and big bulbous boobies. Kind of like an uber-sexy Christmas tree."

Molly smiled. Her long evening gown was slit up one leg to her upper thigh and the neckline plunged. She bought the dress many years ago for another New Year's Eve party, but at that one she had worked as a cocktail waitress. She hadn't felt sexy then, but now she did. Val had taught her that sexiness and confidence went hand-in-hand. Both feelings were new to her.

When Angelina went to retrieve Val's CD, Steve asked, "Everyone there tonight will be gay, right?"

Val nodded. "You only have to worry about the lesbians, and I'll do my best to keep them away from Molly. Promise."

Steve managed a stalwart smile.

Molly thought it was wonderful of Steve to hold down the fort and allow her to honor the long-standing date with Val.

Angelina returned with Val's CD. "Is the party going to be glamorous?"

"Just like Paris in the Twenties," Val said.

Angelina sighed. "Oh, I wish I could go."

"What do you have planned for tonight?" Molly asked Steve.

"We've got movies, popcorn, dog treats, and sparklers. We're going to ring in the New Year with style. You two go and have fun."

Molly kissed Steve, Angelina, Talisman, and Blondie, while Val kissed Angelina, Talisman, and Blondie. He tried to kiss Steve, but Steve grasped his hand and kissed it instead. Molly thought it a rather gallant and daring gesture for her all-American guy. She knew his new life with her was challenging.

Molly followed Val out into the frigid night.

"I like your fella," Val said as he helped her into his Mercedes.

She waited to respond until he slid into the driver's seat. "Besides Angel and you, he's the only person who's ever loved me. I can't get over my good fortune at having all three of you here at the same time. It's taken twenty-nine years for my life to be good, and now it's just perfect."

He started the engine. "Don't cling to things. Everything passes."

Molly knew the advice came from his own experience, but she didn't want to consider what might pass. "Are you thinking about Peter tonight?"

"Kitten, I always think about Peter."

He pulled the car out of her driveway onto the country dirt road that led away from her house. They headed toward town and drove in silence for a long time, each lost in their own thoughts.

Val's blinking cape lit up the night.

*   *   *

Café au Gay was located on Temple Hill, a trendy shopping district located near Blackstone University. Art galleries, chic boutiques, atmospheric coffee houses, and ritzy clubs clustered on a hillside in the shadow of an old, renovated Krishna Temple. The area attracted Blackstone's wealthy and artistic, as well as tourists and students. The sidewalks were wide to encourage pedestrian traffic, and the narrow streets were designated one-way to discourage vehicle traffic. Val's Mercedes inched along Nirvana Street toward their destination on Shakti Lane, while avoiding groups of revelers who spilled out into the road. The snow-shoveled streets and sidewalks were slick, so it didn't surprise Molly to see a wheelchair tip over and a man fall from it. What did surprise her was that no one rushed to the man's aid. Val, intent on driving, hadn't noticed.

"Val," she pointed to the sidewalk where the man lay floundering, his wheelchair on its side. Val eased on his brakes and powered down Molly's window.

"Hey, there!" he shouted to a group of people standing nearby. "Aren't you going to help him?"

"Ain't gonna go near him," a young man shouted. "Too gross."

"Totally," a girl with spiked blue hair said. "He crapped himself."

The man on the ground moaned and flailed about uselessly, trying to reach his wheelchair. "Help me." His voice was desperate.

Men and women decked out in elegant clothes and furs walked by, staring in obvious distaste. The college kids laughed and taunted him.

"Help me! Help me! Help me!" they shouted.

"Someone?" the old man begged.

"For Christ's sake, what's wrong with people?" Val pulled over to the curb and set the brake. Cars behind him honked as they tried to negotiate the tight space beside him to move forward. People leaned out of car windows and cursed.

"I'll call 911," Molly said, reaching for her cell phone.

Val shook his head. "Not yet. Give me a minute."

He got out and walked around the car to the sidewalk. Molly opened her door and joined him but stopped short a few feet away from the man when the stench hit her. The blue-haired girl had been right.

The area was brightly decorated with holiday lights, blinking neon signs, and overhead street lamps. The bum was dirty and disheveled, and there was streak of blood on his forehead.

"I'll call 911," Molly repeated.

"No!" The sharpness in Val's voice was uncharacteristic. He walked up to the man, crouched by his side, and examined the cut on his forehead. "It's not deep."

"Am I dead? Are you an angel?" The bum's words were slurred.

Val smiled, and his white cape twinkled. "No, I'm Cher. Who are you?"

"I'm Spur. You really are Cher, ain't you?"

"You an old cowboy, Spur?"

Spur nodded. "You gonna sing at one of these nearby clubs?"

"Yes, I am." Val helped him sit up, and the man swayed like a ramshackle hut in a tempest.

Molly noticed the reek of liquor mingled with that of human waste. She fought her gag reflex, uncertain what to do. Unwilling to move any closer, she glanced up and noticed the crowd had grown—a blinking Cher crouching by a malodorous bum was certainly attention-grabbing. She tuned out the rude comments.

"Where do you live, Spur?" Val asked. "Is there someone I can call for you?"

"I don't live nowhere." Sudden sobs split the night. "I

don't got no one. I'm alone. Always alone."

Val slipped off his cape and draped it around the man. "Put the wheelchair in my trunk, Molly."

Disbelief mingled with Molly's disgust. "Val?" What was he going to do? He wasn't really going to let the man in his car, was he? Besides the odor, what if he had lice or was diseased? What if Molly carried something awful home and infected Angelina?

Val's face reflected compassion. "If we call the cops, they'll just throw him in the drunk tank. The Butts Out Group supports a warming and detox center called Hope House. I want to take him there. He'll be treated with dignity."

Molly heard his words, but they took a few minutes to filter through her internal storm. The Butts Out Group was his Alcoholics Anonymous club. He really was going to put Spur in his car. Taking a deep breath, she steadied herself, righted the wheelchair, folded it, and carried it to the trunk while trying not to slip on the ice.

No one came to her aid, either.

Val tossed her his car keys. "You drive. I'll sit with him in back."

Val scooped Spur up in his arms and carried him to the car. Molly opened the door, then stood back while he put Spur inside and scooted in next to him.

Molly closed the door, walked to the driver's side, and glanced up to see that the crowd had grown still and silent. No one was heckling now. She wondered if they all felt as shame-filled by their reactions as she did. Taking a deep breath, she got in the car, rolled down the windows, cranked up the heat, and started the engine.

Spur's sobbing began anew. "I'm sorry. So sorry. Oh, God, sorry…."

Val murmured comforting sounds. "Hush. Look, angel wings are holding you. It's going to be all right now."

Molly glanced at them in the rear-view mirror and saw

Val wrap the blinking cape more tightly around him. He tipped Spur's head over onto his shoulder. "I'm alone too. I know how hard it is."

"My wife died," Spur mumbled. "I miss her so much."

"I understand," Val said. "My husband died, and I miss him so badly the pain just tears me up."

"Sonny ran into a tree didn't he?"

"My husband's name was Peter, and a drunk driver ran into him."

Spur moaned. "Oh, I'm sorry. Did I kill him?"

"No, Spur."

"I can't remember, but if I did something bad 'cause of the whiskey, I'm sorry."

"It wasn't you," Val said.

"Did they find who done it?"

"The drunk driver died too."

Spur grunted. "He got what he deserved."

"No, Spur. Every life is precious."

There were a few minutes of silence, and Molly wondered if Spur had passed out. Then he said. "I've wasted my life."

"It's not too late," Val told him. "Make what time you've got left count."

"How come Cher's helping me?"

"The world's a mysterious place."

Spur's tears returned. "I'm so alone."

Val patted his head and began to sing. Softly, he comforted the man with Cher's song "We All Sleep Alone."

Tears poured down Molly's cheeks as she followed Val's directions to Hope House.

*   *   *

Molly and Val never made it to Café au Gay. After Val got Spur cleaned up and settled into Hope House, they went to Val's home. While he showered and changed, Molly fixed him a pot of coffee and poured herself a snifter of brandy. Then she built a fire in his large fireplace and settled in on the couch. Her thoughts were confused, her emotions chaotic.

Val reappeared dressed in jeans and a sweater. His short, dark hair was damp, and his unadorned face movie-star handsome.

As always, Molly's heart did a tap dance when she saw him. "You're such a sexy man."

"Yeah, I know." His bright smile banished Molly's shadows.

He fixed himself a cup of coffee, sat down, and slipped an arm around her.

She snuggled into him, burying her face into his chest. "I've always loved your cologne. It's classy."

"It's Peter's. After he died I started wearing it. Scent is the sense most tied to memory."

"Have you dated at all since he died?"

He shook his head.

"You must be so lonely."

"Oh, kitten, I miss Peter, but I'm not lonely. I've got Tali and the best friends anyone could ask for. I'm close to God. Peter and I still share love—some things never die."

Molly took another deep breath and felt herself relax. The fire crackled and popped, its breath quickening as hers slowed. She always enjoyed the comfortable ambiance of Val's Spanish-style hacienda. Although the tile floors were elegant and the walls wore expensive tapestries, Val's personal touches made the home inviting. Molly especially enjoyed the framed photographs perched on every available surface. Besides pictures of Val and his many loved ones, dozens of images of Val with notable celebrities revealed his fascinating life. Prior to becoming a real estate broker,

Val had been the entertainment editor for *The Blackstone Daily News*.

"Why didn't you go into show business?" Molly asked. "I mean, with your looks, talent, and parents it seems like the obvious path." Val's mother was the head of Blackstone University's drama department, and his father was a famous movie star whose identity was kept secret from all except family members.

"Who knows what the future holds?" He grinned. "I haven't given up on the dream yet."

Molly gave him a playful slug. "Get out. Really?"

"We all need dreams. What about yours?"

That was an easy one for Molly. "I'd like to get married someday. I hate that Angel's father never married me, although it was a blessing given the way he turned out. But I'd like to give her a real family."

"Is Steve the one?"

She shrugged. "Too soon to know. He's good with Angelina, and he loves us. He's safe and solid. We'll see."

Val's eyes studied her for a moment. "Safe is good." His tone indicated mild disapproval.

Or perhaps Molly just imagined it.

"I love how you've come out of your shell since we met," Val said.

"Well, you did help."

He laughed. "I remember the librarian look you started the job with—those shapeless knee-length dresses and the tight little hair bun. Thank God we cured you of that travesty."

Val had conceived her current professional wardrobe: sexy power suits with skirts on the short side, heels on the high side, and a trademark neck scarf. He dubbed her new look "sophisticated saleswoman with a hint of sex kitten."

"It's more than your appearance," Val said. "You've

bloomed, like a rare and precious flower."

Molly took a sip of her brandy and thought about ways she had changed, and ways she still needed to. "I'm so sorry about earlier tonight."

He gave her a curious look. "And what are you sorry for exactly?"

"I was selfish. I didn't want to help Spur because he was dirty, and stinky, and might have something contagious. What kind of person am I? I mean, you didn't hesitate. Not for a second."

Val studied her for a moment. "Well, let's compare you and me. Let's really look at this carefully. I was raised with love by a mother who's a bit eccentric but who never hurt or judged me. I always lived in this wonderful community with all the advantages one could hope for. From the time you were born you endured the worst kind of abuse, abandonment, and life in a war zone. You've been in total survival mode all your life. I think you were just in survival mode tonight. Don't beat yourself up over it."

"I want to be better than that!" Molly's passion surprised her. "I don't want to live in fear anymore."

"Courage is a choice."

She thought about his words, but they didn't make sense. "Is it wrong to want to be safe? To be sure Angel is safe?"

"You can always try to play it safe, but that keeps you small and earthbound. Most people live that way. I want you to take wing and soar. I pray for that every single day."

Molly didn't believe in God, but—despite everything else that had happened to her—she did believe in love. And she was grateful for Val's love.

Outside, firecrackers exploded and car horns honked. The clock on the wall confirmed that it was midnight.

Val leaned forward and gave her a tender kiss. "May

the New Year be the beginning of a glorious new life for you, Molly O'Malley."

She kissed him back. "And for you too, my most dear and wonderful friend."

CHAPTER TWO

Two weeks after Val died, Molly returned to work at Broker's Best of Blackstone. She had been a real estate broker for five months and was the only one of four original rookies left standing. So the owner of the company, Jake Dalton, moved her from the basement office she had shared with the other rookies to an office of her own.

The final step to getting settled in her new digs was the hanging of a special picture on the wall. The painting had been commissioned at the onset of her career—it featured Molly and her three fellow rookies. She hung it on the wall and struggled to adjust its angle.

"Need help?" Jake asked from the doorway. His presence never failed to cause Molly to catch her breath. When they had first met, Jake was the wind, she was dry grass, and lightning summoned wildfire. Their blaze had been short-lived, but there were still live embers.

Molly adjusted the painting. "Is it straight?"

"Looks good," Jake said. "But are you sure you want the constant reminder?"

"I want to never forget."

"It's unlikely any of us ever will."

Val's murder had forever changed them all.

Jake was normally cowboy cool; Molly was one of the few who understood his vulnerability. Absently, he fondled the rim of his cowboy hat, the heel of his boot tapped the door jamb, and he tugged on his neatly trimmed beard. After a long moment, he cleared his throat. "Do you like your new office?"

"Prime location. Did you put me across the hall from you to keep an eye on me?"

A smile played at his lips. "I wanted to keep you close."

Jake was having trouble accepting the fact that Molly had a new man in her life.

"Is it possible to get a second desk?" she asked.

"So, the rumors are true? You're really going to get an assistant?" He left the obvious unspoken—no rookie broker hired an assistant.

"I don't want to work alone."

Jake's eyes slid to the depiction of Val in the painting, and when they returned to Molly they reflected understanding.

A big, beautiful, Black woman stepped into the doorway, forcing Jake into the room. She threw her hand to her hip. "Say what? Did I hear correctly? You're getting an assistant? After only five months *and* in the midst of this mortgage melt-down theme park we're playing in? I know you've done an unbelievable number of deals so far, but has it gone *completely* to your head, girl?" Coco was the town's top agent, and she never failed to intimidate Molly.

However, Molly had learned to not let the competition witness her insecurity. She tossed her head, gave Coco a defiant look, and said, "Yes. I'm drunk with power."

Coco's eyes grew wide. "Lord have mercy." Muttering under her breath, she turned and stormed down the hall.

Molly was pretty sure she heard Coco call her shameless and comment on her impudence and gall.

Jake's smile removed the chill from the air. "I love your fire."

Molly had just discovered her inner fire. She hoped recent events wouldn't conspire to smother it.

*   *   *

The offices of Broker's Best of Blackstone were in a large, rustic log cabin with flagstone floors and open-beam ceilings. Country music always played in the background, and cowgirl receptionist Jessie—Jake's little sister—was famous for her rhinestone-studded Stetsons, pink cowboy boots, and irreverent loud-speaker announcements. What Jessie was not known for was being speechless.

"Just spit it out," Molly urged. Jessie had buzzed Molly's intercom but was having a struggle.

"Well, um, there's…. Have you ever watched *Rocky and Bullwinkle*?"

Molly wasn't sure she was hearing Jessie correctly so lifted the handset. "What?"

"See, there's this person." There was a second long silence.

"Yes?"

"She says her name is Natasha Fatale."

Natasha Fatale was the Russian spy in *Rocky and Bullwinkle*. "Um, okay." Molly tried to connect the dots.

"She's here to interview for the assistant job."

Molly grinned. Well, at least it was an applicant with an apparent sense of humor. That might come in handy. "Send her in."

Silence.

"Jessie?"

"Is your dog in there with you?"

Molly glanced at Talisman, comfortably ensconced on her plush corner bed. "Her scarf of the day says HUMAN RESOURCES DIRECTOR." It was tied nattily around her neck.

"Good. Then I'll send *Natasha* in."

"I can hardly wait."

Molly's office was right off the main lobby, and within seconds a strange apparition appeared at Molly's door: a large Latina woman wearing huge sunglasses, a platinum blond wig, a long sheepskin coat, and—given the petite nature of her face and hands—a bulky body suit that lent the illusion of weight.

The scent of the coat woke Talisman from her beauty sleep—Australian Shepherds were a herding breed.

The woman closed the door behind her and extended a hand to shake. "My name is really Maria. Maria Madrid."

Molly smiled. "I didn't think it was Natasha Fatale."

Maria removed her sunglasses, and her eyes darted about. "I had to come incognito. The repercussions of being recognized are too frightening to think about."

Molly accepted the résumé, sat behind her desk, and directed Maria to a chair across from her. Talisman leapt from her bed and bounded to the woman's side, giving her the canine once-over: sniffing, snuffling, and eyeing the woman warily.

Maria flinched. "What is it doing?"

"She's human resource directing."

"It makes me nervous," Maria said.

"Well, trust me, Tali is much tamer than whatever it is you're afraid of. And what would that be exactly?"

Maria's brown eyes grew wide, and her voice became a whisper. "Lily Dalton. I work for her."

Fear flooded Molly. "Omigod."

"I'm her assistant."

"Oh, this is bad." Molly's head exploded as images of Molly's nemesis took her mind hostage. Lily Dalton was Jake's ex-wife and the owner of Blackstone's Homestead Realty. Even though Lily and Jake had been divorced for many years before Molly became romantically involved with him, Lily resented their affair and made Molly's life a living hell. Stealing Lily's assistant would be a suicidal move.

"Lily Dalton is a fire-breathing dragon who spews destruction and then dances in the ashes," Maria said.

"Yep," Molly agreed. "That pretty much describes her." She tried not to think of Havana's dire mention of the smell of sulfur.

"I cannot work for her anymore, but good jobs are hard to find right now. I'm raising three children alone. I know you're a single mother, and you must understand my obligations. I would be a valuable employee. My skills are excellent, I am bilingual, and I work hard. Please save me from that devil woman. She is Satan's mistress."

The woman's desperation was matched only by Molly's trepidation.

Talisman stopped sniffing and rested her chin on the arm of Maria's chair, her sky blue eyes fixing her with a steady stare.

Maria shifted uneasily. "What is it doing?"

"She's trying to figure out what you are."

Maria leaned as far away from Talisman as possible and returned her attention to Molly. "I know how badly Lily treated you when you got that high-end listing on Thundermountain Road—especially since she was dating the seller. And then when she found out about you and her ex, oh, that was terrifying. I know she did terrible, awful things to you. Please don't be afraid to hire me. What more could she do to you than she already has?"

"Well...."

Talisman butt-slammed Maria's chair, which caused the frazzled woman to shriek. "What is it doing *now*?"

Molly wasn't exactly sure. "You smell like sheep. Perhaps she's trying to herd you?"

"Please make it stop."

Molly smiled. Lily notwithstanding, she couldn't hire someone afraid of Talisman. It would never work. Quietly, she said, "Tali, you're scaring her."

Talisman stopped, threw Molly a disappointed look, and returned to her bed.

Maria crossed herself. "*Madre de Dios*, it understood what you said. How could that be?"

"Tali is an extraordinary dog."

From Maria's expression, it was clear that Talisman now ranked high among her many fears.

Molly felt compassion for the woman, but sympathy was not enough. "I can't hire you. It took courage to come here, but my advice would be to try and find a job outside this business. Lily will never allow you to go in peace otherwise."

Maria slumped in defeat, but the hefty fat suit buoyed her up. "Ah, you're probably right. She won't even let her employees associate with anyone in the real estate industry because she worries about her secrets. I can't imagine what she would do if a former employee went to work for someone else in the business."

"I'm sorry, Maria."

"I understand."

Molly stood and politely dismissed Maria Madrid.

Natasha Fatale slipped on her sunglasses and made a stealthy escape.

*   *   *

The next job applicant just *loved* Talisman. Brooklyn Green's high-pitched, sing-song voice hurt Molly's ears, so she couldn't imagine how it affected Talisman.

"Who's a pretty wittle girl? Aren't you just a smootchie-wootchy? I just *wuv* you. I bet you're a cookie monster like my own precious puppy baby." Brooklyn offered Talisman a dog biscuit pulled from the pocket of her pink Armani suit.

Talisman looked at Molly with a sick expression, and Molly shared the sentiment. The proud dog rebuffed the biscuit by pushing it away with her nose, then returned to her bed and curled up facing the wall.

Brooklyn's eyes blinked with confusion. "Was it something I said?"

"Yes."

The pretty young woman returned the dog treat to her pocket and settled back in her chair. "I have a dog too. Her name's Sami, and I could bring her to work with me. I just know that she and Talisman would be the best of friends."

Talisman was picky about the company she kept. Molly was too. "Let's talk about you, Brooklyn."

The young woman's appearance was quintessential all-American: honey blond hair, flawless peach complexion, sweet little-girl voice, a mouth upturned with little commas on each cheek. Then there was the pink Armani suit with matching heels. Real estate Barbie. She perked up at the subject of herself. "I just got my real estate license and would be an awesome assistant. I received my bachelor's degree from Blackstone University last year with a major in ecology and a minor in business administration. After graduation, I attended the school of The Secret Power of Intention and Visualization in the Now and received my PMA—Positive Mental Attitude—certification. I could help you apply those principles to growing your business."

"Why do you want to work for me, instead of going out on your own?" Molly asked.

"You're a rock star. I mean, you're legend. I've heard all about how you kicked real estate ass in your first few months on the job. An overnight sensation. I'd love to breathe your air."

Molly's reputation was well-deserved, and she was proud of it. She was also practical. "And after you've oxygenated, I expect you'll hang your license somewhere else and go out on your own?"

Brooklyn's smile widened. "It would be a fair trade—your mentoring for the fruits of my PMA."

Well, at least the girl was honest. And some chipper cheerleading might mitigate Molly's pervasive sadness and anxiety.

"Besides assisting me with real estate, the job description includes helping me out with my daughter and Talisman."

"Oh, kids and dogs just *love* me."

Talisman begged to differ, and did so loudly and in a most unladylike fashion.

Brooklyn's smile never wavered. "Would you like me to open the window? Fresh air is great for the health."

PMA.

*   *   *

When Jessie announced Molly's final applicant, she did so over the loudspeaker to the entire office in her own, unique fashion.

"The house of the day is royal blue and is a charming executive home in excellent condition. This is definitely one you're going to want to see."

Jessie always announced attractive visitors to the office for covert viewing by those who might be interested. Blue houses were men and pink houses were women. Only once had a "house" on display figured out the secret code (and might not have if Jessie hadn't been so enthusiastic in her description). In that particular case, the property had offered himself up to the highest bidder and Jessie won.

Molly was trying to decide if she wanted to join the female brokers and office staff who were casually making their way to the lobby when Jessie buzzed her intercom.

Molly hit the speaker button. "Yes?"

Jessie's voice was hushed. "This house is yours. A Mr.

Robin Knight, here for the job."

Oh, dear. Having a good-looking male assistant would certainly keep the office gossips busy. That wasn't something Molly relished. She sighed. "Well, after he's been properly ogled, send him in."

Ten minutes later Robin Knight sat across from Molly. Her first thought upon seeing him was that she couldn't hire a man as attractive as Robin, or she would never be able to concentrate on work. Her second thought was to question how the first thought managed to slip past the singular devotion she felt for Steve. Before Molly could even begin to sort out the conflict, Talisman shocked her by jumping into Robin's lap and making herself quite at home.

"Tali! What do you think you're doing?" As far as Molly knew, forty-five pound Talisman had never in her life endeavored to be a lap dog, not even with her adored Val. "Tali, get off *right now*."

Talisman rested her cheek on Robin's shoulder and gazed at him.

Molly was horrified to see Talisman's long hair shedding all over Robin's expensive designer suit. "Etro isn't cheap, Tali. You're ruining it."

Robin gave Molly a quizzical look. "Spot on. How did you know my suit's Etro?"

Robin's cultured British accent was another reason Molly couldn't possibly hire him—it was too delightful a distraction.

"My former sister is a fashion designer. I absorb like a sponge." She gestured to the suit. "Dotted pinstripes. The burst of red under the collar."

His smile was dazzling. "Brilliant."

Molly stood up, walked around her desk, and grasped Talisman's collar. "Tali's extremely independent."

Robin fondled Talisman's ears. "She's confident. Confidence is sexy. Besides, I think she fancies me. Will that work in my favor?"

"Well, you are the first applicant I've had whom she's approved."

He flashed that smile again. "Aussies are psychic, you know. You should trust her instincts."

Molly did.

Unable to tug Talisman off Robin's lap, Molly picked her up and deposited her on the dog bed. She started to get up, but Molly stared her down into submission. Talisman didn't say anything, she just gave Molly a pissed off look and resigned herself to her fate.

"Well done," Robin said. "You're leader of your pack."

Molly chuckled. "No, that would probably be my daughter Angelina. She's going through an even more defiant stage than Tali."

"Maybe I can help. All the little ones fancy me."

Molly returned to her desk and took a few minutes to collect herself. She reviewed Robin's résumé: fresh from London, green card, professional background in administration and management, excellent computer skills. The accent would certainly add class to her office, and a man could offer her better protection than a woman.

"I can take dictation." Robin grabbed a notepad and pen from her desk and dashed off a quick letter. He cleared his throat with great flourish before reciting it as if it were a Shakespearean oratorio. "I, Molly O'Malley, real estate agent extraordinaire, bodacious broker, fierce lioness with the wild red mane and magical amber eyes, am writing to inform you that, even though the housing market is cold, I am red hot. I am a force of nature that no mere mortal shall stop or ever deign to control. I have no fear, nor should you as long as you are in my care. I am woman, hear me roar! Signed, yours in over-punctuation, Miss Molly O'Malley."

Molly exploded in laughter—it had been a long time, and it felt good. She glanced at the painting on her wall and realized that Val would have liked Robin.

Robin followed her gaze. The huge surrealistic painting featured five intermingled figures: a red-headed Irish lass sitting on a giant shamrock clutching a pot of gold to her large bosom; a Buddha with a cigarette dangling from his mouth; a blond princess perched high in a tower; and a dashing man wearing a tuxedo, top hat, and carrying a white-tipped cane. A lovely blue merle Australian Shepherd stood at his side. A small hand-lettered plaque beneath it read THE ODDEST BUNCH OF ROOKIES EVER.

"That's obviously you and Miss Tali," Robin said. "Who are the rest of them?"

A kaleidoscope of beautiful memories clashed with the harsh realities, and Molly struggled. "Summer, the lovely princess, quit. Ben the naughty Buddha, was arrested. Val, the toast of Broadway—known to friends and fans as a fabulously unique gay epiphany—was murdered showing one of my listings. It should have been me. He was showing it for me as a favor."

Robin sucked in some air and then a long silence followed. Finally, he said, "I can promise you this, love. If you hire me, I'll always have your back."

*   *   *

As Molly was escorting Robin out of her office they ran into Jake, and Molly took the opportunity to perform introductions.

"Robin this is Jake Dalton, the owner of Broker's Best. Jake, this is Robin Knight, my new assistant."

The two men shook hands and quickly sized each other up—two alpha males assessing the competition. Jake spread his legs and put his hands on his hips. Robin took a step closer to Molly. Both men were marking their territory, which made Molly sigh. This was the reason she had chosen a boyfriend who was a beta male. Steve had a lot less ego to contend with.

"Welcome to *my* company," Jake said.

"I'm looking forward to working *for* Molly."

Molly sighed again. "See you Monday morning." She gave Robin's arm a subtle push.

Women who hadn't been fortunate enough to see Robin earlier when he had been on display watched with pleasure as he made his way to the front door.

Molly turned to go back into her office, but Jake blocked the doorway. "Why him?"

"Tali approved. Besides, I like his voice."

"Is that all you like about him?"

Molly winked. "I'll let you know."

"I'm serious. You're hiring a man so you'll feel safer, but you can't live in fear."

"It is what it is, Jake." She tried to push past him but he didn't budge, and when their bodies connected sparks flew.

He flushed, and his voice softened—his need was evident. "Molly?"

"It is what it is, Jake."

CHAPTER THREE

Angelina had named their new house *Refugio Seguro*—Safe Refuge. Angelina's life had been hard, and Molly was glad she finally felt safe. That it had taken nine precious years of life for Angelina to have achieved a sense of security made Molly feel like she had failed her. However, at least Angelina's childhood hadn't been nearly as horrible as Molly's own.

Although Angelina's grief surrounding Val's death was profound and touched by anger, she didn't seem fearful. On the other hand, Molly's fear was beginning to eclipse her grief. If perfect Blackstone wasn't safe, how could she ever hope to protect Angelina?

Formerly one of Molly's own listings, *Refugio Seguro* was an old, rambling farmhouse located outside of town on five acres. She had bought it from an elderly widow named Rose Hamilton, who had also become a friend.

"Rose is picking me up in a few minutes," Angelina announced. "I'm going to spend the night with her, and then tomorrow we're going to see *The Sound of Music* at Blackstone University." Rose had become Angelina's surrogate grandmother.

Molly was surprised. "You should have asked permission."

"You would have said yes."

"That isn't the point."

Angelina tossed her head, sending her long waves of chestnut hair flying. Her eyes fixed Molly with a hard stare. "What is the point?"

"The point is that lately you've been behaving as if you're nineteen instead of nine. I know Val's death hit you hard, but I'll not put up with you acting out over it."

Angelina's eyes slipped away. "It's not just Val."

Val had been the last in a series of losses for Angelina. Her father was now in prison, and her Aunt Rita had moved away after a fight with Molly. Angelina had no other family.

"Do you remember why Rita and I had a falling out?" Molly asked.

Angelina's harsh stare returned. "Because you were such a bitch to her."

Molly wrestled with anger. "Because I was *disrespectful* to her. Lately, you've been extremely disrespectful to me. We're all we have, Angel. Let's not alienate each other. Please?"

"You have Steve."

That threw Molly. Was Angelina jealous? "I thought you liked Steve. I know he adores you."

Angelina started to reply when the doorbell rang.

"I'm looking forward to spending Sunday with you and Tali at the dog show," Molly said.

"I love spending time with Tali," Angelina said pointedly. She skipped to the front door to let Rose in.

Rose was a tiny woman of seventy who was spry, intelligent, and full of life. She and Angelina greeted each other with hugs and smoochy kisses, while Molly went to the back door to let an insistent Talisman inside.

"Thank you for letting Angel spend time with me." Rose's violet eyes sparkled with anticipation.

Molly bit her tongue and smiled.

Rose tousled Angelina's and Talisman's hair. "Why don't you two give me a few minutes alone with your mom?"

Angelina groaned and shuffled out of the room.

Molly invited Rose into the kitchen. "I just made a pot of tea. Would you like a cup?"

"Yes, dear, that would be nice. It's really chilly today. I think a snowstorm is moving in." Rose slipped out of her long, wool coat and hung it on a hook, then sat down at the kitchen table and patted it. "I miss my old table."

Molly poured them each a cup of tea and sat down across from her. "You want it back?"

"Oh, heavens no. My new place is far too small. I left what I left here for you."

Molly had appreciated the furniture, as she owned none when she bought the house.

Rose started to say something, then stopped. She took a sip of the tea, started to say something, and stopped again.

"I'm all ears," Molly said.

Rose offered a weak smile. "Well, that's good because I really need to talk about something."

Molly waited.

Finally Rose said, "I'm a bad, bad widow."

"Excuse me?"

"Well, you know how much I loved...*love*...Gilbert."

"It's hard to miss." Rose's home was practically a shrine to her late husband, and he was still her favorite topic of conversation.

"I am starting to feel things I shouldn't feel. I'm awful. I'm bad." Rose's hand trembled, and she rushed to set down her cup before spilling its contents. Tears trickled down her face.

Molly grabbed the Kleenex box off the counter and placed it in front of her. "Tell me, honey." She had never seen Rose like this, and it worried her.

"It's Percival."

"Our Percy?" Percival Frasier was the lender to whom Molly referred her clients, an elderly white-haired man who strongly resembled Orville Redenbacher. Percy had been invited into Molly's intimate circle of friends-as-family.

Rose's face crumpled in anguish. "I like him, Molly. I like him a lot. It's so wrong."

Understanding dawned, and Molly suppressed an urge to smile. "You're attracted to Percy?"

Rose nodded and began to sob. "Oh, I'm so ashamed."

Molly moved to take a chair next to Rose, slid an arm around her shuddering shoulders, and drew the fragile woman into her. "Percy is a kind and charming man. Why are you ashamed of liking him?"

"It makes me disloyal to Gilbert."

"Does liking Percy make you love Gilbert less?"

Rose blew her nose. "Well, no, of course not."

"And is your heart so small that it can only hold one love?"

"Well, no, of course not."

Molly patted Rose on the back and gave her some time to consider.

"What am I going to do?" Rose asked.

"Have you told Percy how you feel?"

Rose drew back, a panic-stricken look on her face. "I could never do that."

"Does he have feelings for you?"

Rose blinked. "I have no idea."

"Perhaps that would be a good place to start."

"How do I find out without revealing my shame?"

"Do you want me to try and find out?" Molly asked. "Discreetly, of course."

"I just don't know. If he does, that complicates things."

"If he doesn't, it simplifies things."

"Well, that's true." Rose visibly brightened. "That's absolutely true."

"Tell me, do you think Val would resent the fact that Tali has fallen in love with Angel?"

"No, of course not. He would want her to be happy."

"Gilbert would want you to be happy too."

Rose considered. "Be discreet."

"The soul of it," Molly assured her.

Angelina stuck her head in the kitchen. "Can we go now?"

Rose stood and put on her coat. "Time for angels to fly."

Angelina hugged and kissed Talisman, gave Molly a casual wave, and they were gone.

As they stood in the front door and watched Rose's car pull away, Talisman whimpered.

"At least you got a kiss goodbye," Molly said.

*   *   *

"We have a Friday night all to ourselves," Steve said. "Whatever will we do with all this alone time?" His tone told Molly exactly what they'd be doing. He was building a fire in Molly's fireplace while she picked up Angelina's toys that were scattered around the living room.

As the room heated up, Steve pulled off his STEVE'S HEAVY METAL GARAGE sweatshirt—his uniform for the car repair shop he owned near campus. The tank top he wore beneath it clung to his well-sculpted body, and Molly felt her own heat begin to rise.

Molly studied the load of toys and games she held in her arms. "We could play strip poker."

He grinned. "Five card stud, redheads wild."

"Or maybe naughty Monopoly."

"Well, as a real estate agent, you would have the advantage. That might be fun."

"Oh, oh, oh. How about dirty word Scrabble?"

"I know lots of dirty words."

Molly held up Angelina's paddles from her Wii ping pong video game. "Paddles?"

"Molly, I never knew."

She emptied her arms into Angelina's toy box. "Okay, how about we play studly mechanic? You lube my chassis, service my engine, tweak my transmission, inflate my tires, inspect my air bags—"

Steve's lips silenced her. After a long, luxurious kiss, he whispered, "How about I just make you feel like a woman should?"

Molly melted. He scooped her up, laid her down on a pile of pillows in front of the fireplace, and they stripped away their clothes.

Steve's lips were always gentle and coaxing, and hers enjoyed giving him pleasure as well. Steve was the first man with whom Molly felt relaxed enough to ask for what she wanted, and to experiment with things she had never before had the confidence to attempt. There was also a quality of playfulness about their love-making that she had never experienced. It made her happy.

They took their time, their fingers caressing the other's skin, raising gooseflesh. Their tongues tasted and their mouths aroused. They fought the urge to couple until the fire was so hot neither could wait another second. When he finally entered her, Molly lost herself in the union and rode waves of pleasure that transported her to a place where she knew for certain she was loved and cherished and safe.

Steve had helped her find her very own *Refugio Seguro*, and she hoped it would be her permanent residence.

*   *   *

Later, in the middle of the night, Molly heard a strange sound. It startled her from sleep, and disentangling from Steve's arms, she sat up in bed. The sound was unmistakably the distinctive blood-curdling whine of

Havana's cat, Marina Night—it seemed to be right in the room. Molly shook her head to force herself more awake. The moonlight streaming through the closed window fell on the foot of the bed where Talisman stood at attention, her fur bristled. Next to her, Blondie was oblivious, snoring like a car engine in bad need of service. Steve was in the same condition as his dog.

"Do you hear it too, Tali?" Molly whispered.

Talisman growled.

Molly recalled Robin's comments about an Aussie being psychic, but it didn't explain why she was also hearing it. Somehow, at her core, she felt that it was a warning of some kind. She had never believed in things supernatural until Havana's previous predictions had proven so eerily correct. Now, the universe seemed a place of incomprehensible mystery, and it didn't feel friendly. Too uneasy to fall back asleep, she quietly slipped out of bed and into a warm robe, then went to the kitchen. Talisman followed.

Molly turned on the flame beneath the water kettle and dropped a tea bag into an empty mug. She took the lid off the jar of dog cookies and gave Talisman a treat. The clock on the stove read 2:21 AM. Outside, the snowfall had started and icy shards pelted the window. She shivered and knelt to cuddle Talisman, who leaned into her and nuzzled.

"I want the bad things to stop," Molly said.

Talisman's deep sigh told Molly that she did too.

Molly buried her face in Talisman's fur and breathed deeply the scents of wood smoke mingled with Angelina's honeysuckle shampoo. She pulled away and looked Talisman in the eye. "Oh, Tali, are you taking baths with Angel again?"

Talisman looked away, her expression guilty.

Molly stood, drowned her tea bag in boiling water, and marched up the stairs to Angelina's bathroom. Sure enough, the tub's drain was full of soggy clumps of dog fur. How many times had Molly told them not to indulge in mutual bathfests? The house was old and the plumbing questionable. She knelt by the old clawfoot tub and used her fingers to pull out what she could, but there was more she couldn't grasp. She looked around for a tool of some sort—a pencil would probably do. Going into Angelina's bedroom, she flicked on the light and rummaged in her desk drawer. Not intending to snoop, she was surprised to find an envelope addressed to Angelina in Rita Sanchez's handwriting. Rita, whose *barrio*-dwelling family took Molly in and unofficially adopted her when she was eleven. Rita, whom Molly had driven away with grave disrespect. Rita, once a sister to Molly, and now only an aunt to Angelina. Molly's stomach tightened as a desire to honor Angelina's privacy did battle with her own need to reconnect with her former sister.

Molly slipped the letter out of the envelope.

Angel ~ No snow in LA. Lots of gangs. So many blondes it's gotta be the dumbest place on earth. Nope, haven't met J.Lo yet. Designing upscale *barrio* fashion for rich bitches feels like a kind of revenge against the privileged class. Just call me The Caliente Latina Avenger. Nope, you can't come live with me—don't care how pissed off you are at your *mamá*. Deal with it. Life ain't fair. Love you. *Vaya con Dios*. ~ Rita

Short and not sweet, that was Rita. Once a gangster, Rita always cut to the chase. Life as a fashion designer in Los Angeles didn't appear to be dulling her edge.

Molly trembled as she returned the letter to its place. Angelina asked to live with Rita? Why? What had Molly done to alienate her so badly? They went through some rough times together when they first moved to Blackstone, but Molly worked hard to make things right.

Angelina's bad attitude had only resurfaced in recent weeks.

As she was about to close the drawer, Molly noticed a letter addressed to her in Rita's handwriting. Confused, she picked it up and examined it. Unopened, it was dated a week ago. Why hadn't Angelina given it her?

Molly tore it open. The message was also short but not-so-sweet.

Molly ~ Rumor on the street is that the gangsters Miguel ripped off are out for vengeance. Watch your back. ~ Rita

Molly's knees gave out, and she sank into the desk chair. Angelina's father, Miguel, had betrayed a gang of drug dealers before being arrested. The gangs in the *barrio* were known for exacting revenge on family, and while Miguel was now in prison, Molly and Angelina were easy marks due to Molly's high-profile real estate career. She wondered how far afield the Denver-based gang members would travel. She glanced up and cursed the photo of Miguel that was among the framed pictures lined up on the shelf above the desk. Next to it was a picture of Miguel and Angelina. The two looked so much alike it never failed to amaze Molly—Miguel's Latin genes had totally overwhelmed Molly's Irish ones. Next to that was a picture of Rita with her brother Juan and her daughter Yvonne, taken the day before the two were gunned down in a gang war. Then there was a photo of Val with Talisman. However, the photo of Molly and Angelina taken just this past Christmas was now mysteriously gone. Could it have fallen? Molly looked behind the desk, then underneath the desk. Disbelief drove her to rifle through the desk until she found it face down in the bottom drawer. The early morning revelations stole her breath.

"I love her," she told Talisman. "Everything I do, I do for her. Isn't that enough?"

Talisman had no answers to give.

*   *   *

Talisman led an interesting life, had a meaningful job, a myriad of fascinating friends and social activities, was doted on by adoring assistants, pampered by a staff of experts, and her love life was lifted straight from the pages of an epic romance novel. Spiritsong's Lucky Talisman of DeMitri was a most special Australian Shepherd.

Val had bequeathed Talisman to Molly upon his death—along with a list of detailed instructions for care and feeding. Molly found the task overwhelming, but Angelina had embraced the mission with passion, and it became a way for them all to cope with their loss. Val's untimely passing had left behind a gigantic black hole whose gravitational pull threatened everyone who had loved him. Talisman was the anchor that now kept them all grounded.

Talisman had been unanimously elected as official mascot of The Valentino DeMitri Gay Epiphany Fan Club. Angelina accepted the position of her personal assistant. Val's best friend, Toby Fletcher, became her social secretary. Molly, who had a snazzy BMW and good driving record, donned the hat of official chauffer. Today the fan club delegation made a formal appearance at an AKC dog show in Denver.

The National Western Complex sprawled over eighty acres, and the conformation events were held in a spacious indoor hall. Hundreds of people and dogs swarmed the facility, which was set up with vendor booths and rings for the various competitions. Molly found the press of people and general bedlam disorienting, but Toby appeared quite at home. She was glad for his presence on her first dog show field trip with Talisman.

Talisman had once been a show queen, but Val retired her after she won Best in Show at Westminster. Although Val said he wanted her to go out in a blaze of glory, the fact that Peter died shortly after she took her crown was the real reason. Peter had been Talisman's handler, and the shows were a family affair. However, every time major dog shows were held near their home, Talisman made an appearance to visit old friends and lovers.

Talisman always wore a scarf around her neck that declared her sentiments. Today's scarf read JUST LIKE ROMEO & JULIET.

"It's quite tragic, really," was all Toby would say by way of explanation. He led them through the wild maze of people and dogs who were milling about between shows.

Where Val had been a dashing and dapper gay man, Toby reminded Molly of bright Little Orphan Annie with his huge halo of curly, orange hair and patchwork-style clothes—ever-wrinkled and paint-stained. Toby was a flaming gay artist.

Talisman led their little parade. She appeared intent on some important mission and tugged hard on the leash that Angelina grasped with both hands. Toby followed, scanning the crowd for familiar faces. Molly, Steve, and Blondie lagged behind. Blondie's greatest joy in life was sniffing people's crotches, and Steve had to struggle to keep her moving.

Toby grew animated as they approached herding dog territory. He pointed to a Puli. "Oh, look, there's Tassel. Her registered name is Twin Peaks Bosom Buddy." A pretty Collie caught his attention. "And there's Spot— The G Spot. Oh, oh, and that Briard is Jacob Black—Kiss the Girls and Make Them Howl." Toby stood up on tiptoes and craned his neck to see above the crowd. "That itty bitty Corgi is Pia—Passion in Action. And the Bouvier des Flandres over there is Flame—Desire Lights Up the Night. The GSD is Dusty—Lust in the Dust." He waved his hand frantically to get an Old English Sheepdog's attention, "Hi, Hot to Trot Scratch My Itch. You look so handsome today."

Molly laughed. "These herding dogs seem like a wild bunch."

Toby rolled his eyes. "Oh, you don't know the half of it, honey. And let me warn you to beware of the Border Collies. They're the bad boys of the herding breeds, a scrappy band of rebels who live by their own rules. All the bitches gravitate to them. Well, except Tali, of course. There was only one for Tali and, well, it's a tragic tale of tailless tragedy."

Molly had never before had a dog and was discovering a whole new world. It was quite an adventure.

Toby's eyes darted to a striking black and white Border Collie. "That's Studly—The Sex Machine. Do *not* let Blondie see him. Trust me, he'll break her heart."

Molly glanced at Blondie, who seemed much more interested in people's private parts than Studly's.

"How come you know all these dogs so well?" Angelina asked.

"I used to travel the dog show circuit with Val and Peter. I painted portraits of the dogs. They all love me."

Studly The Sex Machine growled at Toby as they passed.

"Well, most of them anyway," Toby whispered.

Suddenly, Talisman screamed—a wild screech that shocked everyone in the area to silence except Angelina, whose shriek echoed Talisman's as the dog ripped the leash from her hands. Talisman charged into the crowd and disappeared in a blur of fur.

"Tali!" Molly's adrenaline surged, she released

Steve's hand, and raced after her. The sea of people parted to allow passage, but the dogs weren't so accommodating. Molly tripped over Passion in Action and came down hard on the concrete floor. The searing pain stole her breath, and before she could regain her footing, Steve was hovering over her.

"You okay?" he asked.

Molly groaned and allowed him to help her up. "Did I hurt Pia?"

The little Corgi sat unscathed a few feet away, her person seemingly oblivious on the other end of the leash.

Steve shook his head. "But you're bleeding."

Molly glanced down, more dismayed to see the rip in her new jeans than the skinned knee. "We've got to find Tali." She couldn't imagine how Angelina could survive yet another loss.

Angelina and Toby caught up with them.

Toby gave Molly's back a gentle pat. "Don't worry. I know right where she is. Follow me."

They traipsed off in search of her.

Talisman's beauty was spectacular. Her long, full coat was a marbled swirl of black and silver with copper highlights, and she had a lush white collar and gorgeous white markings on her face, chest, and legs. Her sky blue eyes reflected extraordinary intelligence, and right now those eyes were staring into her mirror image.

"It's a boy version of Tali," Angelina said with wonder.

"It's Chance," Toby said. "Tali's forbidden love."

Molly had known Talisman for almost six months, and never before had she witnessed the prim, prissy dog exhibit anything other than ladylike behavior—except when she was lifting her leg to pee like a boy dog. (Val had once observed that Talisman could be somewhat gender-confused.) However, in the presence of Chance, gender-confusion was most definitely not an issue.

In a wanton display of canine coquettishness, Talisman danced for Chance. She dipped low in a coy play bow and then bounced up and butt-slammed him. In response, Chance smiled and twisted his body into a U-shape and wiggled toward her. She chirped and trilled, and he chattered his teeth. Talisman stared at him with a wild gleam in her eyes, batting her eyelashes in a decidedly come-hither manner. Chance smacked his lips and nuzzled her ear. Both shook their tailless bottoms shamelessly.

"Tali is spayed, right?" Molly asked.

Toby nodded. "She is now, but their passion goes much deeper than hormones."

"She's acting like he's some kind of rock star," Angelina said.

"He is. Champion Caitland Isle Take A Chance—the first Aussie to win Best In Show at Crufts, the most prestigious dog show in the world." Toby placed his hand over his heart. "I remember when they met. It was love at first sight."

"So, what's the tragic tale of tailless tragedy?" Steve asked.

Toby looked at them all like they were imbeciles. "Well, they're both blue *merles*, and *merles* aren't allowed to mate with each other—it's a genetic thing. Their babies could be blind and deaf."

Angelina gasped. "Oh, poor Tali and Chance. How sad."

There were so many things Molly still had to learn about being a mom to an Australian Shepherd. She glanced at Chance's handler and he gave her a conspiratorial wink as if to say, "Let them have their fun."

Suddenly, Talisman threw back her head and let loose a feral howl. Her body went rigid, her fur stood at attention, and her eyes slid past Chance to narrowly focus on a beautiful red, white, and copper Australian Shepherd who stood nearby.

"Uh oh," Toby said.

"Why 'uh oh?'" Molly took a few protective steps in Talisman's direction.

"The redheaded bitch is the other woman who came between them," Toby said. "She's a tri-color, so she and Chance weren't forbidden. Her name is Vixen—I'm Too Sexy for My Fur."

Chance, apparently sensing the awkwardness of the situation, sat down and averted his gaze.

Vixen's amber eyes and coppery red fur shimmered in the bright overhead light. Her face was delicate and pretty. She was undeniably ravishing, in a canine sort of way.

Steve gave both Vixen and Molly an appreciative once-over. "Well, there is something to be said for sexy redheads."

"Your eyes and hair are the exact same color as hers," Angelina said to Molly, her tone reproachful.

Molly noticed that everyone was staring at her. "What?" Both bitches had her in their sights as well. "I don't want him. I swear." She pulled Steve closer and made a point to snuggle into him. "I'm very happy with the stud I've got."

Chance sighed, lay down, and rested his chin on his paws.

Angelina always took her role as Talisman's personal assistant very seriously. She marched right over to Vixen's handler and said, "Please take your dog somewhere else because she's simply ruining everything."

Startled, the woman glanced at Molly.

Molly struggled to keep a straight face. "What she said."

The woman tossed her head, muttered something

about their impertinence, and quickly led Vixen away.

Angelina patted Talisman, and the two of them shared a high-five. Then Talisman lay down next to Chance and licked his ear, which set his teeth to chattering, and then their angst-filled reunion began anew.

Steve hugged Molly. "They've got a passion that rivals ours."

"Yes, but theirs has an unhappy ending," she said.

"Ours won't. I have an entirely different ending planned for us."

His words reminded Molly of an old family saying, but she didn't voice it. Instead it bounced around inside her head like Talisman's flirtatious little dance.

You know how to make God laugh? You tell Him your plans.

CHAPTER FOUR

Robin smelled really good. His cologne wasn't a classic men's cologne like Val used to wear, but reminded Molly of a cross between pine trees and musk. It was invigorating. Despite herself, she found his presence to be stimulating in general. He was attractive and charming.

Molly's office wasn't large, so they positioned Robin's desk to face hers and placed two client chairs in between them. Other office furnishings included a brass coat rack, a file cabinet, and a wall of built-in bookshelves. She had provided Robin a new computer, and he immediately demonstrated brilliant organizational skills by setting up a client data base, updating her website, and designing a newsletter to mail to her sphere of influence. His first day was going more smoothly than she had expected.

Until Fang Chang showed up.

"What he doing here? Why he no fill out paperwork?" Despite her four-and-a-half foot stature, Fang loomed large in the doorway.

Molly jumped. In all the time she had worked at Broker's Best, she had never seen the unpleasant little bookkeeper outside of her own office. "What?"

Fang sniffed and pointed to Robin, who was standing at the filing cabinet. "You just sleep with him or he work for you?"

Molly narrowed her eyes. "Robin is my new assistant."

"You pay his taxes?"

"Like me, he's an independent contractor."

Fang stomped her foot. "Like you, he need to fill out paperwork. Jake not responsible if your dog bite your pretty new boy under this roof. "

Molly looked at Talisman. Her scarf of the day said I'M JUST A PUSSY CAT.

"If he not pay taxes, Jake not responsible. If he do something illegal, Jake not responsible. If you sleep with him and give him disease, Jake not responsible."

A silent pall fell over the room.

Finally, Robin said, "Just ring when you're ready for me to sign the paperwork, and I'll come round."

Fang gasped. "You British colonial opium warring Englishman!"

Robin appeared unflustered by the attack. "Actually, that would be my ancestors."

Fang waved her bony finger between him and Molly. "You two made for each other. Your boss is *chòu biǎozi*." An eerie smile lit up her face and she shuffled away.

Molly sighed. "I wonder what she called me today."

"'Stinking whore,' actually."

Her face flushed. "The fact you understand Chinese could prove quite useful."

"I expect to be quite useful."

"Fang hates me. Her half-sister, Lily, is Jake's ex-wife. Jake and I had a relationship—long after their divorce, I hasten to add."

"And you gave him a disease?"

Molly's eyes shot to him, and she was relieved to see amusement rather than condemnation on his face. She would have to get used to his dry humor. "I gave him myself. He didn't know it was something he wanted until it was too late."

"What a silly bugger he was."

Molly thought so too.

*   *   *

Liberty True wore a jaunty American flag beret, and her Basset Hound, Ross, sported a flashy American flag ensemble. Molly greeted them in the lobby and led the way to her office past dozens of curious eyes.

"We're very patriotic," Liberty said. "People never quite know what to make of us." Her silver-streaked dark hair was tucked up into the hat, and wisps curled out and framed her handsome face. She wore blue jeans, a sweatshirt that said FREEDOM FIGHTER, hiking boots, and a fur-lined camouflage parka.

Ross's insulated red, white, and blue vest matched the snood that contained his long ears. "They were dragging in the snow," Liberty explained as she stooped down to adjust the hat.

Ross's loud sigh seemed infinitely patient.

They were an interesting couple.

Liberty was a history professor at Blackstone University and in the market to buy a home. Val's mother, Margo, had referred her to Molly.

When they entered Molly's office, Talisman leapt from her cushy bed and eagerly gave Ross the once-over, sniffing and snuffling every square inch of him.

Ross was unmoved and had no apparent interest in returning the canine courtesy greeting ritual.

"Liberty, this is my assistant, Robin Knight."

Robin stood and took her hand. "My pleasure, madam."

Liberty fixed her steel-blue eyes on him. "Oh, you're from the mother country. We kicked your asses, didn't we?"

Robin didn't miss a beat. "Yes, you certainly did. May I offer you a spot of tea?"

Liberty smiled, reached into her coat, pulled out a

small book, and shoved it into his hand. "Here's a pocket constitution. Read about what makes America great."

"Fabulous."

Liberty fished around in her pockets until she found another one to offer Molly. "Freedom isn't a spectator sport."

Molly accepted the booklet and nodded politely. What had she gotten herself into? "Please have a seat." She directed Liberty to the chair on the other side of her desk.

Before Liberty sat down she walked to Robin's desk, ripped a Post-it note from a pad, and slapped it across the eye of his webcam. Then she did the same on Molly's laptop. "Big Brother is watching you."

"Thank you?" Molly ventured.

"Government snoops have grown more bold through the years, but none have been so brazen as those in the current regime," Liberty said as she settled into the chair. Ross plopped down next to her. Talisman lay down next to him and continued to sniff. From where Molly sat, he smelled like corn chips.

"So, did you find me some houses to look at today?" Liberty asked.

Molly nodded. "We have quite a few lined up. However, I'm concerned that you wouldn't allow me to have you prequalified by a lender." The only reason Molly had agreed to show her property was because of Margo's recommendation. Normally, she would never proceed without prior lender approval.

"The oligarchs are taking over the world. You'll be a slave if you let others control your currency. I don't use banks; I keep my money in gold."

"So, you plan to pay for your new home with gold?" Molly asked. The concept was stunning.

"You betcha. I've been converting my cash into gold for most of my fifty-odd years, and gold is worth a hell of a lot right now. I can buy my new place outright. Then no one can take it from me. It's my dream."

Molly enjoyed helping others realize their dreams. "Dreams are good."

When Liberty smiled, she lit up the room. "When you cease to dream, you cease to live."

*   *   *

Liberty was looking for a home on acreage that was remote—somewhere she could be self-sustaining when the country collapsed due to financial depression, government tyranny, the destruction of the middle class, and the end of freedom. Molly listened to Liberty's philosophy while they drove around town looking at property.

"We've got to learn to be self-sufficient," Liberty said. "When all hell breaks loose we aren't going to be able to count on the government, which when an emergency strikes is absurdly inept."

Molly couldn't disagree.

They had left Ross at the office in the care of Robin and Talisman. Molly scheduled showings for homes in eastern Blackstone on rural farmland and up in the more rugged foothills. However, the farmhouses didn't appeal to Liberty because, "They're not a defensible position for when the social order collapses."

So, Molly chose to focus on showing her the properties in the foothills.

"It's got to have a well, so I have my own source of water," Liberty said. "And fertile ground, so I can plant a survival garden. And a fireplace or wood stove, in case the power grid goes down."

They rode in Molly's car. The roads were icy, but her BMW handled it well. When Molly glanced over at Liberty she was tickled by how excited her client seemed to be. Despite the many drawbacks of her new profession—impossibly long hours, financial risk, physical danger—Molly experienced a sense of satisfaction in helping people. It sure beat her previous occupation as a cocktail waitress. "I'm glad I can help you, Liberty."

Liberty's intelligent eyes sized her up. "What's most important to you in life?"

Molly didn't hesitate. "Keeping my daughter safe."

Liberty grunted. "Then it's a damn good thing you met me. Stick with me, and I'll teach you everything you need to know."

Molly's life had always been about survival but not the same kind Liberty spoke about. She was curious about what Liberty's life had been like. "Did you learn these things from your parents?"

Liberty's laugh was loud and hearty. "I learned about living off the land from them, but not much else. My parents were hippies who tuned in, turned on, and dropped out. My brother and I were both born in a tipi up in the mountains. They named him Good Karma and me Astral Plane."

Well, that answered the burning question Molly had about whether Liberty was her birth name, though now it created new questions. "How long did you live like that?"

"Until I was eight. My aunt went to court and got custody of Good and me."

"Your parents?"

"Don't ever be caught stoned out of your mind in a freak summer snowstorm."

Startled, Molly glanced over at her. The smile was still on Liberty's face but no longer in her eyes.

"I'm sorry," Molly said.

"Hedonism is a fool's paradise."

"Well, at least the hippie culture gave way to one more practical."

Liberty shook her head. "The beast has merely shapeshifted—our society is more concerned with pleasure-seeking than ever before. As with Rome, it will be our fall. The populace is fiddling while our great nation burns."

Molly didn't want to consider bigger societal issues. She had her own problems to worry about.

"Don't you smell the smoke, O'Malley?"

Molly was determined not to inhale.

*   *   *

The house on Rocky Road was a small modular located on ten acres, tucked into a remote corner of the foothills. The winding road leading to it was not well-plowed, but Molly's trusty car managed a valiant, albeit rough, ascent. She glanced at the sky and noticed storm clouds moving in. Already mid-afternoon, they had seen numerous houses, but none met Liberty's requirements. Molly was tired and hungry, and she hoped that this house might be the one.

Liberty had been nibbling on a bag of trail mix and offered it to Molly, who was grateful. She took a handful of nuts, seeds, and raisins and munched on them as they made their way through the snow to the house.

Molly knocked on the front door. Normally, sellers were not supposed to be home during showings, but she always made sure before letting herself in with the key from the lockbox. The door swung wide almost immediately, and they were greeted by a tall, thin man with a bad complexion and a nervous smile that revealed a mouthful of broken, rotting teeth.

Ever since she was sexually assaulted at one of her open houses, Molly's danger radar had been dialed to ten—and his darting eyes told her something wasn't quite right. She fished her business card out of her coat pocket and handed it to him. "I have an appointment to show this house."

"I know, they said you'd be here between two and four, but we didn't want to take little Lisa out in the cold." He stepped aside to reveal a frail girl, perhaps five years old, standing in the middle of the room. She had a rubber-backed kitchen throw rug wrapped around her, and tiny fists held it closed. Despite her efforts, she trembled.

When Molly stepped into the house, the strong smell of cat urine assailed her. She also noticed that it was nearly as cold inside as outside.

Liberty followed Molly inside, and the man slammed the door shut.

Already ill at ease, the sudden noise startled Molly. She struggled to slow her racing heart.

The man leaned back against the door. "I and the missus—I'm Ronnie and she's Gina—we'll stay out of your way. Go ahead and look."

A woman appeared out of the kitchen. Her jeans and sweatshirt hung like loose skin on a thin frame, and her short blond hair had been hacked off in blunt, uneven layers that stuck out in all directions. She didn't smile but merely saluted them with a toothbrush and said, "I'm still cleaning the floor in here, but, yeah, okay, look."

As Molly fumbled with the showing notes, some of the trail mix fell from her hand. Before she could bend down to pick it up, Lisa pounced on it like a wild animal and shoved it into her mouth. The desperate look in her red-rimmed eyes stole Molly's breath. "Are you hungry, Lisa?"

Gina grunted. "Yeah, I guess time got away from me while I was cleaning, and I forgot to make lunch."

Molly knelt down, cupped the girl's frigid hand, and filled it with more food. Lisa frantically shoved it into her mouth. The child had obviously missed more meals than a single lunch.

Liberty handed Lisa the sack of trail mix. The child snatched it and dashed off to one of the bedrooms.

Molly gave Ronnie a reproachful look.

He began to pick at a sore on his face with one hand, while the other gestured to a desk on which a dismantled computer lay. "I was busy too, working on fixing that."

"What's wrong with it?" Liberty asked.

"The shadow people got inside and made it go berserk."

Molly was totally creeped out. "It's so cold in here. Is there something wrong with the furnace?"

Ronnie used the back of his hand to wipe a film of sweat off his forehead. "Are you crazy? It's an oven in here."

Molly wasn't the one who was crazy.

"The place smells like cat pee," Liberty said. "What's with that?"

Ronnie and Gina exchanged nervous glances.

"Cats?" Gina said uncertainly.

"It's okay for them to look around, right?" Ronnie asked Gina.

Gina saluted them with the toothbrush. "Yeah, okay, look."

Molly and Liberty began a cautious exploration of the house. Ronnie and Gina didn't stay out of the way but followed close on their heels. It wasn't legal for a real estate agent to ask another's clients why they were selling their house, so she was glad when Liberty thought to ask the question.

"The shadow people told us something bad would happen if we stay," Ronnie said.

"Just 'cause you're paranoid, doesn't mean they're not out to get you," Liberty told him.

"Right on, sister."

The home was immaculately clean, sparsely furnished,

and smelled awful. The scents of nail polish, Freon, and drain cleaner floated in the air and made Molly's nose burn, so she was relieved when they stepped outside to look at the backyard.

The wind had picked up and whipped the snow into drifts. As Molly exited the house, quick reflexes allowed her to dodge an airborne plastic trash can lid. A raised arm protected her face from being struck, and the lid landed at her feet. She picked it up and trudged over to the can, but Gina wrenched it from her hands, shoved her out of the way, and slapped the cover into place.

However, Gina hadn't done it quickly enough to keep Molly from seeing what was in the trash: empty cans of Drano, dozens of batteries, hundreds of match book covers, and boxes and boxes of Sudafed.

Molly quickly glanced away and tried to keep her voice steady. "Is there a well on the property?"

Ronnie moved to his wife's side as she stood guard at the trash can. Both suddenly wore hostile, challenging expressions, and even though neither had their coats on, they were still sweating. Meth will do that to a person, Molly realized.

"Yeah," Ronnie said. He looked down at the business card he still held. "Yeah, Miss Molly O'Malley of Broker's Best, located at 1601 Main Street in the heart of Blackstone." His eyes no longer darted, but met hers with unmistakable challenge.

Gina grasped the head of her toothbrush and pointed the handle of it toward her as if it were the barrel of a gun. "Miss Molly O'Malley of Broker's Best, located at 1601 Main Street in the heart of Blackstone."

Molly's heart pounded so hard it hurt.

"I'll buy the house," Liberty said.

Ronnie and Gina both blinked, the evil spell broken.

Gina saluted her with the toothbrush. "I'll clean the house for you before we leave."

Liberty smiled. "I can't wait." She grasped Molly's arm and tugged her toward the driveway.

When they were safely inside Molly's car and headed back down the hill, Liberty said, "Wish I'd had my gun."

"Me too," Molly said, surprised by her own sentiment. She was passionately anti-gun. "Thanks for getting us out of there. Your offer to buy the place was quick thinking."

"So, what was the deal?" Liberty asked.

"It's a meth lab." Molly had learned all about meth houses in real estate school.

"What are you going to do about it?"

Molly hesitated for only a few seconds. "I'm going to call the police."

"I'm proud of you, O'Malley. Doing the right thing in life takes courage."

Molly felt the presence of the shadow people and knew they were following her. She didn't feel the least bit courageous.

*   *   *

Liberty collected Ross, who apparently spent a day of luxury sprawled on Talisman's cushy bed.

"It's not like you to give up your throne, Tali," Molly said.

Talisman sighed with great flourish.

"Tali doesn't know what to make of a dog who isn't instantly over-the-moon about her," Robin said. "She's rather flummoxed."

Molly smiled at Talisman. "It's good for her out-of-control ego."

Liberty jotted down some times and dates on a piece of paper and handed it to Molly. "Here's my teaching schedule. Please set up more places to look at, and let me know."

"Will do, Liberty." Molly shook the other woman's

hand.

"*Semper fi*, O'Malley."

Liberty and Ross left the building.

"What's she like?" Robin asked.

"One of a kind."

Molly went to the kitchen and fixed a cup of strong, hot coffee. Then she returned to her desk and phoned the detective she knew at the Blackstone Police Department. Detective Luis Mendoza had taken the report of her sexual assault and was also handling Val's murder investigation.

Detective Mendoza took the report on the meth house without comment.

It was the *without comment* part that bothered Molly.

"I know you think I'm a coward, Detective," she said. "I imagine you're surprised I'm taking this risk in making the report."

"I don't think you're a coward. But yes, I am surprised you're taking this risk."

Molly had been afraid to file a report about her sexual assault, and then when Val's murderers rejected their plea agreement and withdrew their guilty plea, Molly had struggled with whether she would testify against them. The man who had assaulted her at her listing on Thundermountain Road was among those who had gone back later and killed Val in order to rob the mansion.

"I told you I would testify in Val's murder if there was no other way to get a conviction," Molly said. It took her a while to make that decision, but she had finally agreed. Why couldn't he forgive her struggle?

"I know." His voice was gruff.

"I come from the *barrio* where you just don't turn in drug dealers or testify against murderers," she said. "Not if you value the life of your family...of your daughter. In my world, that's where they seek vengeance."

"I know."

Like Talisman, Molly was capable of sighing with great flourish. After a long silence, she asked, "So, when are you going to take action about the house on Rocky Road?"

"Immediately," he said. "There's a child at risk."

Yes, Molly knew there was a child at risk. Possibly—her gut told her—more than one.

*   *   *

Toby and his friend, Danny, were the best of friends, and the best of drag queens. They had once dressed up as magnificent show girls and performed a glorious rendition of "Big Spender" for Val's real estate promotional video. They could sing and dance, and their jazz hands were as good as jazz hands got. That afternoon they swept into Molly's office dressed as twin Carol Channings and belted out a rousing "Hello Molly" version of "Hello Dolly."

A crowd of Broker's Best agents and staff gathered to witness the spectacle. Molly cringed. First Liberty and Ross, and now Carol and Carol. She would be the subject of water cooler gossip for weeks.

When they were done, Robin and Talisman gave them a standing ovation while the rest of the audience drifted away presumably—Molly decided—to gather around the water cooler.

Talisman stood on her hind legs, bottom wiggling joyously, and greeted both Carols with happy kisses.

"Kiss kiss," Toby said to Talisman and kissed her nose.

"Kiss kiss," Toby said to Molly, applying gentle kisses to her cheeks.

"Kiss kiss," Toby said to Robin, then grabbed him with gusto and planted a serious kiss right on his lips. "I have no idea who you are, handsome stranger, but I am *so* happy to see you."

Either Robin was gay, or he was quite secure in his manhood, because he didn't punch Toby. He simply said, "Brilliant."

Danny's hand flew to his massive bosom. "Omigod, did you hear that Hugh Grant accent? Oh, be still my heart. Can I have a kiss, too?"

"Another time, perhaps," Robin said. He grabbed Talisman's leash, clipped it to her collar and led her out the door. "Walkies," he called back over his shoulder.

Molly liked Robin—he hadn't run away screaming yet, despite Fang, Liberty, Ross, Carol, and Carol. That was a hopeful sign.

"Oh, dear, did we chase his cute ass away?" Danny asked.

"Yes," Molly said. "Now sit your fabulous asses down and tell me what you need."

"Our asses are fabulous, aren't they?" Danny said, taking a seat across the desk from Molly. Toby perched next to him.

Both Carols were perfect. It wasn't just the amazing makeup lending the classic wide-eyed expressions, the cute blond hairdos, or the glamorous Dolly gowns. It was the perfectly raspy voices, the brassy styles, and the megawatt smiles. As Robin had so eloquently stated, they were brilliant.

"We're performing tonight at Café au Gay," Danny said.

"You'll knock them dead," Molly said.

"Speaking of dead, we need to talk to you about Val," Toby said. Carol vanished in an instant, eclipsed by a dark orb of pain.

Molly waited.

"The Valentino DeMitri Gay Epiphany Fan Club wants to buy his house. There are enough of us to be able to afford it. There's a lawyer in the group, and he'll incorporate us. We'll own it as a corporation."

Per Val's final will, Molly was the listing agent for the property.

"We want to make it a gathering place where we can celebrate his life," Danny said.

Toby nodded. "We thought we'd call it Falcon Lair. His namesake, Rudolph Valentino, had a house named Falcon Lair, and it was a really big version of Val's house. Spanish-style stucco, red tile roof, courtyard, fireplaces, wrought iron. Elegant, like Rudolph, like Val...." His voice trailed off, and he struggled to collect himself.

"Both Valentinos died at almost the exact same age," Danny said. "Both were canvases on which others painted their dreams."

"That's what Rudolph said about himself, you know," Toby said. "The canvas thing."

Molly struggled to control her own emotions. "I think it's a wonderful idea." She handed them Percy's business card. "If you need a lender, he's great. Have your attorney give him a call." Molly thought of Val's mother. "Have you talked to Margo about this?"

Toby grabbed a Kleenex from the box on Molly's desk and delicately dabbed at his eyes. "She's going in on it with us."

Molly hadn't seen Margo since shortly after Val's death. "How's she doing?"

"Oh, not well," Danny said. "Not well at all." He raised an imaginary bottle and simulated guzzling.

"We're worried about her," Toby said.

A wave of guilt flooded Molly. She should have been more attentive to Margo—she owed Val that much—but she had been too raw and ripped up by her own grief. "What can I do?"

"She gave us permission to have one of Val's traditional Friday movie nights at the house," Toby said.

"We're going to make it a 'Gays of Wine and Roses' event. Show the Jack Lemmon movie *Days of Wine and Roses* that was about, you know...." He raised the imaginary bottle again and chugged.

"Our non-smoking, gay men only AA club—The Butts Out Group—is going to be there and we're going to have a spontaneous, not-too-scripted AA meeting after the movie," Toby said. "It would be great if you could get Margo to show up."

Molly nodded. "Sure, I can do that."

"It won't be easy," Danny said. "She's become an anti-social butterfly."

"I'll figure something out," Molly assured them.

"Bring Hugh Grant." Toby waved toward Robin's desk. "He'd cheer her up."

Danny patted his bosom. "He'd cheer us all up."

Molly would have to offer Robin hazard pay. "I don't think—"

"Molly O'Malley?" An unfamiliar man was standing in her office doorway.

"Yes?"

"You're Molly O'Malley?"

"Yes."

He walked in and handed Molly an envelope. "You've been served," he said, turned, and left.

Confused, Molly ripped it open and reviewed the papers inside. Her stomach turned over as the full import of the documents became clear. She was being sued.

The perfect ending to a perfect day. In her mind she reached for that invisible bottle and chugged.

CHAPTER FIVE

Among Molly's first clients was a family by the name of Wacker. They were New Age nuts who had driven her nutty. She had helped them buy a new home, listed their home and sold it herself to the Hoyt family, listed the Hoyts' home and sold it herself to the Sloan family. It was a triumphant real estate trifecta from which she had made a boatload of money.

While selling their home, the Wackers had received two simultaneous offers—one from the Hoyts, and the other from a family named Ahmed who had been represented by Jake's ex-wife, Lily. The Ahmeds, who were Muslim, were suing Molly and the Wackers for religious discrimination. The government had also begun an investigation into Molly and the Wackers for violation of the Federal Fair Housing Act. And a discrimination complaint had been filed against Molly with the Colorado Real Estate Commission. It was a triple whammy from hell.

"Is it true that the Ahmeds made the better offer?" Jake asked Molly. He was sitting behind his desk, and she was seated across from him. He didn't look happy. She remembered sitting in this same chair her first day on the job when he had told his new rookies, *Try not to get sued or arrested; it makes for bad press.*

Molly nodded. "The Wackers made the decision based on numerology. Something about adding the value of the letters of the buyers' names to the dates of the contracts to the amounts they were offering. They chose the contract with the most auspicious number."

Jake stared at Molly.

"You'd have to understand how loopy these people are, Jake. They chose the house they bought because we found a dead body there, and they thought it would be good for their children to work through the trauma. They demanded an exorcism, a séance, and a medicine woman's blessing prior to closing. The other agent—Ted here in our own office—dubbed them 'total wackmobiles.'"

Jake seemed unmoved. "The complaint says that the Wackers were home when the Ahmeds looked at the house. Mrs. Ahmed was wearing a *burka* and Mrs. Wacker apparently made a comment to her about how the clothing didn't allow something called *chi* to properly flow."

"The Wackers refused to leave for showings after they had some medications stolen during an open house," Molly explained.

"When the Wackers made their decision about which offer to accept, did you advise them of the possible repercussions?"

Molly blinked back insistent tears. "You'd have to know the Wackers. They aren't in the least bit reasonable and don't care about rules."

"You didn't answer my question."

"No." She was unable to meet his eyes. "I didn't advise them of the possibility of a civil rights backlash. I had already told them when we listed the house that they couldn't discriminate."

"What did you say to them when they made their decision?"

Molly thought back. "I guess I told them to trust their feelings and do what they felt was right. I was trying to be supportive of their way of doing things."

Jake groaned. "The fact that your own client bought the house with an inferior offer doesn't look good either. It implies you influenced the decision to benefit your own interests."

"I didn't, Jake." She looked at him with pleading eyes, needing him to acknowledge her integrity.

He softened. "I know, but it doesn't look good."

"What can happen to me if I can't prove my innocence?"

"Steep fines, loss of your real estate license, jail."

The harsh reality knocked the breath out of her.

"Whichever way this goes, your defense costs won't be covered by your E&O insurance. That's only for contract errors or omissions, not ethics issues or violation of federal law."

"Are you going to stand by me in this?"

"Of course. I'm your broker."

Molly wanted more from him. She wanted him to stand with her because of his belief in her, not because of duty. However, all along she had wanted more from him than he had been willing to offer. "I suppose everyone will find out."

He nodded. "I can't protect you. I'm sorry."

The heat rose in Molly's face. Why was this happening to her? Then understanding dawned. "Lily was the Ahmeds' broker."

Jake nodded. "Lily."

Molly considered how much hell Lily had put her through because of her brief romantic relationship with Jake.

All around chew is dragon's breath and smell of sulfur, Havana Santiago had said. *I see a devil woman, fear and loss.*

Molly's inner scream sounded just like Marina Night's blood-curdling whine.

*   *   *

Molly, Angelina, and Talisman went to Steve's home. After Molly's day from hell, he had offered to make them dinner.

Steve lived in a comfortable split-level house at the end of a cul-de-sac; Molly had met him when she first moved to Blackstone and rented the house next door. She had always found his place cozy. Littered with baseball caps, dog toys, softball equipment, car repair manuals, and musical instruments, it felt all-American and safe— just like Steve.

The ginormous-screen TV that filled one entire wall never failed to fascinate Molly. She hadn't even owned a television until long after Angelina was born, and that portable model remained their only television. Sitting on Steve's plush couch, she stared at the muted, high-definition images of a hockey game being played in all its bloody, body-slamming, fist-fighting glory. The players' mood reflected her own, but she wasn't in the position to vent in such spectacular fashion.

Steve made Molly a big cup of hot cocoa, heavily spiked with Kahlua, smothered in whipped cream, and topped off with cinnamon sprinkles. He handed it to her and sat down.

"I've got dinner in the oven. It'll be a while," he said.

Molly worked on the whipped cream, trying to make her way to the Kahlua. She really wanted the Kahlua. "Dinner smells good."

"My mom's famous chicken and dumpling recipe." Steve's domestic skills were way better than Molly's.

Angelina, seated at the dining room table, licked at the mountain of whipped cream atop her cup of hot chocolate. "I just love whipped cream. And dumplings. And Tali. I love soft, fluffy things."

Despite her own mood, Molly smiled. "Are you doing

your homework?"

"I'm helping Tali write a love letter to Chance. Chance's person, Nancy, told me she'd read it to him."

Talisman was curled up at Angelina's feet next to Blondie, who was tenderly licking her ear. Offering solace, Molly supposed.

"We'd love to hear it," Steve said.

Angelina looked down at her notebook. "My dearest most wonderful Chance-man. Seeing you the other day ripped open my heart, and I am so very sad. We not only have identical blue eyes and matching fur coats, we have twin souls. We are true soul mates. Why, oh why, is fate so cruel? As it says in *Romeo and Juliet*, 'A greater power than we can contradict hath thwarted our intents.' Why can't life be easy? Why can't life be kind? My heart is ripped open, and I am so very sad. *Vaya con Dios*, my most special Chance. Your one true love, forever and ever, Tali."

"Wow," Molly said. "That's an amazing letter."

"Tali's going to sign it with her pawtograph. Steve helped me with the *Romeo and Juliet* part, but the rest came straight from Tali."

Molly regarded Steve with admiration. "I'm impressed."

He grinned. "Yeah, well, I'm just a romantic in jock's clothing."

Steve was great with Angelina and the closest thing to a real father she had ever known. Miguel had showered her with gifts and affection—when he had been around—but he had never taught her anything, or encouraged her, or been someone she could count on.

"You know that recording of your band you let me listen to the other day?" Molly asked.

Steve nodded.

"Why don't you let Angel listen to that? Maybe through those great headphones you've got?"

Steve's eyes reflected understanding. "Want to hear The Cul de Sac Guys' latest practice session, *chica*?" Steve was lead singer and guitarist in a middle-aged rock band.

Angelina was delighted to slip on the headphones. He adjusted the volume, and she bopped and wiggled while slurping her hot cocoa.

"So?" Steve asked.

"I'm in big trouble."

He brushed the hair from her face. "I know."

"The civil case could cost me a fortune, the Real Estate Commission case could cost me my license, and the federal case could cost me my freedom. Wouldn't it be ironic if I ended up in prison right alongside Miguel? Both of Angelina's parents, felons."

"What can I do?"

Molly fumbled for words. "All of the events lately have made me think about what would happen to Angel if something happened to me. Something most definitely could happen to me. The gangsters that Miguel pissed off are looking for vengeance, and I'll probably have to testify against Val's murderers. Today I reported some meth heads to the police. Now there's this...." She faltered, struggling hard to hold back the tears.

Steve took the cup of cocoa from her hand and set it on the coffee table, then gathered her into his arms.

Molly held on tight and struggled for words. "If something happens, Angel has no family. Her Aunt Rita isn't really her aunt, and I wouldn't want Angel raised by her anyway—she's such an angry person. I have no relatives, and God forbid Miguel's parents should try to make a claim for her—they're horrible people." She faltered again. "You've been such a good friend of ours since we moved to Blackstone. I totally trust you. Angel loves you. If something should happen to me, would you consider taking custody of her?"

"Of course. I love her."

It was that easy.

Molly kissed him. Besides Angelina, he was the best thing that had ever happened to her, and despite everything, he made her feel blessed. "I've made an appointment with an attorney about the lawsuit, so I'll find out how this should be handled. With Miguel in prison and the restraining order we have against him, I'm hoping there won't be any problems. I don't understand much about custody law, but I'll find out." A terrible sense of urgency filled her.

"We'll get through this, Molly. We'll get through it together. We—you, me, Angel, and our crazy wonderful dogs—we're a family. We'll get through this. It'll all be okay."

Molly really wanted to believe him.

*   *   *

Jake hired Brooklyn Green as a new rookie real estate broker, along with a Goth girl named Babylon Legend, and a middle-aged housewife named Ruby Rosen. Molly watched as Jake gave them their new broker orientation and then sent the three off to get settled in the shared rookie basement office known as The Dungeon. When Molly, Val, Summer, and Ben had used that office they renamed it Oddworld. Molly figured Brooklyn would probably now dub it, The Secret Power of Intention and Visualization in the Now Real Estate Rookie Success Center.

Molly walked across the hall to Jake's office and stood in the doorway. "So, what's up? I thought you only hired one group of rookies a year."

"Times are tough," he said. "Desperate times call for desperate measures."

"But, a *Goth*? Crazy clothes, tattoos, black makeup,

purple hair?"

"There's a large Goth community in Blackstone. They buy houses too."

"But Jake, what are you thinking? What's she going to do to our company's reputation?"

A slow smile crossed his face. "Do you know how many of my brokers stood right there and said those exact same words when I hired Val the flaming homosexual?"

That shut Molly up.

"Babylon is a tough cookie, Brooklyn's got spirit, and Ruby's very earnest—almost as earnest as you were when I brought you on board. It's a promising group."

Molly shrugged. "Well, I considered hiring Brooklyn myself, so that I understand. As for Ruby, I hope Brooklyn and Babylon don't scare her away."

"She's a good Jewish mother. Guilt is her secret weapon. She'll hold her own."

Molly stepped inside his office. "I saw an attorney this morning."

Jake nodded. "Mine has made contact with the Wackers about the case, so it's okay if you want to connect with them now." He had asked her to wait.

"Do I have to?"

"It would be wise."

She sighed. "I know. I was kidding."

"Darryl, my attorney, said their response about facing a lawsuit by the Ahmeds and being investigated by the feds for discrimination was to suggest that everyone involved in the case get high colonics to rid themselves of toxic energy."

Molly gestured wildly. "See? That's what I was talking about."

"It would be funny if it weren't so serious," Jake said.

"So, what should I do now?"

"Tread lightly. Watch your back."

"The Ahmeds aren't terrorists, are they?"

Jake gave her a sharp look. "Not funny. Don't *ever* let me hear you say anything like that again."

Molly flushed. It had been a rather lame attempt to lighten the mood.

"The only terrorist you need to worry about is Lily," he added.

Molly didn't find that in the least bit reassuring.

*   *   *

Robin made some unauthorized changes in Molly's office. He took down the dartboard that the Oddworld rookies had used to vent their anger. Val always pinned a photo of Ron DeSantis to the bull's-eye and took careful aim. Ben targeted his bank overdraft notices. Summer attacked an image of Coco. And on more than one occasion, Molly found it satisfying to throw darts at Miguel.

Robin replaced the dartboard with a wall calendar that featured beautiful scenes from nature. Then he changed the title on the wall chalkboard from SAFETY TIP OF THE DAY to INSPIRATIONAL TIP OF THE DAY. Today it said, ENERGY FOLLOWS THOUGHT. CHOOSE YOUR THOUGHTS WITH CARE.

"Robin, Robin, Robin," Molly said when she saw his handiwork. "I thought I dodged this bullet when I hired you instead of Brooklyn."

"It's my job, and I'll assist how I want to."

"Robin, Robin, Robin. When I fire you, I think you should apply at the grocery store to be the automated voice in the self-serve checkout line. Women would buy something just to listen to you speak to them. Your voice is very sexy."

He smiled. "Which is why you won't sack me."

"Well, I might not have to. You've set sail on a sinking ship. Flee while you're still in sight of dry land."

"I'm good at bailing water."

"You impress me," her arm waved at the wall, "despite your occasional lapses in judgment."

"I thought I'd make a Starbucks run. What can I get you?"

"How about a triple vodka Xanax latte?"

He grinned and laid some papers on her desk. "I set up your showings for late this afternoon, designed a special advert for St. Patrick's Day, confirmed Tali's appointment with the pet psychic, and started a new blog on your website that has you posting about local real estate trends. Your first post was genius."

Molly regarded him with wonder. "You are a gifted and talented man and should demand a fine dowry and bride price."

His laugh was sexy too.

She pointed to the glorious bouquet of flowers perched on his desk. "You have an admirer?"

"Carol and Carol, actually."

"Oh, dear."

"I'm afraid they're rather smitten with me."

"Well, you can't blame the girls for trying."

"Right."

Jessie's voice came over the loudspeaker. "Today's house of the day is pink and definitely the builder's model. It's a gorgeous show home with custom paint, a huge balcony, all the upgrades, and a deluxe game room."

A low rumble arose in the building as men began to migrate.

Robin gave Molly a quizzical look.

"An attractive woman is in the lobby and available for viewing," Molly explained.

"Whatever is a deluxe game room?"

Molly laughed. "I don't think I want to know."

"Does she know she's on display?"

"Did you know you were the day of your interview?"

Robin thought for a moment, and then realization dawned. "Fancy that."

"Go, before you miss out on all that important male bonding stuff."

Robin walked out the door and met Jake, who was also headed to the lobby. The two paused and sized each other up, testosterone practically shooting out of their ears. Molly had always likened these stampedes of Broker's Best men to a herd of rutting elk. When Robin and Jake stumbled into one another, her first thought was that within seconds their antlers might be locked in mortal combat. And even though it didn't happen right there, right then, Molly had a sense it was inevitable.

*   *   *

Shannon Flanagan and Brian Doyle had met on the Be-in-Harmony.com online dating site. Describing themselves as insanely happy, they were now engaged and wanted to find a home they could purchase on their wedding day. They contacted Molly because of her name, her Irish-themed real estate ad, her professional motto of *Your Lucky Shamrock*, and her photo. With her red hair and green outfit, she totally looked the part of a lucky Irish real estate broker. Having a photo in her ad of her preferred lender, Percy, dressed up as a leprechaun holding a pot of gold didn't hurt either.

Molly greeted them in the lobby.

Brian shook her hand. "We're proud of being Irish."

"I am too," Molly said with as much conviction as she could muster.

"You sure looked a lot younger in your photo," Shannon said.

Molly grimaced. "It was only taken five months ago." Admittedly, the past five months had been very long and hard.

"Well, pictures can be deceiving," Shannon said.

Molly noticed a slight edge to her voice and wondered if chubby Brian had looked skinnier in his online photo.

Molly ushered the couple into her office and introduced Robin.

"We connected on all forty-nine levels of compatibility," Shannon said in greeting.

Robin looked properly impressed. "Well done."

Brian bristled. "Oh, you're an Englishman—an oppressor of the good Irish people."

Molly coughed so she could cover her mouth and hide her smile. Poor Robin. First Fang, then Liberty, and now uber-Irish Be-in-Harmony people. She hadn't realized the English were so universally despised.

"*Erin go bragh?*" Robin said hopefully.

Brian grunted and Shannon glowered. They turned their backs on him, and took seats across the desk from Molly.

"I've set up some showings for today and—"

Shannon interrupted. "Tell me, Molly, how important are the looks of a house to you? Not at all, somewhat, or very important."

"Um, well, very important I suppose."

"Exactly." Shannon seemed quite pleased.

Molly cleared her throat. "Okay, so first we need to sign papers detailing how I'm going to represent you—"

"Please tell us what ethnicities you would be willing to accept as clients," Brian said. "Check all that apply. White non-Hispanic, Hispanic or Latino, African-American, Asian/Pacific Islander, Korean, Japanese, Chinese, Indian, *Arab*, Native American, Other. Remember you cannot go back and change your answers later."

Startled, Molly glanced over their shoulders at Robin, who held up a copy of *The Blackstone Daily News*. The paper had wasted no time broadcasting her shame. "All of the above. I do *not* discriminate."

"Please answer the following statements about yourself as true or false," Shannon said. "'I would never lie.'"

"True," Molly said.

"'Doing what I think is right is more important than what people think about me,'" Brian said.

"True."

"And in the category of living skills, please indicate on a scale of one to seven, one being not skilled and seven being very skilled, how you would rate your ability to remain calm yet resilient during a crisis?" Brian asked.

Molly's entire life had been a crisis—her living skills were well-honed. "Oh, that's easy, definitely an eight."

Shannon blinked. "But that wasn't one of the choices." Both her tone and Brian's expression were reproachful. Obviously these people had no clue how to think outside the box.

"You're absolutely correct," Molly said. "On a scale of one to seven, I would rate myself a seven on my ability to admit my mistakes."

The Be-in-Harmony couple visibly brightened.

"Well, then let's get those papers signed. I would say we're definitely a match," Brian said.

Molly presented the agency agreement to them, but Shannon hesitated when it came time to sign. "How appealing do you find a big house, Molly? On a scale of one through seven, one being 'not at all,' and seven being 'very appealing.'"

Poor Shannon. She really did seem to have an issue with Brian's weight. Molly didn't want them to break up now, right when they were going to buy a house from her. Ignoring her own declaration that she would never lie, but proving her ability to be calm yet resilient in a crisis, Molly said, "Very definitely a seven. Big houses are wonderful."

Shannon signed the papers, Brian smiled his jolly smile, and Molly glanced over to see a look of disappointment on Robin's face. Molly's own face burned, proving that she really did care about what people thought of her after all.

*   *   *

When Molly arrived home, she was surprised to find Percy instead of Steve babysitting Angelina.

"Something happened and Steve wasn't able to pick Angel up from school," Percy said. "He knew you were out showing property, so he called me. I was happy to help."

"What happened?" Molly asked.

"Steve didn't say, but he did assure me that he and Blondie were okay."

Nothing like this had ever happened before, and Molly didn't know what to make of it. "Thanks for stepping in. I don't know what I'd do without you, and Rose, and Steve of course. My work hours are so crazy."

"Tali was moping, so our little Angel decided it would cheer her up to have a bath. They're in the tub together right now."

Molly cringed and chased away fresh visions of hair-clogged drains. "Well, Tali does enjoy being groomed. Weird, but true."

"What are we going to do to pull Tali out of her funk?"

Molly had to smile. Her unusual, extended family had embraced Talisman as one of their own. "I'm going to take her to the pet psychic Val used to consult."

He nodded. "That's a good idea. Animals have feelings too."

"Yes, they certainly do."

"You look rough. Let me make you a cup of tea."

Before she could stop him, Percy trotted off to the kitchen where he ran water and clattered about in the cupboards. His assessment had been correct. She felt rough.

Sinking into the couch cushions, she kicked off her high heels, her toes wiggling in gratitude for the newfound freedom. Looking around her home, a flash of fear shot through her—what if her legal troubles caused her to lose it? That would be such a tragedy for Angelina. And she was starting to love the house too. The big, rambling place had character, unlike so many of the tract homes she showed clients. High ceilings and wood floors made it feel solid. Enduring. The formal dining room, parlor, and library—often considered unnecessary by clients who preferred the more modern great room concept in their homes—appealed to Molly. She enjoyed greeting guests in the formality of the parlor, and eating meals at the big, oak table with the ball-and-claw feet. She really appreciated the built-in bookshelves in the library. Books had always been her passion, and she was working hard to fill those shelves with the classics. During the most difficult years of her life books had been her refuge, and she loved everything about them—especially the smell. She wished it was a scent that could be bottled as a perfume.

The Oriental carpets and antique furnishings Rose had left behind made the house feel like a real home from the moment Molly and Angelina moved their meager belongings into it. Losing the house would be beyond horrible.

Percy returned with a steaming mug of tea, prepared with cream and sugar just like she preferred.

"You're so kind." Molly took a sip of the comforting brew.

"I know you did nothing wrong," he said.

"Thank you for knowing that."

"I'm praying for you."

Molly thought that a former Catholic priest's prayers most likely carried a lot of weight. "Thank you."

"If you ever need to talk...."

Molly appreciated his support. "I'll remember that."

Percy sat in a nearby chair and just watched her. It seemed as if there was something else he wanted to say.

"How are *you* doing, Percy?"

"Okay." He didn't sound in the least bit convincing.

"If you tell me your troubles, then it would help me forget mine for a while."

He brushed back his white hair and glanced away. "Now what makes you think I've got troubles?"

She smiled. "Trouble is the energy I seem to vibrate to—like a tuning fork. I hear a definite hum."

He twisted his wedding band in a nervous manner. "I'm just a bit confused lately."

Molly waited.

"You know that I left the priesthood to marry Sharon. It was one of those loves that defies all reason. I never expected it to happen in the first place, and certainly never expected it to happen again."

"I know."

He sighed. "Well, it hasn't exactly happened again—not with the same intensity, of course. But I'm feeling things I haven't felt in the past decade, not since Sharon died."

A light bulb went on inside Molly. In all her self-absorption, she had forgotten that Rose wanted her to talk to Percy. "Are you feeling affection for Rose?"

He looked startled.

Molly couldn't help but laugh. "I think that's wonderful. I think God wants us to love. I think that's the most important thing in all His creation, and if you feel love for Rose, then it's a blessing. A truly miraculous thing." Here she was giving a former priest a lecture about God, blessings, and miracles. Molly marveled at the irony.

Percy shrugged. "Rose is still so enamored of her late husband that I can't imagine her heart would be open to me too."

"Oh, I think there's more than enough room in that woman's heart for both of you." Molly envied Rose's easy ability to love.

"But what about Sharon?" Percy shook his head. "Wouldn't it be a betrayal of her if I allowed myself to love another woman?"

"No, Percy, I think she would want you to be happy."

He looked doubtful.

For all her talk about God, Molly didn't believe one existed. However, in that moment some inner voice of wisdom gave her an idea. "I think you should invite Rose to dinner and you should make a point to share memories of your spouses with each other. Bring pictures. Share stories. Make Sharon real to her, and let her make Gilbert real to you. Maybe that would be a great place to start. Open your hearts to each other in the presence of your loved ones, and see where that leads."

Percy leapt up from his chair and practically flew to Molly. He kissed her cheek, spun on his heel, and headed for the door. "Thank you, Molly," he called back over his shoulder.

He bounded outside before she could respond.

Love. It really was what mattered most. Molly thought about the fact that despite all her pressing concerns, she had Angelina and Steve. Concerned about Steve, she picked up the phone and dialed his number.

After several rings, a child picked up. "Hello?"

For a moment Molly thought she might have the wrong number. "Is Steve there?"

The little boy's voice was sullen. "Yeah."

"Well, may I speak to him?"

"Not right now."

"Okay." Molly paused. "May I ask who you are?"

"Kyle."

"Are you a friend of Steve's?"

"I'm his son. What's it to you?"

Molly's breath caught. She didn't know Steve had a son. "Where's Steve right now?"

"He's in the bedroom with my mom. He can't talk to you."

While Molly was trying to decide what to say next, the phone line went dead.

However, Molly couldn't hang up—she was too shocked to move. Her inner tuning fork practically shrieked with the sound of trouble.

CHAPTER SIX

Every Wednesday morning a general sales meeting was held in the large conference room at Broker's Best. The meetings were followed by a tour of all the company's new listings, and attendance was mandatory.

The agents provided a breakfast buffet, and the duty rotated alphabetically. Molly had met her obligation shortly after starting at the company, so with the fifty-five agents who now hung their licenses there, it would be a while before her name came up again. She wondered if she would even still be a real estate broker at that time. The future loomed darkly in her mind.

However, these thoughts didn't dim her appetite because she had learned that sustenance was required for the intensity of the house tour. It was, as fellow-rookie Ben had once labeled it, like the running of the bulls. She filled her plate high with breakfast burritos, jalapeno corn cakes, and Mexican fried bananas. For good measure she grabbed a heaping scoop of flan and smothered the bananas.

Ted Borgman sidled up next to her at the flan. "Sorry about your troubles. The Wackers are total wackmobiles. If you need me to testify to that effect, let me know."

"Thank you." Molly thought it kind of him, especially since she had consistently rebuffed his romantic overtures.

"The civil courts are one thing, and the Real Estate Commission is another, but you don't want to fuck with the feds. They're like Q and the Q Continuum—omnipotent and merciless." Ted was all *Star Trek*, all the time.

"That's very comforting, Ted."

"I see you've got a new gay sidekick."

"Robin isn't gay; he's British, just like the actor who played Captain Picard."

Ted grunted. "So what's with the tribbles I've noticed escaping your office?"

Molly blinked as she tried to connect the dots of Ted's crazed mind.

"You know, the big balls of fluff skittering about the halls," he said.

Understanding dawned. "I'm afraid Talisman is blowing her coat—she's shedding her fur like a stripper at closing time. It's an Aussie thing. She's depressed."

"So, what are you going to do about it?"

"I'm taking her to a psychic, like Counselor Troi of the Starship Enterprise."

"Well, may the Force be with you." Ted consistently mixed his sci-fi allusions.

"And also with you," Molly said, and then took a seat at the conference table as far away from Ted as she could get.

After the room was full, Jake stood at the podium in the corner and called the meeting to order. "To begin with, I'd like to say that I know everyone's heard about Molly's lawsuit, and I expect all of you to support her. I realize we aren't a warm and fuzzy group, but she's one of us. Knowing the facts, I can assure you that she's not guilty of the charges. Show some nobility of character and stand by her."

Molly was at once horrified by the attention Jake brought to her and moved by his rallying call. She glanced around the room, and only a few of the brokers met her eyes.

Jake saw it too. He sighed, tugged on his beard, and said, "Remember, what happens to Molly in this matter is going to reflect on all of us in the company. The community will be looking at us very closely through this. A united front can only help us all."

His words made Molly smile. If it took their own selfish interests to keep them from eating her alive, she would be grateful for what she could get.

"This is America," Coco said. "There is the presumption of innocence."

Since Coco was the top powerhouse agent in town, Molly hoped others would follow her lead.

The tension in the room lightened.

"As many of you have heard, I hired three new rookies," Jake said. "I know it's unusual, and won't be a popular decision, but I expect you to be professional and welcome them." He gestured to the newbies. "Please introduce yourselves."

Brooklyn bounced right to her feet and flashed a brilliant smile.

Molly decided that forevermore she would think of her as Brilliant Bouncing Brooklyn.

"I'm Brooklyn Green, and I now realize why the universe has directed me here. I sense a great deal of negative energy. To be truly successful in real estate, as in life, one must embody a positive mental attitude."

The group looked shell-shocked.

Molly covered up a giggle with a cough.

"I just received my PMA—Positive Mental Attitude—certification from the school of The Secret Power of Intention and Visualization in the Now. I have a bachelor's degree in ecology, and I've been certified as an EcoBroker. I'm all about having positive relations with ourselves, each other, and the earth. I've chosen *Go Green* as my real estate motto, and I think we need a theme song here at Broker's Best. I'll get right to work on composing it!" Brilliant Bouncing Brooklyn beamed as she took her seat.

"Lord have mercy," Coco mumbled.

Babylon stood up next. Her wild purple hair was incandescent beneath the bright overhead lights, and the purple powder that dusted her pale skin glittered. Her eye makeup, lipstick, and nail polish were black. She wore a long purple corseted dress that made her ample cleavage pop out of its restraint, and she stood tall in mega-platform black boots. She was a thing of wonder. "I'm Babylon Legend. My real estate motto is *I Am Legend*. I plan to make a shitload of money." She sat down.

"Have they warned you?" Ted asked her.

"About what?"

Ted looked to one side and then the other, then leaned forward and said, "Beware of the purple people eaters."

The tension in the room exploded into laughter.

Babylon didn't flinch. "No, but perhaps I should warn you that I have friends in dark places."

The laughter instantly stopped, and a deadly pall fell over the room.

Molly decided then and there that she liked Babylon. Yes, she was the stuff of which legends were made.

After a few moments of uneasy silence, Ruby stood up. "I'm Mrs. Ruby Rosen, but you may call me Mrs. Rosen. After my husband passed on, God rest his soul, and my son became a big important attorney and has no time for his lonely mother, I decided to get a job. So, here I am. I'm going to adopt the motto *There's No Place Like Home* and use a ruby slipper in my ads. I had a very nice ruby slipper that my late husband gave me before he died, but Brooklyn's dog, Sami, took it off my desk and hid it. I can't imagine a company that allows dogs in the workplace."

"Amen," Coco said. She had been known as The Wicked Witch of Broker's Best ever since she told Val,

I'll get you and your little dog too.

Molly decided that Coco and Mrs. Rosen should get along just fine together in their Land of Oz.

"I told you I'd get you another ruby slipper, Ruby," Brooklyn said cheerfully.

"And I told you that you'll find *my* ruby slipper. I also told you to call me Mrs. Rosen."

Brooklyn's brilliance dimmed.

"Okay, then," Jake said. "As far as announcements go, I'd just like to remind you that this conference room isn't the place to store your FOR SALE signs. If you can't find room in your office, then take them home."

Everyone looked at the dozen of Ted Borgman-inscribed FOR SALE signs stacked in the corner.

"I'm in the process of planning a *Star Trek* convention and needed to clear out my office to make room for the costumes," Ted said.

"A *Star Trek* convention?" Lois asked. "With all those demonic creatures? What would Jesus think?" Lois's own real estate motto was *Find A Home With Jesus.*

For all his *Star Trek* looniness, Ted did have a huge clientele comprised of sci-fi fans and computer geeks. Molly knew it had proven lucrative for him.

"And where do you intend to hold this *Star Trek* convention?" Jake asked.

Ted grinned. "Here of course."

Molly could imagine swarms of intergalactic aliens taking over the place. Well, they would feel right at home with Talisman's tribbles.

"Do you have any *Star Trek* celebrities who'll be making guest appearances?" Brooklyn asked.

"Yes, I do," Ted said. "John Zimmerman, who appeared in the original series as a yeoman who died on an away mission to that barren planet where Kirk was infected by a virus that made him turn into a transvestite Greek god before he got sent back in time to stop Hitler.

You know the episode I'm talking about. Well, boy does Mr. Zimmerman have some stories to tell."

Babylon snorted.

Coco stood and threw her hand to her hip. "Say what?"

Jake sighed. "Is there any other business?"

"Well, on a more *sane* note," Coco said, "I'm going to start a volunteer group of real estate and lending professionals to help people facing foreclosure—we're seeing more and more of it lately. The group will be called *Real Help*. Every Sunday evening after hours Jake's given us permission to use this conference room, and I'll be paying for an ad to announce it to the public. We'll give people negotiation tips to help them deal with their mortgage holders, we'll try to help them find low-cost rentals, we'll locate foster homes for their pets until they can get settled into a place that allows animals. Things like that."

"Why?" Ted asked.

Coco wagged her finger at him. "Because it's the right thing to do, Mr. Go Where No One Has Ever Gone Before." Her challenging eyes swept the room. "I'd appreciate volunteers to help with the project. It's the least we can do for them."

Coco never ceased to surprise Molly. She was horrible to work with. Terrifying really. And then there were moments such as this.

Molly considered volunteering her time but quickly dismissed the notion. She had far more important things to tend to, like keeping *herself* out of foreclosure. The most important thing in her world was taking care of Angelina. Nothing else really mattered. About that, she had no doubt.

*   *   *

After the caravan tour of houses was over, Molly returned to her office to find Lois Templeton waiting for her. She couldn't imagine a reason for the company's resident over-the-top born again Christian to visit her, unless it was to rebuke her again for her short skirts.

"We need to talk," Lois said. She gave Robin an uneasy glance. "Alone."

Molly had not trusted Lois since she stole a client from her. "Anything you've got to say to me may be said in front of my assistant." Whatever it was, Molly wanted a witness.

Lois pursed her lips. "Fine."

Molly gestured for her to sit down across from her, but Lois declined the invitation, thrusting a sheaf of papers at Molly instead. "I'll keep this meeting as short and painless as possible. You're an atheist sinner, and I need someone who won't be raptured to take care of my dear poodle Fluffy when I'm taken up to Heaven. You took in that homosexual's dog and seem to be doing a good job with her, so I figure you know how to do it. This contract was drawn up by my attorney and spells everything out. I'll pay you one thousand dollars up front, and when I'm taken away you'll receive more than enough to take care of my Fluffy for the rest of her little life."

Molly looked at the documents and they seemed entirely legit. It was ridiculously funny, and she tried unsuccessfully to hide a grin.

"Don't be flattered, Molly O'Malley. It's only because I know just what a horrible heathen you are that I trust you'll be left behind."

Molly glanced at Robin, who was also having a difficult time hiding his amusement. She handed the contract back to Lois. "*Val's* dog, Tali, doesn't like toy poodles. She eats them for breakfast."

Lois gasped. "Well, it figures that the dog of a

sodomite would be perverted too." She shook the contract furiously at Talisman, who was resting on her bed. "You're a bad, bad dog. *Bad dog!*"

Talisman sat up and cocked her head with confusion.

Lois headed for the door. "Never mind. I'll go talk to that Goth girl instead. I'm sure she's got sins aplenty I can rely on."

"If I were you, I'd be sure *she* doesn't eat toy poodles for breakfast," Robin said.

"Oh, what would Jesus think?" Lois literally ran out of the room.

Molly and Robin dissolved into hysterical laughter, until Molly noticed Talisman's hurt expression. "Oh, poor sensitive Tali. Come here, girl."

Talisman slunk over to Molly, who kissed her head and ruffled her ears. "You didn't do anything wrong. You're a good good girl." Molly grew pensive. "I should have signed. I just had to give my attorney a ten thousand dollar retainer. Lois's down payment for my sins would sure come in handy right now."

"Have faith. Everything will work out."

Molly didn't have faith—that had just been well-established—and she didn't believe everything would work out.

*   *   *

The rest of Molly's day was jam-packed with work, but all she could think about was Steve. She rifled through the stack of messages on her desk hoping to find one from him. She picked up the phone, dialed his shop, and was told he had taken the day off. She struggled with the urge to call him at home. If he didn't contact her by evening, she would simply drop by his house. The anxiety of not knowing what was going on was unbearable.

Robin's voice broke through her inner chaos. "You said you wanted me to go with you to your Paradise Valley listing?"

Molly's stomach turned over.

"You haven't been back since Val was murdered there?" he asked.

She shook her head. "Chief Waters took it off the market for a respectable time. He's ready to move forward now."

"And you?"

"No. No, I'm not ready at all."

Robin slipped into his jacket, then grabbed Molly's coat off the brass rack and helped her on with it. "Come on, then. Let's go face this thing together."

Molly allowed Robin to steer her out of the building and to his car. She was grateful to slide into the plush seat of his white Audi and let him chauffeur her up into the foothills to the house on Thundermountain Road.

Paradise Valley was what Chief Waters had christened his multi-million dollar estate located high in a secluded valley above town. Ten wooded acres surrounded the house, and a small river guarded it like a moat.

Robin drove his car across a bridge to the cobblestone driveway. "Is Chief Waters here?"

Molly shook her head. "He's in D.C. now. The Intertribal Council tapped him as their point man for federal partnerships. I guess his job is to protect their business interests with the new administration."

"Wouldn't he release you from the listing contract?"

"He offered. It's just that I've spent so much money on marketing this place that I'm in deep. I need to sell it. I've got to think of Angel. And now, with all the new expenses looming, I've got to be practical. I *must* be practical."

Robin pulled up in front of the house, got out of the car, walked around to open Molly's door, and helped her out. Her legs were jelly, and so she clung to him as she ascended the porch stairs to the front door. There were so many bad memories here. The man who had sexually assaulted her right here on this front porch following an open house was now in prison awaiting trial for Val's murder. As she fumbled with the lockbox hanging from the front doorknob, images of the assault replayed themselves in her mind. With shaking hands, she opened the door and peered inside the foyer. She looked at the floor and half-expected to see the blood-splattered albino mountain lion hide on which Val had died, but of course it was gone. However, in her imagination it would always be there. The police had told her the attack on Val was sudden and quick, yet in her mind Molly heard his screams, rhythmic and piercing.

"What's the security code, love?"

It took a moment for her to realize the sound she was hearing was actually coming from the security alarm. "Four, one, six, three."

Robin tapped the numbers on the wall pad right inside the door, and Val's screams were silenced. Molly stepped inside the house, and she made it to a marble bench in the foyer before her legs gave way completely.

Robin shut the front door and sat down beside her.

"Tell me what happened to him," Robin asked.

Molly didn't want to relive it but knew that the healing wouldn't begin until she could stare it in the face. "I got a call from someone wanting to see the house. Angel was sick and I couldn't go. Val came instead. Toby was supposed to meet him so he wouldn't be alone, but he was late. When Toby got here he found Val." Molly pointed to the floor in front of them. "Robbers had hit him over the head with a brass candlestick. He died here."

"You loved him," Robin said.

She nodded. "And no one has ever loved me like he did."

"Nietzsche said 'Love is not consolation. It is light.'"

Tears rimmed Molly's eyes. "He was this bright, brilliant light, and now my life is so much darker."

Robin took her hand. "Light can't be destroyed. It's just that sometimes you can't see it. Can't you still feel him?"

Molly closed her eyes. "Like the background radiation of the big bang."

"I know this might sound daft, but I sense something too. My mum had the psychic gift, and I've a bit of it. I see Val in those tails and top hat from the painting in our office, and he's dancing with another man. Val's body is here on a white rug, but the boys are happy. Over the moon happy."

Molly gasped. She hadn't told Robin about the white fur hide on which Val died, or that after Val's death she had dreamt of him dancing with his late husband, Peter.

Robin squeezed her hand. "Didn't mean to cause a fright."

"No…I'm just startled."

"Life without love is death. Love without life is still love. He's okay. Now you need to be."

Molly nodded and wiped her tears. "The FOR SALE sign is in the garage. Let's put it up and get this place back on the market."

"Right. Off to it." Robin set out to accomplish the task.

Molly stayed for a time on the bench. Finally, she said, "Valentino DeMitri, forever you will stay in my heart."

Somehow, she knew he had heard her.

*   *   *

When they were done at Paradise Valley, it was time to pick Angelina up from school. Molly hadn't been able to reach Steve, and Rose and Percy had made plans to have dinner together that evening—both were in a tizzy trying to get ready. Molly was glad Percy had taken her suggestion, but it did leave Molly in a babysitting dilemma. So, she and Robin swung by Angelina's school and loaded her and her overflowing backpack into the Audi.

"I have lots of homework," Angelina explained as books kept trying to escape their restraint.

"That's good because I'm afraid you're stuck with me the rest of the day," Molly said. "It'll give you something to do."

"It's nice to meet you, Angel," Robin said.

"Omigod I love your accent," she said. "It's so movie starish."

Robin laughed. "I love yours too. It reminds me of J.Lo's."

"Really?"

Molly marveled at Robin's charm—he had remembered that J.Lo was a favorite of Angelina's from something Molly had said. She was sure that Robin was soon to be Angelina's first crush, and as if to confirm that notion, Molly noticed her daughter fussing with her hair.

"Before we head to the office, I need to preview a house for my Be-in-Harmony couple," Molly said. "If it meets all forty-nine levels of compatibility for them, I'll arrange an introduction."

Robin chuckled.

Angelina continued to primp.

The prospective home for Brian and Shannon was an all-brick ranch in a middle-class neighborhood near the university. As they pulled up to it, Molly was dismayed to see a bank-owned property across the street. She had shown that now-abandoned house in January, when the owners were in the final stages of foreclosure. She remembered them as desperate and willing to do anything to sell it before it was put up for sale by the Public Trustee. Molly wished that Coco's *Real Help* endeavor had been in operation then because she didn't know how to advise them. Molly read that a bank purchased the house at the public sale. Now the former real estate FOR SALE sign was gone, and the house stood in a state of limbo until the bank assigned it to one of its preferred real estate brokers.

Molly got out of the car and headed toward the ranch, but Robin lagged behind.

"You can come in with me, if you want," she said.

He stood looking at the abandoned house. "There's something wrong there."

"I know. Every time I see a foreclosed home I feel so sad for the families—"

"No, there's something wrong." He headed across the street, urgency in his voice and his step.

"Robin?"

"Trust me."

Uncertainly, Molly followed him, and Angelina tagged along.

In the time Molly had been a real estate broker she had learned something about houses—they each had their own unique personality. Whether it was born of the architect who conceived it, the builders who birthed it, the decorators who dressed it, or the occupants who loved it, each house was different. This contemporary split-level felt sad to Molly. Maybe it was the big, curtainless windows that resembled large, vacant eyes, or more likely it was her previous encounter with its desperate owners. Whatever it was, she wasn't eager to go near it, but she followed Robin as he walked right past the front porch and headed into the back yard.

"How long do you think it's been vacant?" Robin

asked as he climbed onto the back deck.

Molly did mental calculations. "I would guess probably a month."

Robin stopped a few feet shy of the large bay window. "There he is."

Molly and Angelina came up behind him, and Angelina cried out when she saw the cat lying on the window seat. The emaciated brown and white cat appeared dead. Molly grabbed her daughter and turned her face away from the sight.

The cat's blue eyes were slightly open, but unmoving.

"He's alive," Robin said. "Barely, but there's still life there."

"How can you tell?" Molly asked.

"I just can."

Right, Molly thought. His psychic gift.

Robin tried the back door, but it was locked. He struggled uselessly with a window. "I've got to get in. There's not much time."

"I'll call the police," Molly said. "I left the phone in my car but I can—"

"There isn't time. I'm going to break in."

Molly panicked. She was in enough trouble right now. "I don't think you should do—"

"I'm going to break in now," Robin said, his voice calm. "Take Angel, go to the car, and wait. I'll take full responsibility."

"But—"

Robin turned and froze Molly with his intense eyes. "In life you have to do the right thing no matter what the risk. If I lose my job over this, fine. Please go to the car, and I'll be right there."

Molly wasn't at all sure the cat really was alive, and she didn't want to expose Angelina to the cat if it were dead or involve her in a crime. She took her daughter's hand and led her back to the car.

Angelina was whimpering. "Why would someone just leave their cat behind like that?"

"People who are forced to leave their homes often don't have anywhere to go that allows pets," Molly said.

"But why just leave them in the house like that?"

"They think the bank's going to go right in the house and rescue the pet. They don't understand it can take months for someone to go in."

Angelina's whimpering turned to sobs, and Molly climbed into the back seat of the car to hold her.

Within minutes, Robin opened the car door and handed Molly the cat, who was wrapped in his suit jacket. Hesitantly, Molly accepted it and was surprised to see blue eyes looking at her. They appeared huge in proportion to the gaunt face.

"There's a vet right next to where I live. It's close." Robin jumped in the car, fired up the engine, and sped away from the curb. "It would be good for Angel to touch the cat, to say loving things. All living things respond to love."

Angelina reached for the cat, but Molly stopped her. "I don't think she should touch—"

"Tyler doesn't have the strength to hurt her."

"Tyler?" Angelina asked.

"They left a note behind with his name. They left some food and water too. It just wasn't enough."

"I'll pet him," Molly said.

Robin shook his head. "Since you're probably going to sack me anyway, I'll just say it, Molly. I think you're too uptight. Let Angel do it. Her affection would be more genuine."

Angelina gave Molly a pleading look, so Molly released her hand and tried to muster up some indignation at Robin's words, but she agreed with him.

When Angelina began to gently stroke Tyler and murmur sweet words, his eyes shifted from Molly's face to hers. He watched her intently all the way to the veterinarian's office.

Robin pulled up in front of a small animal hospital, parked, and collected the bundle from Molly's arms. "As soon as I get Tyler checked in, I'll ring a glass company to go repair the damage I did. Why don't you two wait for me at my sister's shop?" He gestured to a huge Victorian home on the corner. A sign on the front said PAGAN PLACE. "Her name's Rowan. Tell her what's happened." With that, he was gone.

"I want to go with them," Angelina said.

"Robin asked us to wait with his sister." If the vet's assessment was grim, she didn't want Angelina there.

They locked Robin's car and walked to the house on the corner. A sign on the door said it was a metaphysical bookstore and curio shop. When Molly opened the door, she and Angelina were welcomed by fragile fingers of incense that smelled remarkably like the pine and musk cologne Robin wore. Two cats sat on a high bookshelf like bookends and greeted them with musical meows. A lovely young woman sitting behind the counter said, "Hello." Her accent was British.

"I'm Molly O'Malley, and this is my daughter Angelina Castillo. Robin asked us to wait for him here."

The young woman smiled and waved them in. "I'm Rowan. Come, make yourself at home." Rowan was tiny and delicate, with a creamy complexion and long, pale blond hair captured in a huge braid that draped over her shoulder. She wore a lavender chiffon caftan and several fresh flowers in her hair.

Molly stepped in and closed the door behind them. "Robin's at the animal hospital next door. He found a cat that's in pretty dire shape."

Rowan's green eyes flashed. "A Snowshoe?"

Molly shook her head. "Excuse me?"

"Part Siamese? With blue eyes and a white triangle on

his forehead?"

"Wow," Angelina said. "How did you know?"

"It's a gift. Got it from my mum."

Molly looked around the shop at the metaphysical books, jars of herbs, and a glass case full of magical charms. Understanding began to dawn.

Rowan gestured to her two cats. "My girls, Rhiannon and Bronwyn, told me he was coming. They're eager for a boy to play with."

"His name's Tyler," Angelina said.

"That's a good name," Rowan said.

"You understand what your cats say?" Angelina asked, her eyes wide with wonder.

"Of course. Don't you understand your dog?"

Angelina shrugged. "Well, yeah, I guess I do."

"There you are."

Molly noticed that the shop was very small, given the size of the home. "Do you live here too?"

"I have a boarding house. I live here, Robin lives here. A number of others do as well."

Pagan Place. Molly wondered about the nature of her boarders.

"Robin likes working for you," Rowan said.

Angelina sniffed. "Mom's going to fire him."

Rowan cocked her head and looked at Molly with curiosity.

"No...no I'm not. We had a disagreement, but he was right."

"He usually is." Rowan gestured to a steaming tea pot on the counter. "I just brewed some strawberry leaf tea. Would you fancy some?"

"Smells good." Angelina scrambled up onto a stool in front of the counter. "Talisman, my dog, has a sister named Strawberry. They call her Berry. And another one named Sassyfras who they call Sassy."

"What great names. Are they red dogs?"

Angelina nodded. "What they call red merle. Tali is a blue merle. So is her other sister, Maddie. They're Australian Shepherds."

"Lovely dogs, Aussies. They're psychic you know."

"Really?" Angelina nodded. "That sure explains a lot."

Rowan filled a teacup, added a spoonful of honey, and handed it to her.

Angelina took a sip. "Yum."

Molly politely accepted a cup. "Does your mother live here as well?"

"Mum's passed over. It's just me and Robin now."

"I'm sorry," Molly said.

"She was a good old gal. We miss her, but we get on."

"Does Robin have a girlfriend?" Angelina asked.

Molly smiled. Angelina definitely had her first crush.

"Not at the moment." Rowan winked at Angelina. "Why? You interested?"

Angelina dissolved into uncontrollable giggles.

Rowan opened a nearby display case, removed a small pink satin drawstring bag, and handed it to Angelina. "Here's an old English love charm. It's filled with special herbs designed to someday attract your true love to you. Put it under your mattress, and you'll dream of him so you'll know him when you meet."

Angelina inhaled deeply and then stuck it in Molly's face for her to smell.

It was a delightful bouquet that smelled like violet, rose, lavender, and vanilla. "Very nice," Molly said.

Rowan handed Molly a small purple satin drawstring bag. "Why don't you take this one?"

Molly looked at the bag and then at Rowan's face. She was startled by the sudden seriousness of her expression.

"I don't need a love spell," Molly said.

"It's not a love spell."

Molly sniffed the bag and noticed that the scents weren't flowery, but sharp: cloves, dill, nettle, bay laurel.

"What's it for?"

"Protection. You're in strong need of protection. Trust me. It's a gift."

Molly thought she heard Marina Night's whine, and her eyes flew to where Rhiannan and Bronwyn sat. Their fur was fluffed up, as if they had heard it too.

Molly tucked the charm into her pocket. Right now, she would take all the help she could get.

*   *   *

Tyler was hospitalized, and it appeared as if he would survive. The vet said that they rescued him with no time to spare. Molly was impressed with the unusual gift Robin had inherited from his mother, which made Rowan's warning all the more unsettling. Despite her two consultations with Havana Santiago, Molly had always been firmly grounded in the natural world—the realm of the supernatural was foreign territory. Val had introduced her to spiritual concepts, and now Robin seemed determined to convince her of the verity of things metaphysical. However, she had enough trouble just traversing the world she knew and entertained no desire to explore others.

It was late afternoon by the time the three of them made it back to the office, just in time to awaken Talisman from a long nap and greet Liberty True and Ross.

Liberty's sweatshirt declared her allegiance in bold letters: PROUD MEMBER OF THE AMERICAN RESISTANCE! Wearing an American flag with REBEL PATRIOT shimmering in gold sequins, Ross made his own unique statement.

Angelina was instantly enthralled by Ross. "He's a blond."

"They call his coloring lemon and white," Liberty

said.

Angelina crouched down and greeted him with baby talk. "Aren't you just the most handsome-wandsome Basset Hound ever?"

Ross turned his back to her, flopped on the floor, and grunted.

"Don't take it personally," Liberty said. "Ross doesn't understand the concept of affection."

"Why do you dress him in the flag?" Angelina asked.

"We're very patriotic," Liberty said. "I named him after Betsy Ross, the designer of the American flag. And it makes it so easy for me to say the Pledge of Allegiance every day. I stand him up in the corner, place my hand over my heart, and go for it. Have you said the Pledge today, Castillo?"

"Well, I stood respectfully for it in class, but we're not required to say it."

Liberty looked shocked. "Why *wouldn't* you say it?"

Angelina shrugged. "I dunno. I guess it feels silly to me."

Uh, oh, Molly thought.

"Don't you love America?"

Angelina shrugged again. "I dunno."

Liberty adjusted her signature beret and gave Molly an exasperated look. "So, what are your thoughts on the issue of patriotism?"

Molly felt like shrugging her shoulders and saying, *I dunno.* Instead she said, "Frankly, I've not really thought about it too much." She had always been more concerned about her own little world than the larger one that surrounded her.

Liberty raised an eyebrow and turned her attention to Robin. "What are your thoughts, Knight?"

Robin didn't hesitate. "I think patriotism is a dangerous form of tribalism that encourages separatism and war."

Molly suddenly didn't feel so good. She hoped she wouldn't lose Liberty as a client because of political controversy.

Liberty crossed her arms and leveled each person in the room with a look of assessment. After a few minutes, she pointed at Robin. "I disagree with you, but I respect you more than I do O'Malley." She pointed at Molly. "You have to stand for something in life. Figure it out, and help your daughter figure it out too."

Properly chastened, Molly herded everyone out to her car to go look at property. Robin would be leaving the office soon and couldn't dogsit, so Talisman and Ross rode in the back seat of Molly's car with Angelina. Molly knew that Talisman was a good passenger but was a bit concerned about Ross. To Molly, it appeared that if he decided to turn a piece of her fine leather interior into a chew toy, no one would be able to dissuade him. Plus he drooled. A lot.

"The drool. Is Ross okay?" Molly asked Liberty.

"Except for the rabies, he's just fine."

Despite her concern, Molly smiled. "Keep a careful eye on the dogs for me, Angel."

"Ross is kinda hard to ignore, Mom."

Liberty smiled like a proud mama. "My little flag is a force of nature. You should see him on the hunt. His nose is spectacular."

"You hunt?" Angelina asked.

"And fish. I could live entirely off the land, if need be. Everyone should learn to be self-sufficient for when society collapses."

"Society is going to collapse?" Angelina asked.

"It can't go on like it is much longer. The financial crisis we're facing will be much worse than the one in the last century because people are so much more dependent now. Somewhere between several thousand and several million Americans starved to death during the Great

Depression. If we're going to survive another one, we need to be more independent. Tell me, O'Malley, how much food do you have in your house right now?"

"Well, I was going to go grocery shopping tomorrow."

"Good grief!" Liberty shook her head wildly. "Do you know that if a natural or manmade disaster struck, the grocery stores would have their shelves wiped bare in less than three days? Then what would you do?"

"Well, I'm not exactly sure." Molly had never thought about it.

"Do *not* be caught with your pantry down, O'Malley. It's suicide. Our forefathers knew. They always had food put up. We're lazy, we take our welfare for granted, we rely on the government. Such foolishness."

"I couldn't shoot an animal," Angelina said.

"I bet you could fish," Liberty said. "Do you know how?"

"No."

Liberty twisted around to face Angelina. "Do you know that you can eat dandelions—the flower and the root? Very nutritious. Do you know what berries are safe and what ones aren't? Roses, sunflowers, lilacs are edible. Rose hips are a great source of Vitamin C. Do you know how to grow vegetables in your own garden, Castillo?"

"No."

Liberty looked at Molly with a raised eyebrow.

"Up until recently we were inner city people," Molly explained.

Liberty shook her head again. "Even city folk can plant container gardens and harvest dandelions in an emergency. Stick with me, girls, and I'll teach you what you need to know to survive the dark times ahead. In the meantime, get that pantry stocked with food you can eat right out of the can, for when the electrical power goes out. And don't forget to get an old-fashioned non-electric can opener."

"We're going to lose our electricity?" Angelina asked.

Liberty nodded. "Terrorist events, heatwaves, blizzards, sunspots and space storms, an EMP caused by a nuclear bomb set off over America—lots of ways we could lose the power grid. We gotta be prepared."

Molly glanced back at Angelina and noticed her look of alarm.

"Oh, and store lots of dog food," Liberty added. "And don't forget bottled water."

"We won't have water, either?" Angelina asked.

"When the power grid goes down they won't be able to pump the water to your home." Her eyes widened with alarm. "You don't drink the municipal water straight from the tap, do you?"

Molly nodded. "Well, yeah."

"*Never* do that." Liberty waved her hands about like a crazy woman. "There are so many contaminants in the public water supply, you should be purifying it. And if the system gets compromised you're going to have to get creative. You need to get a good water purifier— something like the Big Berkey. It's used by the Red Cross, Peace Corps, and relief workers all over the world to clean nasty water and make it drinkable. You gotta have water or you die fast. The Berkey doesn't need electricity, so you can use it when the power grid goes down."

After a long silence, punctuated only by Ross's loud snores, Angelina asked, "What does it mean that you're a member of the American Resistance?"

Liberty adjusted her beret. "This country is in the midst of the worst constitutional crisis in its history, and we the people are rising up to restore the republic. As a teacher, it's my solemn duty to speak the truth no matter how hard the tyrants try to silence me. As Thomas Jefferson said, 'All tyranny needs to gain a foothold is for men of good conscience to remain silent.'"

Molly couldn't imagine anyone silencing someone as zealous as Liberty.

"What don't they want you to say?" Angelina asked.

Liberty grew pensive. After a few moments she said, "There's so much that needs to be said, but I suppose the takeaway for today is that hate will not make America great again."

"So, you're like a champion for liberty and justice for all?" Angelina asked.

Liberty's laugh was loud and hearty. "Out of the mouth of babes. I like you Castillo. We're going to be great friends, you and me."

"Will you teach me to fish?"

"I'll teach you everything I know."

With Angelina's penchant for idolizing female superheroes, Molly wondered if that would turn out to be a blessing or a curse.

*   *   *

When Liberty first saw the property on Thundermountain Road, she wept. Even Mr. Unenthusiastic Ross managed an energetic scamper through the brush, his nose reading the ground like an issue of *American Hunting Magazine*.

Located on a hill between Chief Waters' Paradise Valley estate and Jake and Jessie's Double J Ranch, the five-acre spread had a small, two bedroom stone cottage with a big wood stove, wide plank wood floors, and drop beam ceilings. A picturesque, old barn stood by the river, drinking water came from a well, and the secluded location made the property defensible. Fruit trees shaded the house, a section of woodland on the other side of the river sheltered wildlife, and open land provided space for a huge survival garden.

"It's what I've been dreaming of my whole life," Liberty said through the tears. "Everything I've ever wanted."

Angelina took her hand and squeezed it. "You deserve it, Liberty. You're a good person, and you've worked so hard to get it."

Molly marveled at her daughter's sweetness.

"I'll teach you to fish right here," Liberty told Angelina, leading her to the edge of the water. She walked to the crest of the hill and pointed beyond the valley below to a distant outcropping of rocks high on a ridge. "That's where I've spent every single Easter my entire life. My parents started taking us to those caves when we were kids. You can see the most spectacular sunrise from there. There's one cave that has a hot spring inside. It's the best kept secret in the area. Actually, I've never met anyone else up there. And the way the morning sun angles into the hot spring cave is spectacular. The walls are lined with crystals and the light strikes them just right so they glitter like a thousand stars. It's a spiritual experience."

"How do you get up there?" Angelina asked.

"I hike. There's a back way to get in there from the west, but from here it'll be much easier." She gestured to the log cabin below on the Dalton land that belonged to Jessie. "If you go due west from there to the backside of the ranch, it's a direct line-of-sight up the mountain. Maybe I can become friends with those ranchers and they'll let me cut through."

If the deal closed, Molly would introduce her to Jake and Jessie. She was sure they would accommodate their new, eccentric neighbor.

"I want this place, O'Malley. Whatever it takes. Write it up. I'll bring the gold."

Molly thought about the gold. "You do realize that you'll need to convert it into good funds for the purchase, right? You can't walk into a closing with sacks of gold."

"Well, we'll have to have a discussion someday about the phrase 'good funds,' the Federal Reserve, and the banksters. But for this piece of heaven, I'll do what it takes."

Molly smiled. "Then let's write up your offer."

They all climbed back into Molly's car and headed to her office.

"What do you love about America most, Liberty?" Angelina asked.

Liberty turned to face her. "This country's founders declared that 'all men are created equal and endowed by their Creator with certain unalienable rights, including life, liberty, and the pursuit of happiness.' In the grand scheme of history, that was huge. Simply huge."

"We learned in school that the government gave us our rights, not God," Angelina said.

Liberty shook her head so hard her beret nearly fell off. "Not true. The role of government is to protect individual rights—not grant them. And the role of the people is to insist the government fulfills its duty. When the government goes astray, like it is now, you have to stand up to it. That's what I do."

"But isn't that scary?" Angelina asked. "I mean, the government is so powerful."

"President Woodrow Wilson said, 'Liberty has never come from the government. Liberty has always come from the subjects of it. The history of liberty is the history of resistance.' I'm a freedom fighter, Castillo. I refuse to surrender to government tyranny."

"But aren't you afraid?" Angelina pressed.

"Yes, but once you decide what you stand for in life, you have to be willing to risk everything for it."

Molly looked at her daughter's face in the rear view mirror and was surprised to see a fierce expression of admiration. Molly had seen Angelina regard only one other person with that look, and that was Rita, another rebel with radical ideas. It was unsettling. Who was her daughter, and how could they be so different from one another? Molly had no desire to stand for anything or defend any cause. She just wanted a life of comfort and safety for her family. It didn't seem too much to ask for, so why did that simple goal always remain beyond her reach?

*   *   *

After Molly and Liberty wrote the contract offer, Molly loaded Angelina and Talisman in the back seat of her car, where they promptly curled up together and fell asleep. It was late.

Molly debated what to do. She still hadn't heard from Steve. Nothing. It had been two days. The anxiety of not knowing seemed worse than facing whatever truth was lurking, so she decided to drive to his house.

She parked and slipped out of the car as quietly as she could. The night was dark and cold, but the houselights were on. Even though Molly had a key, she didn't want to use it. Within moments of knocking, the porch light flipped on and a young boy opened the door.

"Who are you?" His tone was hostile.

"I'm Molly. Who are you?"

"I'm none of your business." He slammed the door shut.

Molly recognized the voice as Kyle's. He appeared to be around ten years old and had Steve's curly blond hair and bright blue eyes.

Molly debated using her key after all, but before she could decide, Steve opened the door. He stepped outside and closed the door behind him.

"You look like hell," she said. It was a lame greeting but was honest. The only other time she had ever seen him look so distressed was when Angelina had gone missing for three days. His eyes reflected the same look of fear and anguish.

He managed a wan smile, slipped his arms around her, and pulled her close. "It's a bad situation, Molly."

She melted into the warmth of him while struggling with the cold sense of dread that settled inside.

Kyle opened the front door. "Go away, lady."

Steve tensed. "Leave us alone for a few minutes."

Kyle stomped his foot. "No!"

Steve released Molly, turned, gently pushed Kyle back and closed the door.

Kyle immediately reopened it.

Steve closed it again and held the doorknob, while Kyle shrieked and fought to pull the door open.

"He told me that he's your son," Molly said.

"I won't have the paternity test results back until tomorrow, but yes I believe he is. I didn't know about him until two days ago."

Molly waited. The porch light began to turn on and off, and the odd strobe effect lent eeriness to the already surreal situation.

Steve exhaled, and his breath became a cloud in the frigid night. "I've told you about Amber."

Amber was Steve's high school sweetheart who had left him a decade earlier for another man.

Molly nodded.

"Well, she showed up out of the blue the other day. Her boyfriend, a drug addict, recently died of AIDS. She has it now and her family has disowned her. She says she was pregnant with my baby when she left me."

Molly's heart skipped a beat. "Kyle."

Steve nodded.

Kyle began kicking the door from the inside.

"Amber's here?"

"She has nowhere else to go, Molly. She's not

responding to the drug cocktail. She's dying."

"Kyle?"

"I'm the only family he'll have when she's gone."

As the full impact of the facts hit Molly, her knees gave way and she reached out to him. With his free arm, he steadied her.

"I was going to wait until I got the test results before letting you know," he said.

"Let me out! Come back in! Make her go or I'll kill her!" Inside, Kyle wailed, kicked the door, and flicked the lights.

"Do you still love her?" Molly asked.

"I've loved her since I was fifteen years old, but that's not what this is about. This is about doing the right thing. I won't let her die alone, and I will assume responsibility for my son."

Molly clutched at straws as tenuous as the clouds of breath floating around them. "What if the test shows he's not your son?"

"Whatever the results, I'll do the right thing."

There was a loud crash inside, and Blondie started barking.

Alarm flashed across Steve's face. "I've got to go before Kyle hurts Blondie. He's very troubled."

Steve quickly stepped back into the house and locked the door behind him. No goodbye, no kiss, no desperately needed assurances.

Dizzy, Molly stumbled toward the car. A strangely familiar cat darted across her path. It looked like Marina Night. Startled, Molly stopped and peered into the shadows beyond the streetlight for a better look.

The cat sat with its luminous eyes fixed on her, and Molly remembered Havana's words.

Spirits, dey say bad blood and a berry bad seed.

CHAPTER SEVEN

Molly met with Charles and Leah Wacker the following morning to discuss the discrimination lawsuit. It was the first time they had spoken together about the situation, and Molly was not looking forward to it.

They requested to meet at Mr. Wacker's health food store, The Back to Eden Tree Hugging Organic Granola Shoppe. A pale young woman who wore the nametag BEGONIA led Molly from the front of the sprawling store to a back office. On the way, Begonia faltered and grasped Molly's arm for support.

"Are you okay?" Molly asked.

Begonia managed a wan smile. "I'm doing a total body detox program right now. I'm just having a cleansing reaction."

She examined the girl whose acne, dull eyes, and sallow complexion made Molly question the wisdom of whatever health regimen she was practicing.

Another employee, a young man whose nametag read ALADDIN, noticed Begonia's distress. "You okay?"

Begonia nodded. "Just a cleansing reaction."

"Oh, I know how that goes. Been throwing up all week myself. That new herbal blend I've been taking to purify my blood takes some getting used to." He grimaced and rubbed his stomach.

Molly hoped there would be no imminent genies popping out of his lamp.

"I heard they pulled Dawn off the register because her

nose was running like a faucet and customers were complaining," Begonia said.

Aladdin nodded. "She quit eating dairy and is having a cleansing reaction."

Molly glanced around at the appearance of the other store employees, and they all looked pretty grim. She decided that even if her own admittedly unhealthy comfort foods ultimately killed her, she would be willing to remain blissfully unaware of her toxic condition until the bitter end.

Begonia waved Molly onward, and together they made a painfully slow journey to the back office.

Charles ran the store, and Leah worked as a psychologist. Their children—Kachina, Athena, and Thor—were wild demon trolls from hell who had driven Molly crazy when she showed the family homes. She knew that no member of the family was inclined to play by society's rules, which made the lawsuit they were facing together a daunting prospect.

Charles and Leah were New Age retro hippies whose clothes were psychedelic and whose feel-good drugs were prescription. Today, from their glowing countenances, Molly could tell they were well-medicated. She was grateful because when they weren't so happy, they behaved like brutish tyrants.

"Welcome to our nest away from the tree," Leah said in greeting. "Our bean bag is your bean bag." She gestured to a huge pink blob with tentacles. It looked like a giant jellyfish.

Dressed in a short skirt and high heels, Molly tried to ease down into the chair as best she could.

Charles sat cross-legged on the floor behind a table made from a giant slab of tree trunk. Leah lounged on a futon next to him. In one corner of the office, water flowed from the nipples of a mermaid fountain. A nearby three-foot erect-penis incense burner had patchouli-scented smoke rising from its head, and a lava lamp burped colorful goo. A chubby white cat perched on a high ledge above a large gurgling aquarium. Molly didn't notice any fish in the tank and made the obvious correlation.

"Did the cat eat the fish?" Molly asked.

A look of horror flashed across Leah's face. "No! We're converting her into a vegetarian."

"If she would only stop eating the mice, we'd be further along in that process," Charles added.

"We recently adopted Serenity from the shelter," Leah said. "She's pregnant and no one wanted her."

Molly was surprised by their uncharacteristic generosity.

"I'm going to conduct an experiment on the psychological effects of cat birthing tanks," Leah said. "I plan to write a book."

Alarmed, Molly's eyes flew to Serenity and the giant aquarium. Serenity's expression did not look at all serene, and her tail swished back and forth peevishly.

Molly decided she would tell Robin about the situation and see if he'd be willing to use his gifts to rescue the poor cat and find her a decent home. "About the lawsuit—"

"We have nothing to worry about because we're innocent." Leah flapped her arms for emphasis, and her voluminous tie-dyed sleeves made her look like a psychedelic duck.

"Yes, but we have to mount a defense," Molly said.

"No, we don't," Charles said. "We don't acknowledge negativity and certainly won't give it power by engaging it."

"*The Course in Miracles* teaches that evil does not exist and is only real if you believe in it," Leah said. "Ergo, evil is an illusion that must be overcome by right thinking."

Molly struggled to make sense of her bizarre logic. "Please understand that the consequences of this for all of us could be dreadful. My boss and I—"

"You and your boss have insurance to cover your losses," Charles said.

"Our insurance doesn't cover this sort of thing."

"You and your boss need to adopt a positive mantra," Leah said. "We've been using, 'We are light. Light dispels the night.' If we all say it in unity, we shall prevail."

Together, as if on cue, Leah and Charles began chanting, "We are light. Light dispels the night. We are light. Light dispels the night."

"Come on, Molly," Charles said. "You must join us. We must be in harmony. We are light. Light dispels the night."

"Serenity, you join us too," Leah said. "Your attitude hasn't been very positive lately either."

Both Molly and Serenity just stared at them.

After a few minutes, Charles and Leah stopped chanting.

"You and your boss should do a cleanse. It'll raise your energy." Charles stood and grabbed a large plastic jar off a shelf. "Ten types of fiber and twenty-five special detox herbs. Coffee enemas and wheatgrass suppositories will help too. And, of course, a high colonic using twenty gallons of warm water will flush all that negativity right down the drain." He handed the jar to Molly.

The label on the container said FLUSH WITH SUCCESS. As Molly stared at it, the desperation she felt reached critical mass. Her money, career, and very freedom were on the line, and the only things they could respond with were crazy chants and bowel hygiene? Adrenaline surged, and she threw the jar across the room. It landed inside the birthing tank, where the cap popped off, and the water filled with gelatinous glop.

Leah's hand flew to her mouth, and she regarded the tank with an expression of horror.

Charles scratched his head and looked at the mess with confusion.

It appeared to Molly as if Serenity smiled.

Molly struggled to escape the clutch of the bean bag chair. "What's *wrong* with you two? This lawsuit isn't just going to go away if you *ignore* it. We could all go to *jail*. What will happen to our *children*? We have to work together in the courts, not have a Kumbaya-fest in the bathroom."

Leah gasped.

"We are light? Light dispels the night?" Charles asked.

"We are light. Light dispels the night," Leah said. She scrambled to her feet and rushed into her husband's arms.

The blood drained from Molly's face. What had she done? She couldn't afford to alienate them. Her mind raced as she tried to think of a way to backpedal.

Charles and Leah shared hushed whispers, then Charles grabbed another jar off the shelf and thrust it in Molly's hand. "This is Jolly Juice, my own special home brew," he said. "It's a fermented blend of kava kava, valerian, and catnip. It'll make you feel really groovy."

Leah fumbled in her pocket, pulled out a prescription bottle, and slapped it into Molly's other hand. "You really do need to lighten up, or you're going to ruin everything for all of us."

"*Me?* I'm going to ruin everything for us?" Molly resisted the urge to hurl the gifts in their faces. Instead, her fists clutched the items, she stormed out of the store, and marched to her car. Once inside, she sat for a long time and tried to still her violent trembling. How could she successfully defend herself against the charges when her co-defendants were idiotic fools? Taking a deep breath, she fought back insistent tears. All her life she had tried to do everything right, but the Fates never seemed to smile on her. The situation with the Wackers, Angelina's inexplicable anger toward her, the looming threat from the gangs, and the unsettling situation with Steve were dragging her down into such a dark place that she could no longer see light.

The stress of it all seemed beyond her ability to bear.

She looked at the bottle of Xanax Leah had given her. After Val's death, Molly's doctor had urged her to take the anti-anxiety drug—and even written a prescription for this very same strength—but she refused. Drugs had destroyed the lives of too many people she loved and created in her an extreme distaste for them, legal or otherwise.

The longer she sat there, the worse her panic attack grew. Every possible horrible outcome to her multiple, dire life situations threatened to suck her into a pit from which she imagined no escape. After a half hour of frantically flailing about in the quicksand, she decided to take a Xanax, and washed it down with the only thing on hand—the bottle of Jolly Juice.

*   *   *

By the time Molly returned to the office, she was glad she had taken a happy pill and drank the Jolly Juice because she no longer cared about anything. It was such a relief.

Robin gave her a quizzical look when she walked in. "Well, now. I would have thought you'd be a mess, but you're smiling."

Molly shook the bottle of pills in his face. "All my life I've resisted taking drugs, but today this probably kept me from committing hippiecide."

Robin read the label, shook his head, and held out an open hand.

Reluctantly, Molly surrendered the bottle.

"I'll pour them down the loo," he said.

"What is it today with all you people and toilets?" She giggled and plopped down into her desk chair. "So, what'd I miss so far this morning?"

"Your friend Rose called. She fancied my accent and so told me the story of her life, including all about how well her romantic supper went last night with her new fella Percy, and how now her dead husband's spirit has shown up on her porch and won't go home. She wants you to fix it."

Molly snorted. "Of *course* she wants me to fix it. Um. Fix what?"

"It seems Percy's dog, a very handsome hound named Rex, was waiting for her when she got up this morning and won't budge. Neither she nor Percy have a clue how he got there or why he doesn't want to leave. She's sure it's the reincarnation of her dear late husband, Gilbert, and is in a tizzy about it all. Rose is convinced that Gilbert doesn't want her and Percy to be together."

"Bummer. They're *such* a cute couple too. Incredibly old, but cute." She pointed an unsteady finger at Robin. "And, speaking of cute, have I ever mentioned that you are the total shock and awe of cute?"

He smiled his charming smile and deftly changed the subject. "Rose, Percy, Rex?"

Molly slapped her desk. "Right! Um. So, how'm I supposed to fix it?"

"What if Rex accompanies Tali to the pet psychic? We can find out if Rex is indeed Gilbert, or just a hound named Rex."

Molly was glad she hired Robin. "You're *so* the best assistant I've ever had."

"I'm the only assistant you've ever had."

Molly thought that was hysterically funny and laughed so hard she got the hiccups.

Robin picked up the bottle of Xanax and read the label

again. "Molly, I think these are just supposed to relax you. You seem to be having a bit of an odd reaction."

"Well, I did wash the pill down with a home-brewed bottle of Jolly Juice."

"Right. Okay then. Time for coffee." He stood to get it for her, but she stopped him.

"No, no. I should probably move around a bit 'cause I'm feeling *really* relaxed. Sit. Stay. Down boy." Pet psychic. Dead husbands reincarnated as dogs. Hippy dippy wackmobile clients. She lived in an utter loony bin. No wonder she was losing it.

Unsteadily, she got to her feet and headed for the coffee room. On the way, she noticed a small group of brokers huddled around the mailboxes, whispering amongst themselves. Molly instantly decided they must be gossiping about her because that's what they'd been doing ever since she came onboard. From her early days as a rookie, the old-timers had picked on her; they had resented her quick success and she had never been able to win their approval. Fueled by righteous indignation, Xanax, and Jolly Juice, she marched right up to the women, ready to do battle.

Coco greeted her by holding up a brochure and shaking it in her face. "Have you seen what Brooklyn put in our mailboxes?"

Molly was so relieved that they were upset with Brooklyn instead of her she fought back the sudden urge to weep. It would be so wonderful if they found someone else to hate.

"Are you crying?" Coco asked.

Molly blinked away tears. "No, not at all. Not me. Nope." She reached into her mailbox for Brooklyn's brochure. It was a product catalog called *Lust Ladies: Products for Passionate Women*. Inside were pages of sex toys, glow-in-the-dark condoms, naughty costumes, and personal lubricants in a variety of flavors. A small sample of Joy Jelly was included with the brochure. The package said it was designed for "the discriminating palate."

Molly tried to hide her amusement but wasn't successful.

"Are you laughing?" Coco asked.

Molly's titter turned into a roar, tears began to flow again, and all she could do was nod.

"Well, I don't think it's funny at all," Lois said. "This is just so evil. What would Jesus think?"

On the back of the brochure was an invitation to a private Lust Lady party at Brooklyn's house.

Jessie tapped her invitation. "I've been to parties like this. They're like Tupperware parties with a special twist. They're a hoot."

Molly always did like Jessie.

"Lord have mercy," Coco said.

Lois emitted a shriek and pointed to a photo of a complex penile contraption with multiple projections and vibrating capabilities. "It's demonic."

Paula Parry, known for being generally paranoid, shook her head. "This is obviously an attempt to entrap us in a vice sting."

Jessie read the disclaimer on the back to them. "'Lust Ladies is a proud member in good standing of AHPA, the Adult Home Party Association, and subscribes to a specific Code of Ethics for best practices in customer service, ethical conduct, and professionalism.'"

Molly's eyes caught an interesting item in the catalog. "I wouldn't mind playing solitaire with this pack of cards featuring naked men who have giant penises." Startled, she looked up. Had she actually said that out loud?

"How could Brooklyn invite us to something so tawdry?" Coco asked.

Molly read the invitation. "She thinks it would be a good bonding experience for the women of Broker's

Best."

"It is a billion dollar industry, you know," Jessie said. "My friend, Tammy, is a rep for the Naughty Babes Club and makes more money than any of you do."

That silenced the women for a moment.

Molly was fascinated by the fine print in the invitation. "The food menu includes Better Than Sex Cake, which apparently is a big, gooey, sinful mess. There'll be a pickle tray with various sizes to appeal to every taste. Um, Wieners and Balls, which are cocktail sausages and meatballs in sauce. Oh, and anatomically correct gingerbread people. Beverages will include Sex on the Beach, Slow Comfortable Screw up Against the Wall, and Screaming Orgasms."

Coco paled to a shade that made her look practically Caucasian. Lois leaned up against the wall and screamed, which caused Paula to reach into her pocket and withdraw the small Derringer she always carried.

Molly wondered who or what she was considering shooting.

Coco threw her brochure in the trash on top of a pile of others that had been discarded. "Well, I think Brooklyn Green should just go do this and leave real estate to the professionals." She stomped off in a huff.

Lois and Paula tossed their brochures and followed Coco.

After a moment, Jessie held up her foil package of Joy Jelly. "Mine's cherry."

Molly examined hers. "Mine's passion fruit."

Jessie winked.

They both raided the trash can hunting for a variety of flavors designed to appeal to the most discriminating of palates.

*   *   *

Molly awoke in her own bed, her head throbbing. The room was dark, but light sneaked through from the edges of the closed shades. She jumped when someone took her hand, and her eyes struggled to focus. "Omigod, Steve, you scared the hell out of me."

"Sorry. Are you okay? I called your office and Jessie said you and Robin left before lunch. So, I called your cell and Robin answered. He said you had taken ill and were here."

Molly struggled to sit up and remember what happened. "Well, there was the Xanax and Jolly Juice, and then I remember telling Robin about the Joy Jelly. That's when he brought me home and tucked me in. He must have taken my phone with him so he could field my calls. He's such a good assistant." The clock by her bed said 2:12 PM.

Steve didn't say anything.

Molly's smile was embarrassed. "If I were you, I'd be asking a lot of questions."

"Molly...."

Her fuzzy vision was clearing, but something about his face didn't look right. She turned on the lamp and gasped when she saw the ugly raised purple bruise high on his left cheek. "What happened?"

He hesitated. "Kyle hit me with a baseball bat. I saw it coming and almost dodged it, but not quite."

Molly didn't know how to respond. A bad seed indeed.

He squeezed her hand. "The paternity test came back. He is my son."

Molly wasn't surprised. She reached out to his face and her fingers caressed him. "You can't keep him, Steve."

His jaw clenched. "What would you have me do, Molly? Take him to the pound?"

Her fingers recoiled at his sharp tone. Her other hand

withdrew from his.

Steve groaned. "When Amber and Kyle first showed up on my doorstep, this little movie played out in my head. I saw all of us blending into a family. Kyle and Angel developing a relationship that would sustain him after his mother died. You and Amber getting to know one another—I even imagined you becoming friends. Amber would die in peace knowing her son would be raised by a good woman."

"You do understand that isn't going to happen?" Molly could never risk the safety of Angelina or Talisman in the presence of a bat-wielding monster child.

"Yes, Molly, I do understand that."

His tone was harsh and that offended her. How could he expect anything else?

She sighed. "So, what do we do now?"

"I guess I divide my time as best as possible between my two families."

Molly's mind and heart rebelled. "You want me to share you with another woman and her child?"

"It's not like I'm having sex with her."

"But you're sharing your heart with her. You've been in love with her for twenty years. She's living in your house. She's the mother of your son. You do realize that makes me the classic other woman."

"Don't be ridiculous."

Her Irish temper performed a nasty jig. "Don't you *dare* call me ridiculous. I was going to give you custody of Angel if something happened to me. You promised me that we were a family and everything would be okay. How do I explain this to Angel? You, me, our crazy dogs…this is the first real family she has ever had."

"Life throws us curve balls and we need to learn how to—"

"Dodge baseball bats?"

"What do you want me to do?"

Molly's internal dance was wild and she couldn't control it. "I want you to give me your key to my house. I want you to go take care of your real family. You can check back with us down the road if and when things change." She pushed him out of the way, scrambled from the bed, and grabbed her keys off the dresser. Despite her shaking hand, she managed to take Steve's house key off her chain and throw it at him.

He looked at her with an expression of infinite sadness. "But I love you."

"I love you too, Steve, but sometimes love just isn't enough." *What am I doing?*

"Molly?"

"Go now." Before I change my mind.

As if in slow motion, Steve set the key on Molly's nightstand and walked out of her life.

*   *   *

Robin brought Angelina home from school. They arrived within minutes of Steve's departure.

Angelina and Talisman bounced into the house together, and Robin followed.

"I saw Steve, but he ignored me when I waved," Angelina said.

Molly struggled to hide her trembling and fought to hold back tears. She cleared her throat and tried to reply, but it came out as a croak.

"You still feeling poorly?" Robin said.

She nodded.

He took off his suit jacket and hung it over the back of a chair in the living room, then walked into the kitchen. "Everyone sit down at the table, and I'll set out some milk and biscuits. A little nourishment might help." He rummaged through the pantry, pulling out boxes of cookies.

Molly and Angelina sat at the kitchen table, while Talisman sat on the floor between them looking expectant.

Robin placed a platter of Oreos and Fig Newtons in the middle of the table, poured three glasses of milk, and sat down with them. But not before giving Talisman a special biscuit of her own.

Molly noticed Talisman's neck scarf was different than the one she had started the day wearing. It now said VAL IS MY CO-PILOT. "I see Tali changed clothes."

"Toby dropped it off at the office this afternoon," Robin said. "He made it for her himself."

"So you saw Toby. How did that go?"

"He brought me a rose."

Molly smiled. "The message on Tali's scarf does seem appropriate for her visit to the pet psychic this afternoon."

"Do you want me to go with?" Robin asked.

Relief flooded Molly. She really wasn't feeling at all well. "Yes. Actually, that would be great."

"I made arrangements to take Rex along. We can pick him up on the way."

"Is he still on Rose's porch?"

Robin nodded. "And she's still in a total tizzy about it."

"Couldn't you just use your gift and talk to Tali and Rex, instead of us hauling them into Dr. Joe's office?"

"At this stage of the game, I think it's best if Tali sees the person she already has a relationship with."

"Why didn't Steve wave at me?" Angelina asked. "Blondie barked hello to Tali. He looked right at me and looked mad."

Molly didn't want to talk about it but knew she had to. "Something bad happened between us."

Angelina's Oreo paused above the glass of milk. "What?"

How did Molly explain dying ex-girlfriends and

homicidal little boys? "Steve and I broke up." The less said the better.

Angelina's eyes grew wide. "Forever?"

Molly didn't want to give her false hope. "I believe so."

"Why?"

Molly struggled. "Someone moved in with him who I think would be dangerous for you to be around. I did it because I love you, Angel."

Angelina's face paled, and she threw the cookie across the room. "I hate you. I hate you *so much*." She ran out of the room, Talisman close on her heels.

"Why won't she understand I do everything I do because I love her?" Molly asked Robin.

"That's an awful big responsibility to put on a little girl's shoulders, don't you think?"

Molly was startled. "What do you mean?"

"Think about it, love. Just think about it."

*　　*　　*

Dr. Joseph McNeill was an internationally famous animal communicator with three best-selling books on the subject. Talisman had been one of his clients for years, but this was the first time Molly had taken her to visit him. Molly's only previous experiences with psychics had been Havana, Robin, and Rowan, so she had definite preconceived ideas. However, nothing about this psychic was what she expected.

His office was on the third floor of a new bank building in downtown Blackstone. Molly, Robin, Talisman, and Rex took the elevator. Angelina, too upset to come, had stayed behind with Rose.

A receptionist greeted and escorted them to a waiting room. The floor was wood, the couches were leather, and the artwork was elegant. No, not at all what Molly had expected.

"What kind of doctor is he?" Robin asked Molly.

"A veterinarian with an advanced degree in animal behavior."

Robin shook his head. "Sounds more like a doggy psychiatrist than psychic to me. When you see him, be careful what you say. Don't give him anything to work with."

"Skeptical much?"

"There are lots of pretenders around. It's unforgivable to prey on people like that."

When Dr. Joe entered the waiting room, Talisman was giddy. She shimmied her tailless bottom and leapt with joy. He knelt and gave her a big hug followed by a gentle kiss on the nose. "Miss Tali, how's my pretty girl?"

She uttered a tiny squeal and licked his nose.

Molly laughed at Talisman's shamelessness.

Dr. Joe stood and greeted Rex by extending his hand to him. "Shake?"

Rex shook it.

Only then did the doctor greet the people in the room. He was around forty years old and wore slacks, a shirt, and a tie. Molly liked his smile.

"I'm so sorry to hear about Val," Dr. Joe said.

Molly nodded. "He left Tali to me."

"Well, I imagine she and I have a lot to talk about today. And what about Rex? What does he need to discuss?"

Molly glanced at Robin.

Robin said, "He's having an identity crisis. We just want to know who he really is."

Dr. Joe studied the dogs. "Okay. Since we're squeezing him in on Tali's time, and his issue sounds pretty simple, I'll take Tali first and then come get Rex for the last ten minutes of her session."

Talisman snorted.

Dr. Joe shook his head. "She's not happy with that. Quite the princess, isn't she?" He took her leash from Molly, and Talisman trotted after him.

"I imagine finding a human who speaks your own language must be pretty heady stuff for a dog," Molly said.

Robin raised an eyebrow. "We'll see."

Molly and Robin sat down together on the leather couch. She thought about what a roller-coaster week it had been. "You've only been on the job for a few days and have had quite an adventure so far. I imagine it wasn't what you expected."

"Actually, I did have an idea of what it would be like," he said.

His gift. "And you signed on anyway? You're such a daredevil."

"There was a method to my madness."

She looked at him. "And that would be?"

"I'm on a mission."

Molly waited, hoping he would explain, but the mystery remained.

*   *   *

Dr. Joe and Talisman returned to the waiting room twenty minutes later. The doctor sat down on the couch with Molly and Robin. "Tali misses Val horribly. Val and Peter took Tali from her mother when she was eight weeks old, then Peter died, and now Val. That's a lot of loss for anyone to process. And even though Val visits her sometimes in spirit and has been helping her try to make the adjustment, her heart is shattered. Also, she's extremely upset about another relationship she wants that she can't have."

Molly nodded. "That would be with Chance."

"I tried to explain to her that she can't have everything

she wants in life, but that's a concept she just can't wrap her hypothetical tail around."

Talisman sighed.

"She's also distraught about the problems you and your daughter are having with one another. It upsets her to see you two at odds, and she desperately wants peace in the family."

Molly hadn't told Dr. Joe that she had a daughter. His skill impressed her.

"What can I do to help her?" Molly asked.

"I remember that Val used to take her for regularly scheduled play dates with her sister who lives on a ranch near here. Have you ever taken her?"

Molly shook her head. "Val left a list of things like that he wanted us to do for her, but it's been a crazy time and we haven't gotten around to it yet."

"I think you should do it soon. It would help. No one gives much thought to a dog's feelings about family ties. They're with their mother and siblings from the time of conception until they're suddenly taken away to go live with strangers. It's a complete change of pack. And now Tali's suddenly part of another brand new pack. It would help to allow her to reconnect with her roots."

"All right." On one hand it seemed a bit silly to Molly, but on the other it made perfect sense.

Dr. Joe stood and took Rex's lead. "Let's see what's going on with this guy."

Rex barked and pawed at him.

"What?" Dr. Joe asked.

Rex barked again.

Dr. Joe sat back down. "Okay, let's just do it here. Who are you Rex, and what do you want to say?"

Doctor and dog stared at each other in silence for a few minutes.

"I see," Dr. Joe said. He turned to Molly and Robin. "Rex is a dog and not a person, despite accusations to the contrary. He feels an intense urge to protect someone and keep her safe. His human has strong feelings for this woman, and Rex wants to be sure everything works out for everyone."

Molly was so impressed she almost fell off the couch. "Can you tell Rex that what he's doing is upsetting the woman, and it would be best for him not to be so intense?"

"He heard you. They can understand us just fine. It's just that not many of us can understand them." He turned to Rex. "So?"

It was Rex's turn to sigh.

Dr. Joe gave him a hearty pat. "Good boy." He smiled at Molly. "He said he'd lighten up."

After a lot of handshaking, pawshaking, and canine kissing, Molly paid the hefty bill.

"The doctor is the real deal," Robin said as he drove them home.

Molly shook her head. "I am totally blown away."

"Miracles are everywhere if you just have the eyes to see. It's a mystical, magical world where fairy tales do come true."

"The thing about fairy tales, Robin, is that they are supposed to have happy endings. Mine never do."

He glanced at her. "Perhaps the answer lies in changing your definition of happiness."

Molly had no clue how to do that.

*   *   *

Every night Angelina tucked Talisman into bed beside her, where the pampered dog would fall asleep with her head on the pillow. Thrilled with the bond that the two girls were forging, Molly had come to accept that she was never going to be terribly important to Talisman. And that was okay.

So, Molly was surprised to wake up in the middle of the night to find Talisman lying next to her, her head sharing Molly's pillow. Talisman's bright blue eyes stared at her intently in the dim light, and her nose—inches from Molly's face—twitched and quivered.

Molly reached out to touch her. "What is it, Tali?"

Talisman uttered a guttural sound.

Alarm shot through Molly, and she scrambled from her bed to check on Angelina.

Angelina was snug under the covers with no sign of trouble, so Molly closed her daughter's door and returned to her own room.

Molly crawled back into bed next to Talisman. "Are you sick?"

Talisman whimpered.

Molly sat up and urged Talisman to sit as well. She ran her hands over her, looking for something wrong.

Talisman pressed her forehead into Molly's chest.

Molly could find nothing obviously wrong her. Talisman's nose was cold and wet, her eyes were clear, and there appeared to be no pain. "What is it, Tali?"

Talisman whined.

Molly patted her.

Talisman trembled and pressed her forehead into her harder.

"What can I do?"

Talisman pulled away, threw her head back, and howled.

Molly suddenly understood. She didn't need to be psychic to recognize that Talisman was howling for her lost packs. She didn't need to have any special gifts to see the anguish in Talisman's eyes.

Molly pulled Talisman closer, wrapped her arms around her, and gently rocked. "I know, Tali. I'm sad too. I want Val back. I want Steve. I know. Is that why you've come to me? Did you know I'm feeling the same way?"

Molly marveled at the capacity to love that humans and dogs shared. From the time the two species had found each other in the dark shadows of history, it was this shared quality that forged their special bond.

Talisman relaxed and surrendered to Molly, while Molly's tears joined Talisman's whimpering. Their two broken hearts merged in search of healing, and they comforted each other until the morning sun chased away the night.

CHAPTER EIGHT

Talisman's scarf of the day said MY HEART IS MY MOST BEAUTIFUL PART. Molly had picked it out for her.

When Molly arrived for work her eyes were red and puffy, and Robin greeted her with an expression of concern. He stood up from his desk, helped her off with her coat, and gave her a hug. "I'm sorry you're hurting," he whispered in her ear.

Molly appreciated his compassion.

A man cleared his throat, and Molly disentangled herself from Robin's arms to see Jake standing in the doorway. "When you have a moment," he said before returning to his office.

Robin handed her a cup of Starbucks coffee that was waiting for her on her desk, and she walked across the hall.

"Close the door," Jake said. His manner was unusually gruff.

Molly did so and took a seat across from him. She hoped he was upset about what he had just witnessed, instead of some more bad news.

"I see your new assistant is making himself right at home. How does your boyfriend feel about that?"

Jake's behavior was so typically male that it almost made Molly smile. "Steve and I broke up yesterday."

"Didn't like the other man in your life, huh?"

"Actually, I didn't like the other woman."

That knocked Jake off his horse, and he stumbled for a

few moments. Then—like a good cowboy—he quickly recovered. "Well, I imagine your new assistant will make the most out of your bad situation."

Molly took a sip of her coffee. It was good. Robin really did know how to take care of her, but she pushed away the catty urge to say so. "Was there some *business* you wanted to discuss?"

Jake just stared at her for a few minutes. Molly was unnerved by his silence and apparent struggle to say what was on his mind. Finally, he said, "I'm sorry for how hard everything has been for you. You're a good woman and deserve better."

"Yes, and in our relationship I deserved better too." They had broken up when she found him in bed with Lily, and in all this time they had never discussed it.

"Yes, you did," he said.

She waited for more.

"How did your meeting with the Wackers go yesterday?" he asked.

Molly took another sip of coffee before responding, swallowing with it the disappointment she felt at his change in topic. It seemed they would never really achieve closure. "The Wackers aren't going to cooperate. It's all just going to go away because they have good internal hygiene and a positive mantra."

"Well, depositions will begin soon, and if they don't show up for theirs, they'll be in contempt of court. Ignoring it will just get them fined and/or arrested."

"I realize Lily hates me, Jake, but why put everyone through all this just to get back at me?"

He shook his head. "Don't take it so personally. This is way more complex than it appears. It's possible that I could lose my license too. If that happens, every other agent in this office will have to find somewhere else to work. Guess what agency most of them will end up at?"

The only other large real estate company in town was

Lily's.

Molly was shocked. "I didn't realize that you could get into trouble."

"Because you're a rookie, I'm legally obligated to provide close supervision—which makes what you do my responsibility. And Lily? She went straight for the weak link. If that chain snaps, we all go down."

Molly hung her head. Thankfully, she had drained her tear bucket hours ago or there would have been a flood. "Is there any hope, Jake?"

"There's always hope."

"Are you scared?"

"Only a damn fool wouldn't be scared."

*   *   *

Liberty's offer to purchase her dream home was accepted, and Molly wanted to deliver the good news and signed contract to her personally. Besides, she needed to get out of the office. She found the fate of all of her Broker's Best colleagues resting on her shoulders to be an overwhelming concept to assimilate. So, she grabbed her file and practically ran out of the building.

The roads surrounding the college were packed with cars and it took longer than expected for Molly to arrive at Liberty's office. She parked between news vans from CNN and Fox News and was curious about what was happening on campus. Everyone seemed to be migrating to the plaza outside the auditorium, but she didn't take the time to follow them. Instead, she wove through the crowd toward the history building where she found Liberty in her office, sitting on the floor in the middle of dozens of handmade protest signs.

In greeting, Liberty thrust a placard that said DEMOCRACY DIES IN IGNORANCE! into Molly's free hand. "Congressman Spearing is here today to give a speech. Members of the Resistance are here to tell him what we really think. You should join us."

It had been a rough week, and Molly didn't want to play. "I can't stay for the rally, I just came by to let you know they accepted your offer and to deliver the signed contract."

Liberty leapt to her feet and snatched the papers from Molly. "Hallelujah! Woo-hoo!" She danced around the room, leaping and pirouetting quite gracefully for a woman wearing combat boots. She even belted out a chorus of "The Battle Hymn of the Republic."

Ross, who had been sleeping on the couch, managed to wake up and seem mildly enthused for a few moments before he yawned and promptly fell back to sleep.

Breathless, Liberty finally collapsed in the chair behind her desk. "Thank you, O'Malley. I've never been this happy. Ever."

Molly loved it when her clients were happy.

Liberty waved to the couch. "Sit. We need to talk."

Still holding the sign, Molly took a seat next to Ross, who was already snoring like a tuba-playing chainsaw.

"You love your daughter, this I know," Liberty said.

Molly nodded. "More than anything in the world."

"So, why don't you care what kind of a world she's going to grow up in?"

"Excuse me?"

"You have to do more for her than you're doing." There was an unusual tenderness in Liberty's voice. "We live under a system of government that's supposed to be by the people, for the people. If the people don't get involved, don't participate in that government, then they surrender their lives and the lives of their loved ones to the control of others."

Molly was irritated. "I do the best I can."

"No, you don't."

Molly tossed the protest sign on the pile of others with

a little more flourish than intended.

Liberty sat back in her chair and leveled her with assessing eyes. "They're gutting education, O'Malley. Whitewashing history, banning books, stripping students of their rights—and that's just the tip of the fascist iceberg." She leaned forward, her voice sharpening. "They don't want kids to think critically. They don't want them to question authority. That's why they're censoring discussions about race, gender, and even basic history. They're rewriting the past to control the future." She uttered a bitter laugh. "They've turned teachers into the enemy. Criminalizing us for teaching facts. Pushing laws that let parents sue if they don't like what we say in class. Hell, they want kids to report on their teachers like we're living in some dystopian police state."

Molly had no idea this was happening. "But why?"

Liberty's eyes darkened. "An ignorant population is easier to control. That's the goal. Starve the schools, silence the teachers, and keep kids too uninformed to fight back. But we can fight back. Please join us today. Stand up for your daughter's future."

Emotionally, Molly's stress level was in orbit. But she loved Angelina more than anything in the world, and there wasn't anything she wouldn't do for her. "Okay, Liberty. I'll do it for Angel."

Liberty gave a loud war whoop. "That's my girl, O'Malley. We'll make a freedom fighter out of you yet. And maybe a time will come when you won't do it just for Angel, but for America too."

There was a knock on Liberty's open door. The man standing in the doorway didn't look happy. "I'd like to talk with you, Liberty."

"So talk, Warner."

"Alone."

Liberty cocked her head. "This is my friend Molly O'Malley, and you can talk to me in front of her.

O'Malley, this is my department head, Dr. Warner."

He cleared his throat and straightened his tie.

Molly stood. "Do you want to sit here?"

He ignored her, so she sat back down.

"There have been some complaints from your students about you again, Liberty."

She smiled.

"Is it true that you're offering extra credit to those who attend today's rally?"

"Absolutely."

"Those who don't want to attend, who have no desire to protest, feel as if they're being compelled," he said.

"They don't have to go."

"Then they are at a disadvantage in their grade."

Liberty shook her head. "They don't have to protest anything. It would just be good for them to see democracy in action."

"You really shouldn't be attending this rally yourself. We don't like our professors to engage in controversy."

"This is America."

Dr. Warner sighed and shuffled his feet. "The federal government has started withholding funding from universities that speak up against its new policies."

"You sound scared," Liberty said.

He fiddled with his tie, his expression grim. "The majority of your students like you, Liberty. Adore you, really. But the faction who find your eccentricities offensive? They have friends—and family—in high places. As you know, we're one of the most prestigious universities in the state, and many government officials send their children here. We are...quite concerned."

"Your concern is noted."

He walked away without another word.

Liberty looked at Molly and said, "'To avoid criticism, do nothing, say nothing, be nothing.' I may be many things, O'Malley, but nothing ain't one of them."

*   *   *

Molly stayed for an hour of the rally. Surprisingly, she found it invigorating. She didn't know if her participation had made the slightest difference in influencing the course of the country, but there was a sense of satisfaction in the effort. As she left, Liberty was being interviewed by the media. Molly imagined that Dr. Warner wasn't going to be happy.

She returned the placard to Liberty's office and then walked to the Theater Arts building to see Val's mother. After fifteen minutes of searching, Molly found her backstage in The Matthew D. Klauza Center for the Performing Arts, overseeing the set design on her upcoming production.

Molly hadn't seen Margo since Val's funeral, and she almost didn't recognize her. Grief had eclipsed her beauty, and the transformation was shocking. Margo had always reminded Molly of a Mediterranean goddess. Now her finely chiseled face was gaunt, her olive skin had lost its luster, her normally luminous brown eyes were hollow and vacant—her vibrant spirit was completely shrouded in darkness. How could this have happened in such a short period of time?

"Do you have a few minutes?" Molly asked.

Margo appeared startled to see her. She tucked greasy strands of loose hair up under her black cap and nodded. "Let's go to my office."

They wove through dozens of students hard at work sawing, hammering, and painting.

"What show are you working on?" Molly asked.

"*Guys and Dolls.*" Margo didn't seem excited, which was uncharacteristic. She walked slowly, her perfect dancer's posture gone and her lush figure diminished. Raggedy clothes no longer found curves on which to cling.

Margo's office was just as unkempt as its owner. Papers scattered, trash littered, books languished, and a sour smell hovered.

Margo walked in, closed and locked the door, then removed a pint of vanilla vodka from inside a trophy on her bookshelf. The trophy was one of Val's, awarded to him by The Great Dames Club for his impersonation of Mae West. She sat down at her desk and took a long swig straight from the bottle, then leveled Molly with sad eyes. "It's been awhile."

"Too long. I was here to deliver papers to Liberty and thought I'd drop in."

"What do you think of our Liberty True?"

Molly smiled. "She's eccentric and wonderful. Thank you for referring her to me."

"So, tell the truth. Did the boys send you?"

Molly wasn't a good liar. "Yes. They love you and are worried. They've decided to carry on Val's Friday night movie event tradition and want you to come."

"What's the movie tonight?"

Molly hesitated. "It'll be a 'Gays of Wine and Roses' event."

A sharp, humorless laugh burst from Margo. "A movie about alcoholism...they aren't subtle are they? *They are not long, the days of wine and roses: Out of a misty dream our path emerges for a while, then closes. Within a dream.*" She shook her head. "So, they'll all be there as Jack Lemmon's character Joe Clay—the reformed alcoholic—and I'm the hopeless, drunken wife?"

"Well, they have invited the entire non-smoking, gay men only, Butts Out group of AAers." Molly sighed and tried to think of a positive spin. "You're the only woman they've ever invited to their special closed group. You should be flattered maybe?"

"Would you be?" Margo asked.

"Being loved is never a bad thing."

Margo took another long swing of the vodka and closed her eyes. "I miss him so much."

Molly thought of a myriad of platitudes, but they all seemed so meaningless in the face of the other woman's raw pain. "Last year when Angel went missing, I felt that if she were found dead I wouldn't survive. She's my reason for living. I understand wanting to give up. I really do."

Margo didn't respond.

"Val stayed with me for all three of those hellish days Angel was gone. He held me, bathed me, fed me, and cried with me. I remember that he wouldn't let me succumb to my self-pity. He told me that Angel would want me to be okay. Val would want you to be okay too."

"Well, I'm not."

"I can see that." Molly's mind struggled for something else. Anything else. "Tali saw her pet psychic yesterday. She told Dr. Joe that Val appears to her sometimes and he's trying to help her adjust. I would presume that if he's helping her, he's most certainly trying to help you. Maybe he was the inspiration behind his friends organizing this event tonight."

Margo's expression changed, and a softness crept in. "I was so proud of him when he got sober. He even stayed sober after Peter died, and Val was utterly devastated by that."

"He would be proud of you if you're able to work this out, don't you think? Perhaps he's hanging around until he's sure you and Tali will be okay. Don't you want him to be able to move on?"

Margo's eyes narrowed. "Do you really believe all that spiritual mumbo jumbo?"

Molly hesitated. "I honestly don't know, but I do know that Val did."

There was a long silence.

Finally, Margo said, "If I don't numb the pain, I don't know how I'll survive it. I mean that literally. It will rip me apart from within and I'll die."

"Better to die and just get it over with than do this." Molly was surprised at her own harsh tone. Perhaps it was a natural response to the horrors inflicted on her by her own alcoholic mother. She took a breath and tried again, "A lot of people love you, Margo. Let that be your strength."

Margo set the bottle down, her reluctance obvious.

"Let me take you home, help you get ready for tonight, and then drop you off at Val's house," Molly said. "Please? Please let me help you."

Reluctantly, Margo allowed her to help.

*   *   *

Molly called Robin and asked him to pick up Angelina at school. After Margo was safely delivered to the gays, she swung by Pagan Place.

Angelina and Talisman scrambled into Molly's car, while Robin loaded Angelina's backpack and Talisman's travel bag—Talisman never traveled anywhere without her bag full of bottled water, organic dog food, and special treats.

"Thank you so much," Molly said to Robin. "I appreciate you helping out like this."

"My pleasure. I always enjoy the company of a pretty girl."

Angelina blushed and giggled.

"Do you need me tomorrow?" he asked Molly.

"No thanks. I'm showing the Be-in-Harmony couple some homes and then, hopefully, I'm done for the day. I thought Angel and I could go to a movie or something together."

"That would be a nice thing for you two. I went

through Val's file of Tali instructions today and found her sister, Maddie. She lives on a ranch owned by a Preacher Levi. I rang him and left a message with your office and cell numbers. Hopefully, he'll ring back soon so we can get our furry girl out of the grump."

From the back seat, Talisman managed a perfectly timed sigh.

"Call if you need me for anything," Robin said in parting.

Angelina waved to him as they pulled away. "He is *so* cute."

Angelina's first crush. She was growing up fast.

"You look like you had a good time," Molly said.

"We brought Tyler home from the vet today and got him all settled in. He's going to be okay. He even purred for me."

"I'm so glad."

"Robin told me about what Miss Coco's doing to help people who lose their houses. We want to help her create the foster program for pets of people who lose their homes, you know, until they can find a place where they can have them."

"You and Robin are going to do this?"

Angelina nodded. "And Rowan. And some of their friends. And people who come into the store. The veterinarian next door said he would volunteer some with their doctoring."

"Wow. That's wonderful." Molly considered. "What a nice thing for you to do."

"I don't want anything like what happened to Tyler to happen again."

"What if the people can't come back and get their pets?"

"Then we'll find forever homes for them."

Selfishly, Molly hoped their own home wouldn't become a forever home to an abundance of creatures.

"Did you eat dinner?"

"Rowan's a vegetarian. She made a walnut and brown rice loaf with mushroom gravy and mashed potatoes. It was yummy."

"Sounds yummy." Molly was grateful to Robin and Rowan for Angelina's good mood. It was the most her daughter had spoken to her in a long time. But she rejoiced too soon. Angelina slid into sudden silence, and Molly couldn't get her to open up again.

When they got home, Angelina settled in front of the television and Talisman stretched out on the couch.

Molly fixed herself a ham sandwich and a cup of coffee, then sat down in the living room to eat. She wanted to be close to her daughter, even if the feelings weren't mutual.

"So, what movie would you like to go see tomorrow?" Molly asked.

Angelina pushed buttons on the remote, flipping through channels, and didn't respond.

"Angel?"

"I dunno." She continued to change the channels.

The noise was irritating, and Molly was about to reprimand her when she heard a familiar voice. She glanced at the TV and saw a familiar face. "Stop there," Molly said.

Angelina paused on CNN. "Is that Liberty?"

"Yes. Oh, my goodness. Turn it up."

Liberty was saying, "...I didn't come here today because it's easy. I came because my students, my community, and my country are worth fighting for. I came because our right to pursue an uncensored education is something I will never let the government take away."

Liberty was wearing her trademark patriotic beret and FREEDOM FIGHTER sweatshirt. Her protest sign said THE HISTORY OF LIBERTY IS A HISTORY OF RESISTANCE.

"You can't shut us up. You can't lock us down. We will speak the truth, we will teach the truth, and if you try to stop us, we will rise. No regime has ever succeeded in silencing the voice of the people forever."

The camera momentarily panned down to Ross—proudly dressed in the American flag—and then returned its focus to the interview.

The reporter nodded his head, his expression earnest. "I hear your passion. And you are?"

Molly cringed.

Liberty looked right at the camera and said, "Dr. Liberty True, Professor of History at Blackstone University, and I am a freedom fighter."

"Uh, oh," Molly said.

"Why 'uh, oh?'" Angelina asked.

"Her boss told her not to participate in the rally. She not only did, but now she's famous for it."

"She's brave to speak out."

"Foolish, if you ask me. She could lose her job."

Angelina swung around and glared at Molly. "No! She's *brave*. And Robin was *brave* for going into that house to rescue Tyler. And you're not. You're a *coward*."

Molly caught her breath. "What did you call me?"

Angelia stood up and scrunched her fists at her side. Veins popped out of her forehead, and her voice was shrill. "You wouldn't risk getting in trouble to save a cat's life, and you broke up with Steve because you were afraid, and you told the police you wouldn't go to court about Val's murder because it was too risky. You're a coward, and I'm ashamed of you."

Suddenly, everything fell into place for Molly. Angelina's contempt toward her began around the time she had first told Detective Mendoza that she didn't want to testify against Val's murderers. She didn't know Angelina had overheard that conversation. "I did decide to testify in Val's murder trial." Molly didn't mention that she had offered to only if there was no other choice.

"Why weren't you willing to at first? It was for *Val*."

"I was concerned for your safety, Angel. I was afraid his murderers or their friends would come hurt you if I testified."

Angelina continued to glare at her.

"And about the cat, I was concerned that if I got in trouble I would lose my real estate license for breaking and entering and not be able to support you anymore."

Angelina seemed unmoved.

A sense of helpless arose in Molly. "Steve has a little boy living with him now who is violent, and I am concerned he could hurt you."

"Why didn't you tell me you were arrested?"

Molly paled. "I haven't been arrested, I'm being sued. Where did you hear that?"

"At school."

"I should have told you the facts so you would be prepared for the gossip. I was afraid...I mean, I didn't want to upset you."

Molly's explanations were met with stony silence, which grew like a great impassable mountain rising from the depths of the emotional sea that churned between them. Finally, very softly, Angelina said, "I don't want to be the reason you're a coward."

Angelina called Talisman, and they both disappeared up the stairs into their room. The door slammed shut behind them.

Angelina had been raised in the Latino culture where respect was everything. Now Molly understood that as far as her daughter was concerned, she was nothing at all.

CHAPTER NINE

Molly dropped Angelina and Talisman off at Rose's house for the day. Angelina was silently unrepentant, and Molly was at a loss as to how to handle the situation. Talisman took pity on her and actually gave her a kiss goodbye, which she appreciated. It was better than nothing.

As Molly was preparing to pull away, Rose trotted out to the car and slid into the passenger's seat. "Do you have a moment, dear?"

Molly turned off the engine. "For you, always."

"I want to thank you so much for clearing up the mystery of Rex, but I have another problem now that I need your help with."

Molly waited.

Rose lowered her voice. "It's Percy's Lump. It just lies there. It's very unnerving. And when it does wake up, it's only for about thirty-seven seconds. I also think I may be allergic to it."

Molly was surprised that sexual relations had happened so quickly between Rose and Percy. It seemed out of character. "Um, well there's always Viagra."

"Is that for allergies?"

"Has Percy seen a doctor?"

Rose shook her head. "Why would Percy see a doctor?"

"For his, you know, lump?"

"Oh, you mean a vet. Yes, and supposedly

everything's fine. So, I was hoping you could have the pet psychic talk to Lump for us."

Molly realized they were having a serious case of miscommunication. "What kind of lump are we talking about here?"

"Percy's cat, Lump. The laziest thing I've ever met. Either that, or it's depression. Could you arrange something with the psychic? As I said, it's very unnerving."

Molly began to laugh and gently beat her head against the steering wheel. Finally, when she could talk, she said, "Robin's sister is a pet psychic who specializes in cats. I would guess she's way cheaper than Dr. Joe. I'll ask."

"Thank you, dear."

"And talk to your doctor about your allergies. I'm sure he can prescribe something. Love Percy, love his Lump too."

Rose beamed. "You're so right about that. Have a nice day." With that, she bounced out of the car and into the house. Since Rose and Percy had connected, she had reclaimed a youthful energy. It was delightful to witness.

On the other hand, Molly felt way older than her twenty-nine years.

She started up her car and headed out into traffic.

When she had been a child, she had been her own mother. There was never a period of innocence or nurturing because her drunken mother had been lost in a bottle from her earliest memories. Then came her abandonment at eleven, the eventual incorporation into the Sanchez family, and her ultimate rejection by them. Now here she was, alone again except for a daughter who disrespected her, and everything she'd worked her entire life to achieve was teetering on the edge of annihilation. Yes, she felt very old indeed.

Molly stopped at a light and the black Mustang in the lane on her right caught her attention. Her heart skipped a beat when she realized it was Steve. He was looking away from her at his passenger, a delicately beautiful blonde who was crying. Steve reached to brush away the woman's tears, his hand rested on her cheek, and she reached up to cup it. Molly had never seen a photo of Amber and was unprepared for how lovely she was. Witnessing the tender scene was a shock to her system, and when the light changed and the Mustang sped away, she was paralyzed. An insistent honking behind her finally set her in motion.

She had no choice but to move forward.

*   *   *

When Molly walked into the Broker's Best lobby, Jessie practically pounced on her.

"You *never* told *me* you knew Preacher Levi."

Molly blinked. "Who?"

Jessie made a sound of impatience. "Preacher *Levi*. He called for you a few minutes ago. I took the message, and he said you could bring Tali to his ranch tomorrow. What's that about?"

It took Molly a moment to put the pieces together. "Oh, he owns Tali's sister. Robin was trying to set up a play date between the two dogs."

"Preacher Levi owns Tali's sister? That practically makes you related to him. Oh my God, you are *so* lucky."

Molly had to smile. She hadn't known that the famous cowboy preacher was now a relation.

"He invited you to attend his sermon after you drop off Tali. And there's going to be a barbeque after the service. Please, please, *please* let me go with you."

Molly nodded. "Sure."

"He's so hot—the man of my dreams. Can I call him back and let him know we'll be coming?"

"Knock yourself out. Don't forget to get directions."

Molly headed toward her office.

"Oh, I forgot to tell you that Percy's in there waiting for you." Jessie cocked her head. "Well, at least I think it's Percy."

A distinguished black-haired gentleman was sitting at Robin's desk.

Molly did a double-take. "Percy?"

He looked up with a bashful smile and ran his fingers through his newly dyed hair. "Is it too much?"

Molly struggled to hold back her laughter. All she could do was shake her head.

"Do you think Rose will like it?"

Molly nodded. "But you don't need to change for her, Percy. She's crazy about you."

"I just thought my hair was too...well, white."

"I'm glad you two found each other. It's wonderful to see you both so happy."

"God works in mysterious ways."

She envied him his faith.

Molly glanced at her watch. "Brian and Shannon should be here soon."

Percy removed a file folder from his briefcase. "I just need them to sign these documents so I can issue that prequal letter for when they find their dream house."

"Hopefully, that'll be today." Molly sat at her desk and rifled through papers, organizing her showing instructions for the day. After a few minutes she glanced up to see Percy staring at her.

"Are you okay?" he asked.

She forced a smile. "No, but I'll survive."

"You're in my prayers every day."

Molly didn't put much stock in prayers, but she thanked him anyway.

"A lot of people love you," he added.

She wished that were true.

*   *   *

The house at 69 Wildfire Way had been staged, and it had been staged by someone who knew that sex sells. The dining room table was set for a romantic dinner for two, complete with burning candles and a bottle of champagne in a frosty ice bucket. The kitchen crock pot filled the house with mouth-watering smells of delicately seasoned roast beef, and the whole-house sound system played classic 1960's love songs. A path of rose petals led to the master bedroom where the huge four-poster bed was turned back to reveal black satin sheets. A bath was drawn in the deep, jetted tub, and scented candles perched on every available surface. The place was staged as if the sellers were waiting breathlessly for the showing to end so they could rush back home and commence a romantic evening of dining, dancing, and lust. However, Molly had shown the house before, and this was how it always looked. The clever gambit hadn't inspired her previous clients to jump at the chance to own their own little slice of erotic heaven, but it had only been a matter of time.

Brian and Shannon had no problem making themselves right at home. As the Righteous Brothers crooned "You're My Soul and Inspiration," Shannon gleefully rifled through the sexy lingerie that hung in the master closet: luxurious silk and satin sleepwear, sweet and sassy baby dolls, flirty chemises, and gorgeous corsets and bustiers. She held one of the more erotic items up to herself and performed a seductive dance around the bedroom.

"Oh, I could so live here!" she shouted.

Molly didn't have the heart to point out that the lingerie didn't come with the house.

Brian's laughter was wild. "We'll take it."

Molly wasted no time in writing up the offer, and

within hours the Be-in-Harmony couple had a contract for their own little slice of romantic heaven pie.

*   *   *

Sunday was Talisman's scheduled playdate with her sister, Maddie. Molly was hopeful the visit would lift Talisman's spirits, and even though going to a church service wasn't high on her personal list of favorite things to do, she was glad it provided an opportunity for her to spend the day with Angelina.

Angelina and Rose spent hours on Saturday primping Talisman for the occasion. Her hair was washed and styled, her teeth were brushed, her toenails painted pink, and Rose embroidered a new scarf for her to wear which read I'M QUEEN OF THE SHOW RING.

Molly noticed Talisman's violet-scented hair conditioner as she loaded her into the car on Sunday morning. "Angelina, you do realize that we're taking Tali to a working ranch so she can romp around in the mud with a hardcore cowdog...right?"

Angelina tossed her head. "Tali wanted to look her best to see her sister."

Molly sighed.

So Angelina sighed.

Then Talisman sighed.

Molly didn't want to rain on their parade. "Well, Tali will certainly wow Maddie with her sassy show dog style."

That seemed to appease the girls, and Molly was relieved. She placed Talisman's travel bag in the car, waited until Angelina had secured herself into her seat—she had chosen to ride in back with The Queen—and started the car. They were headed to The Double J Ranch first to pick up Jessie.

The early morning March air was brisk, but the bright

sun and southern winds had melted the snow. Molly hadn't been sure how to dress for Preacher Levi's church service, but she decided on an outfit she used to wear when she was a cocktail waitress at a country western bar in Denver: a simple denim skirt and pearl-button shirt, with a snazzy pair of cowboy boots. She stuffed her long, wild curls up into a white cowboy hat and eschewed lipstick in favor of plain lip gloss. It was the best down-home look she could manage.

Molly had rarely attended church. She had been baptized Catholic, but her mother never took her to Mass. When Molly became part of the Sanchez family, she had occasionally accompanied them to Catholic services. Then Rita's daughter and brother were shot and killed while playing on the front lawn in the shadow of a statue of the Virgin Mary. That was the day Molly had lost her faith.

Her thoughts drifted to Val as she realized he would have been thrilled by her plans to attend a religious service—he had always worried about her lack of spiritual direction. If he was taking notice of her life from the other side, she hoped that he could also see how hard she was trying to be a good mom to Talisman—and she hoped he wouldn't notice what a bad mom she had become to Angelina.

Molly glanced back at her daughter and was surprised to see her biting her fingernails. She had never noticed her doing that before. "Are you nervous about something, Angel?"

Angelina shrugged. "It's just strange to drop Tali off at a ranch for the day. I mean, she's used to being pampered and everything. What if a cow steps on her?"

Molly thought about it. "Well, according to Toby, this has been a monthly event her whole life. Val wouldn't have done anything to put her at risk."

"But Tali's a beauty queen. How come her sister is so

different?"

"Val and Peter thought Tali had what it took to compete in show, so they trained her to do that. If she'd been raised on a ranch, I'm sure her stockdog instincts would have been nurtured and the two girls would be more alike."

Angelina shrugged. "I guess it was nice of Val to make sure Tali and her sister had regular visits."

"Val understood the importance of family." Molly's words were well-chosen. She wished her daughter could grasp hold of the same concept.

*   *   *

The Double J Ranch was a two-hundred-forty-acre spread where Jake and Jessie Dalton raised award-winning horses. Inherited from their late parents, the ranch was located in a lush valley in the foothills above Blackstone. Molly had not been back to The Double J since the day she walked in on Jake and Lily in bed together. The unwelcome emotions that now flowed through her rose like the overflowing banks of the river that ran through these foothills. During Molly's relationship with Jake, he had never denied he still loved his ex-wife, and their relationship didn't prevent him from reconciling with Lily when the opportunity arose. However, Molly wished his short-lived reunion with Lily had been handled with more respect for her own feelings.

She took a deep breath and turned into the driveway, driving past Jake's house to get to Jessie's. Jake's stone and glass house featured many Asian touches that were Lily's brand from their six years together. Jessie, on the other hand, had a rustic log cabin to call her own that was as classic American as it could be. Just like Jessie.

Jessie stood on her porch, dressed cowgirl chic, entirely in hot pink and rhinestones. She ran from the house, hopped into the front passenger seat, and slammed the door shut. "Let's get to gettin'. I've been having wet dreams all week about the preacher."

Molly gave her a horrified look.

Jessie's eyes grew wide and she whipped around to face Angelina. "I'm expecting to be baptized by Preacher Levi, if he's offering them today."

Jessie covertly mouthed the word, *Sorry*, to Molly.

Molly made a U-turn and was dismayed to see Jake step out of his house and walk toward them. Reluctantly, she stopped and rolled down her window.

At the sight of her, he took off his cowboy hat and held it to his heart. "Why, Molly O'Malley, you make a ravishing cowgirl." He reached out and tugged a few red curls from under her hat, letting them fall free to decorate her face.

His electric touch shocked Molly, and she was glad he couldn't hear her rapid heartbeat. "And you've always been a studly cowboy, Jake Dalton,"

Jessie winked at Jake. "No offense big brother, but you don't hold a candle to Preacher Levi. Just sayin'."

"You coming with us?" Angelina asked.

Jake shook his head. "My soul's beyond saving, I'm afraid." He put his hat on and stepped back from the car. "You ladies all have a fine time today. And Jessie, try to behave yourself."

Eager to insulate herself, Molly rolled up the window and sped off in a cloud of dust.

"You goin' to date him again now you and Steve broke up?" Jessie asked.

Molly shook her head. "Electrical burns are painful."

"What you two have is powerful. I'd give anything to experience that even once in my life."

Molly chuckled. "Be careful what you wish for."

They pulled back onto Thundermountain Road and drove past the small home that stood between The

Double J and Paradise Valley. Molly pointed to the SOLD notice on the real estate sign out front. "My client, Liberty True, is going to be your new neighbor."

Jessie's eyes grew wide. "The one with the flag-wearing dog?"

Molly nodded.

"She won't be having militia meetings there, or anything, will she?"

Molly thought about it. "She's expressed nothing but non-violent resistance. But she does have guns."

Jessie shrugged. "We're ranchers. Guns I can deal with. Bombs are a whole different animal."

"Her weapons are words and ideas. She's a wonderful woman."

"That's good enough for me. The world needs all the wonderful women it can get."

"I Googled Preacher Levi and saw a picture of him with a woman they said was his wife," Angelina said.

Jessie nodded. "That was Montana. She was a barrel racer. A few months after she married Levi, she ran off with a rodeo star. Levi was just a rancher then. She broke him hard, so he turned to drink and supposedly it was God who turned him around again. That's when he became a preacher. If you ask me, Montana was just a damn fool. But God healed Levi's heart."

In Molly's mind, it wasn't a matter of God saving a man from a broken heart, but of a man simply trying to attribute meaning to his pain. That was a survival mechanism that Molly understood all too well.

*   *   *

Preacher Levi's 5,000 acre sheep and cattle ranch was called Heavenly Acres, and it was located on the plains east of Blackstone. The farther from the foothills Molly drove to get there, the more magnificent the mountains appeared—it was hard to truly grasp their majesty when one lived nestled in their bosom. She kept looking in her rear-view mirror, astounded at the sight. It caused her to wonder how her own life would appear if she could get far enough away from it. She entertained a brief fantasy of dropping Jessie off at the ranch and driving to some new and distant town where she, Angelina, and Talisman could start life over.

Jessie jabbered the entire trip about how sexy Preacher Levi was, but although Molly had seen him on TV, she really wasn't prepared for his charisma. When they pulled up in front of the ranch house and he stepped outside to greet them, she was startled by his intensity. He was beautiful, majestic, and solid—just like a mountain. As he neared and she felt his shadow fall over her, the thought crossed her mind that, like the mountains, he might be best admired from a distance.

He tipped his hat as they climbed out of the BMW. "Ladies."

Jessie giggled.

Molly extended her hand to shake his. "I'm Molly O'Malley and this is my daughter, Angelina." She gestured to Jessie. "My friend, Jessie Dalton."

Jessie took his hand and performed an awkward curtsy, then giggled some more.

Preacher Levi didn't bat an eye—he was probably used to love-crazed cowgirls. "Nice to meet you, ma'am." He touched the brim of his hat and tipped his head.

Jessie practically swooned.

Levi knelt to greet Angelina and Talisman.

"You're getting mud on your jeans," Angelina said.

"This is a ranch. I could be getting worse stuff on my jeans."

Angelina tossed her head and sniffed. "I guess that's true."

The sun rose over the mountain range when Levi smiled at Talisman, and as if the warmth was powerful enough to thaw the heart of winter, Talisman actually smiled and licked his face in greeting.

"It's been a while, Miss Tali. We've missed you. I'm sorry for all your sorrow." Levi pulled her head into his chest, then bent and whispered something to her that no one else could hear. She responded with a soft whine. He kissed her ear, they smiled at each other again, and Talisman seemed more relaxed than she had been in a long time.

Molly wondered if his prayers could ease her own sorrow.

Levi stood, whistled, and another Australian Shepherd raced toward them from the barn, her ears laid flat against her head, her tongue flapping in the wind. Like Talisman, she was a blue merle, but she had brown eyes instead of blue and more white on her face. At least Molly thought it was white. Unlike Talisman, Maddie obviously hadn't recently been groomed. Her white was gray with dirt, her silver and black locks were tangled, and her toenails were definitely not painted pink. But there was one thing the two Aussies had in common—they were both beautiful bitches who were queens of their respective domains. The two girls briefly touched noses in greeting, then Maddie turned her back to Talisman and gazed out at her vast realm, as if to say, "I'm queen of all I see."

Talisman shook her head, which fluffed up her I'M QUEEN OF THE SHOW RING scarf, then sat down a respectable distance away.

"Is Tali going to be okay?" Angelina asked. "She doesn't look very happy."

Preacher Levi smiled. "She'll be just fine. My new ranch hand will make sure of it. Won't you Josh?"

A cowboy stepped down from the front porch of the house. A cowgirl was at his side. The man knocked the dust off his cowboy hat, spat tobacco juice at the ground, and said, "Yep."

Levi performed the introductions. "This is Josh and his wife, Cheyenne. They'll be in charge while everyone else heads into town for the service."

Molly nodded in greeting. "Please take care of Tali. She's...well, she's special."

"Yes, ma'am," Josh said.

"Remember that the two Aussie girls get to play for an hour, and then you put Tali in the house and let her relax for the rest of the day," Levi said. "She's a fancy beauty queen and is used to the easy life."

Cheyenne nodded. "I'll make sure she gets pampered right fine. She can keep me company inside while I do some chores."

"Then let's get on to the prayer meeting," Levi said. "After the service there'll be a big barbeque. We won't be back 'til late."

Josh spat some more tobacco juice. "No worries. Cheyenne and me will hold down the fort."

Angelina handed Talisman's travel bag to Cheyenne. "This has her special treats, bottled water, and organic kibble. She eats three times a day. She's already had breakfast, but she'll need lunch before we get back. Oh, and be sure to give her one of the multiple vitamins with her food. And there's her plush throw to lie on. She just got groomed and doesn't like getting dirty."

Cheyenne's eyes grew wide and she looked at Talisman as if she were from Mars. "She is a dog, right?"

"A very pampered one," Levi said with a wink.

"Okey-dokey," Cheyenne said.

Angelina knelt and smothered Talisman with kisses, then adjusted her neck scarf. "Have a good visit with your sister." She glanced at Maddie, who was still sitting with her back to them. "They do like each other, right?"

Levi chuckled. "They love each other. I've watched

them play from the house. They get on fine when they think no one's looking. Trust me."

Angelina didn't seem at all convinced. "Maybe this isn't such a good idea."

Jessie threw Molly a panicked look. Molly's mind raced to think of something to comfort Angelina so she wouldn't insist on calling the whole thing off and heading home. However, Talisman came to the rescue. She gave Angelina a kiss as if to say everything was okay.

"Y'all want to ride with me?" Levi asked.

Jessie beamed. "You betcha."

"Well, then let's git to gittin', 'cause the Lord's awaitin'."

Jessie scrambled into the cab of the pickup truck next to Levi, while Molly and Angelina climbed into the back seat. As they pulled away, Molly turned around to see Talisman and Maddie suddenly paying attention to one another, sniffing each other from the top of their heads to their tailless bottoms. Molly nudged Angelina, so she could see.

Angelina didn't appear comforted. "It's an awful big ranch, and she's not used to the outdoors, and there's a lot of ways she could get hurt. What if coyotes come?"

"Maddie is hell-on-paws," Levi said. "No coyote's goin' to mess with her or any of her friends."

Angelina shook her head. "A ranch is a dangerous place. I would just die if something happened to her, Mom. I simply wouldn't survive it."

Molly's breath caught, and she fought the urge to demand they return to rescue Talisman from any and all potential danger right then and there because how would Angelina survive if something bad were to happen? And how would Molly survive if Angelina didn't? She glanced up and saw Levi's eyes watching them in the rearview mirror.

"Val dropped Tali off once a month from the time she

was a pup," Levi said. "At first he was nervous and would hover like an old mother hen. But eventually he figured out that Tali needed some space to grow outside his shadow."

"But what if *something* happens to her?" Angelina asked. There was an edge of hysteria to her voice that worried Molly.

"Val was a man of faith. He knew he couldn't control everything, that somethin' much bigger is in charge."

"You mean God, and I don't believe in God," Angelina said.

Molly was startled. "The last time we discussed it, you did believe in God."

Angelina kicked the seat in front of her. "Yeah, well, we haven't talked about it in a while."

"And you, Molly?" Levi asked. "Do you believe?"

She sighed. "No."

Molly braced for condemnation or ridicule, but instead he grinned. "Well, hot damn, ain't it a miracle you're headed for a Sunday go-to-meetin'? How wondrous the ways of the Lord."

*   *   *

Molly wasn't sure what kind of church she had been expecting, but it wasn't a big old barn with a dirt floor at the county fairgrounds. Cowboys, cowgirls, cowkids, and cowdogs wandered everywhere, while a country band played "The Devil Went Down To Georgia." Right inside the front door was a bench with two beat-up tin buckets on it. There was a sign by one that said THIS IS FOR CASH OFFERINGS—THE ONE ON THE OTHER SIDE IS THE SPITTOON. Molly dug around in her purse, found a twenty dollar bill, and dropped it into the proper bucket. Then she took a moment to marvel at how well some of the tobacco-chewing men could aim their spit at the nearby

spittoon bucket. Levi stopped, pulled a wad of cash out of
his pocket, and tossed it on top of Molly's.

"You donate to your own church?" Molly asked.

"It's a community church. I just preach here."

"Does anyone ever get the two buckets mixed up?"
Angelina asked.

Levi nodded. "It's happened a time or two. Not
everyone who comes to these meetings can read real well,
and some are hung over and not seein' so good. I'm
thinkin' we need to start using a boot for the offerings."

"That might be a good idea," Angelina said.

A small group of cowgirls surrounded them and
jostled Molly, Angelina, and Jessie out of the way to get
closer to Levi.

"Where's your pretty little Maddie?" a tall, shapely
blonde asked.

"She's got company today and won't be comin'," Levi
said.

"So, you gotta a date for the barbeque?" a pretty
brunette asked. "'Cause if not, I'm available."

"I do, indeed." Levi managed to pass through the wall
of women and take Angelina's hand. "But thanks for the
most kind offer."

Angelina beamed.

The cowgirls looked as if they'd been bucked off their
broncs.

After the crowd thinned, Angelina said, "The girls all
seem to like you. It must make you feel real special."

Levi laughed. "Darlin', I'm special to God. That's the
only kind of special that counts."

Molly studied his face and voice for signs of false
modesty but couldn't discern any.

"But all the girls like you," Angelina said.

Levi shrugged. "The one I loved chose another. So, if
I was the prize bull, that wouldn't have happened now,
would it?"

Molly listened for a trace of self-pity, but it wasn't there. She glanced at Jessie, whose shock mirrored her own. Was it possible he really didn't understand the effect he had on women?

"You're not very smart, are you?" Angelina asked.

Out of the mouths of babes. Embarrassment mingled with amusement as Molly struggled to maintain a straight face while chastising her. "Apologize to Preacher Levi right this minute."

"Sorry," Angelina said.

Levi grinned. "I gotta admire a gal who speaks her mind." He took off his hat and ran fingers through his dark hair. "About some things, I'm okay smart. About others, probably not so much." He plopped the hat back on his head. "That pretty much describes everyone though, don't you think?"

Angelina gave it a moment of serious thought. "I guess you're right."

Levi held his hand out to her and said, "Now we got that straight, let's get you ladies seated so I can commence to preachin'."

Molly and Jessie fell in step behind them.

"Unbelievable," Jessie said. "Now I want him even more."

"Some advice?" Molly asked.

"If it'll get me the man."

Molly lowered her voice. "Don't chase because he won't let you catch him. If you really like him, become his friend and see where that leads."

"You're pretty smart."

Molly grinned. "About some things I'm okay smart. About others, not so much."

Levi led Molly, Angelina, and Jessie to a row of folding chairs in front of the makeshift stage and left them alone. Their row had been cordoned off by a rope, and a hand-lettered sign said BY INVITE ONLY. Lights, cameras, and a film crew were positioned in front of the stage.

"How did Preacher Levi get so famous?" Molly asked Jessie.

"Someone filmed one of his sermons, it ended up on YouTube, and, well, he's just got a mighty gift for inspiring devotion. Important people took notice. God works in mysterious ways."

It was the second time someone had said that to Molly recently. She wished she could believe it.

"That is so cool," Angelina said. "How old is he?"

"He's thirty-five, which is much too old for you," Jessie said.

Angelina and Jessie stared at each other with narrowed eyes, and Molly wondered if her daughter was poised for a new crush.

The lights dimmed, the rollicking band softened their tone, and the lights fell on a trio of gospel singers performing "Amazing Grace."

Then the lights shifted to illumine Preacher Levi, who was sitting in the middle of the stage on a rough-hewn bench, his hat in his hands. A small microphone attached to his shirt helped his soft voice carry, and the bright light made his green eyes sparkle.

"Grace is indeed amazin'," he said. "Grace is God's love come to roost in our hearts. We can't make it come, but only build a welcomin' nest and pray for God's mercy. Of course, some don't believe in God." His eyes slid to where Molly and Angelina sat, and a smile played at his lips. "When you live close to nature like we cowfolk do, it's easier to witness God's hand. The sky, the earth, the critters. Is the beauty of all that from some random toss of the poker dice? Not hardly. For city folk, God's hand is a mite harder to see. But they can always look at, say, their own young'uns or critters and see somethin' so powerful, so smart, so loveable that no way, no how, could they be just some clumsy cosmic accident. That bein' said, if there's a Creator with the heart to create such beauty, doesn't it figure that the love in that heart wants to find a place to roost in ours? So, we gotta be humble enough to get out of the way, make space inside us, and ask for that space to be filled. Amen?"

The crowd shouted, "Amen!"

Molly's mind rebelled. Could the truth possibly be so simple? His words made perfect sense to her in a way none before ever had. She felt stunned and disoriented. Her rational brain struggled to regain control, reminding her about all the horrible things that happened in life, which was why she didn't believe in God in the first place. Then the new voice suggested that perhaps those were questions best pondered at a later time. It told her that a journey had to begin somewhere, and perhaps she might consider just taking it a step at a time. Tentatively, Molly took a step and, surprisingly, felt as if she had finally found some solid ground on which to begin a journey of faith.

*   *   *

Late that afternoon, following a sumptuous barbeque and wonderful entertainment by Preacher Levi's gospel singers, they headed back to Heavenly Acres. On the drive, Angelina gave Preacher Levi the third degree about all things God. Apparently, Molly wasn't the only one touched by his sermon.

Molly felt the day had been a perfect family outing.

When they pulled up to Levi's house, Molly didn't even have her seatbelt off before Angelina jumped out of the truck and called for Talisman. Molly hadn't even opened the door before she heard Angelina's frantic screams.

Dozens of dire possibilities crashed through Molly as

she, Levi, and Jessie scrambled to Angelina's side.

Angelina was crouched in the mud, her arms around a filthy Australian Shepherd. Molly's mind rejected the possibility that it was Talisman. Not perfect, pampered, ever-groomed Talisman.

"What did they do to you, Tali?" Angelina's voice was tremulous. "Oh, my poor sweet Tali, whatever did they *do*?"

It took a moment for Molly to realize it really was Talisman. The dog sat rigidly, staring straight ahead, not making eye contact, and most definitely not happy to see them.

"Is she hurt?" Molly's hands frantically patted Talisman down, and she scanned for any trace of blood.

Talisman stood and wiggled out of their grasp, moved two feet away, and sat down again. This time she leveled them both with a reproachful glare.

"She looks really pissed off," Jessie said.

A pickup truck rumbled toward them, parked, and Josh and Cheyenne jumped out. "We heard a scream," Josh said.

Angelina stood up and pointed at Talisman with one hand and them with the other. "*What* did you *do* to my dog?"

The couple appeared confused.

"What are you talking about? Tali's in the house all safe and sound like I promised," Cheyenne said. She climbed the porch stairs, opened the door, and looked inside. "Come on, girl, your folks are here for you."

There was no movement from the house.

Cheyenne's voice turned impatient. "Well, come on, Tali."

Very slowly, almost reluctantly, an Australian Shepherd walked out onto the porch. She looked so different all nice and clean with a pretty pink bow tied to a curly lock of hair atop her head, that it took a moment for Molly to realize it was Maddie.

Maddie sat down at the top of the stairs and gave everyone the evil eye.

"She looks really pissed too," Jessie said.

"Why should she?" Cheyenne asked. "I pampered her right good today."

Angelina's hand trembled as she pointed at Maddie. "*That's* Maddie." Her finger jabbed toward Talisman. "*This* is Tali."

"Whoops," Cheyenne said.

"Oh, Lord," Levi said.

Josh frowned. "Well, that sure as hell explains a lot." A tentative grin played at his lips. "I just thought you had the worst cowdog this side of the Rocky Mountains."

"You made Tali work cattle?" Levi asked.

Josh grinned. "Well, she didn't exactly work them. More like she caused a bit of a stampede."

"Stampede?" Levi asked.

"Well, the dog kinda spooked them. See, the bulls scared her, she did this crazy little dance, and, well, we had a bit of a situation. But it worked out okay."

In a flash Molly understood. She imagined Talisman's rousing celebratory tribal dance of success complete with play bows, leaps, spins, rolls, bounces, prancing, and shimmying. Yes, she could see how that would spook cattle. Poor Talisman was just trying to conjure some courage. Molly used a cough to hide her smile.

Angelina was indignant. "Tali is a *show* dog, not a *cow* dog."

Josh's grin widened. "So, that's why she kept posing for me. And why she didn't want to drink puddle water. And why she howled when I hosed her down."

"You turned a *hose* on her? Show dogs do *not* get hosed down." Angelina was beside herself.

Out of the corner of her eye, Molly noticed Jessie making a valiant effort to hide her bubbling laughter.

"Didn't you notice her blue eyes and her pink toenails?" Angelina asked.

Josh took off his hat and scratched his head. "Well, no, but she did keep battin' her eyes at me and raising her paw. Maybe she was trying to show me. I just thought she had something stuck in them."

Jessie couldn't contain herself any longer, and laughter burst from her like water gushing from a hose.

"It's *not* funny," Angelina insisted.

Jessie fought to catch her breath. "Yeah, honey, I'm afraid it is."

Angelina stamped her foot. "What about Tali's QUEEN OF THE SHOW RING scarf? That should have been a clue."

Cheyenne pointed at Maddie. "When they came back from playing, both were real muddy, and she had the scarf in her mouth."

They all stared at Maddie.

Cheyenne giggled. "Hell, that would explain why she didn't want to be groomed. And why she kept pawing at the inside of the windows all afternoon. She was so nervous that her paws got sweaty and left streaks— must've been scared about what her city sister was doin' to her ranch."

Levi moved to pluck the pink bow from Maddie's hair. "I'm sorry girl. I bet you're a mite humiliated by all this." Despite his comforting words, he chuckled.

Maddie tossed her head and issued a loud sigh.

Talisman tossed her head in exactly the same manner and echoed Maddie's sigh with perfection.

Even though—especially at the moment—the two dogs looked nothing alike, their attitudes and mannerisms were identical. They were both proud queens who had been dethroned, and their indignation was as thick as the mud that coated Talisman. It was classic. Molly found it hilarious, and despite her best efforts she erupted in a belly laugh that had a ripple effect. Within moments all of the adults were in hysterics.

Talisman and Maddie looked at each with pained expressions. Then—at the very same moment—they took off together at a hard run, their ears laid back, their direction toward the rise of a distant hill.

Angelina's scream was so piercing and frantic that it commanded instant silence. "What's wrong with you? How can you make fun of them after what they've been through?" She started to sob. "Tali is so proud, and you laugh at her? I'm sure she did her best. Shame on you all."

Guilt washed over Molly, and she dug around in her pockets for a Kleenex to offer Angelina.

Josh cleared his throat. "Actually, Tali did better than her best. Knowing what I know now, I gotta say she cowdoged up big time." His chin jutted toward a distant field. "We was moving the sheep and one of the newborn lambs got away from its ma. I didn't know, but Tali did. She disappeared and I thought she was slackin'. I was so damn mad at her. I brought the sheep in myself, then I went lookin' for that dog to give her hell and heard her bark. Found her standing over that baby lamb and fending off coyotes. She saved that young'un all by herself. Where she got the guts or knowhow to do it, well, ain't that somethin'?"

Angelina stopped crying, and her face paled. Molly moved to her side, uncertain of what dire reaction she would have to the news.

Angelina's voice was soft and full of wonder. "My Tali was a hero?"

"A damn fine one," Josh said, shaking his head. "Criminy. Ain't it something?"

"Now, there's a miracle for your next sermon, Preacher," Cheyenne said.

Molly considered the possibilities and uttered a silent prayer to her potentially newfound God for keeping

Talisman and that lamb safe. The alternative would have been inconceivable.

"I'll round the dogs up," Josh said, heading for his truck.

"I'll go in and draw a bath for Tali, so we can get her all clean before you head home." Cheyenne turned to Angelina. "I'm sorry about the mix-up. I tried real hard to do everything right."

Angelina nodded but stopped short of offering absolution.

Levi sat down on the porch steps and stretched his long legs. For a time he studied Molly and Angelina in silence. Finally, he said, "Sometimes people wonder how come bad things happen. Now, I don't think God lets bad things happen, but I think He can write straight with crooked lines. Today was a bad thing for Tali, but look at what she got from it. She discovered she was much more than just a pretty face."

"She was a hero," Angelina said. "If she can be a hero, then anyone can."

"Inspirin', ain't it?" Levi said.

Angelina nodded. "Are you going to talk about her at your next sermon?"

"Yep."

"Can Tali and I come hear?" Angelina asked him.

"Sure."

Jessie was quick to jump in. "I'll bring you, if your ma has to work."

Molly decided she would find something to do next Sunday, to give Jessie that opportunity.

"Then I have just the thing for Miss Tali to wear for the occasion," Levi said. "Wait here." He disappeared into the house for a moment and returned with a blue denim neckscarf. "Val gave this to Maddie for Christmas last year, but I think he'd want Tali to have it now."

Angelina accepted it almost reverently. The words

inscribed on it were MORDE DIEM.

"It's the cattle dog credo," Levi explained. "*Bite the day*."

CHAPTER TEN

On Monday morning Talisman's scarf said DON'T BOTHER ME, I'M VERY BUSY & IMPORTANT. Molly thought it should actually have stated that she was very TIRED and important. The events of the day before had taken a toll.

Robin met Molly in the parking lot as she pulled in, and lifted Talisman from the BMW so she wouldn't have to climb out. He put her down and watched as she limped toward the building. "We need to set an appointment for Tali to see her massage therapist," he said. "Her muscles are in need of some tender, loving care. Being a hero is hard work."

"How did you hear about it?" Molly asked.

"Angel rang me last night and filled me in on all the details. She also rang Rowan. Angel's very proud of her girl. I think she's planning a ticker-tape parade down Main Street."

Molly grabbed her briefcase from the trunk and locked up the car. She and Robin followed Talisman as she gingerly made her way up the porch steps.

"I noticed a Reiki Master also listed in the instructions Val left for Tali's care," Robin said. "Maybe we should get her in to see him too."

"Reiki?" Molly asked.

"Reiki works with healing energy that goes beyond the physical. I'm sure Tali went through a lot of fear yesterday. It might help her process it."

Molly nodded. "Massage therapist and Reiki Master it is. Nothing is too good for Superdog."

Robin paused before opening the front door. "I've got to warn you to be prepared to enter The Enchanted Forest, or as Coco has already dubbed it, The Seventh Circle of Eco-Friendly Hell."

"What?"

"Another extreme manifestation of one of Brooklyn's many colorful personalities."

Molly stepped into the lobby—a very green lobby, overflowing with plants of every description.

"Howdy." A voice said from somewhere amidst the greenery. "Can I help you?"

"It's just us, Jessie," Robin said.

"For crissakes. How the hell am I supposed to be a receptionist when I can't see the forest for the trees?" There was a frantic rustling of leaves, then a hand poked through a wall of ivy and waved a file around like a lost flag. "This contract was in the drop box this morning. It's for Molly."

Robin took it and grasped Jessie's hand, giving it a squeeze for comfort. "Hang in there. We'll survive this if we stick together."

"Ha!" Jessie said from somewhere. "The Eco-Broker of Doom has struck with a vengeance. Beware The Green Police. God help us all."

Molly glanced down at Talisman, who was sniffing the trunk of a potted tree with obvious confusion. "Um, Robin, I don't think you know this about Tali, but she is prone to raising her leg like a boy dog."

Robin nodded. "Right-o. I'll keep an eye on her."

Molly handed Talisman's leash to him. "I'll be in after I use the restroom."

Robin and Talisman headed off in one direction, while Molly tried to find a clear path to the ladies room. The trip was harrowing, and Molly was so relieved to find the door that she pushed it open and stepped inside before she realized the room was dark. "Damn." She shifted her briefcase to her left hand and reached out with her right one to try to locate a light switch on the wall. After a few minutes she found it, flipped it on, and nothing happened. "What the—"

"Who's there?" The disembodied voice belonged to Coco.

"It's Molly. What's going on with the lights?"

"I have no idea and can't find the door to get back out."

Molly flailed around with her free hand to try and locate the door handle. She couldn't find it, but did locate a warm body standing like a statue in the corner. Her heart performed a wild tap dance. Was this a trap? "Who is it?" she whispered.

"Babylon."

Molly wasn't sure whether to be relieved or not. "Do you know what's happening?"

"We're lost in the dark."

Molly had already figured that part out.

A blinding light from the hallway flooded the room as someone stepped inside. Molly was about to shout a warning when the new arrival slapped her hands twice, and the bathroom lights came on.

Brooklyn Green gave them all her most perky smile. "What are you doing in the dark?"

"Having a séance," Babylon said.

Brooklyn apparently didn't have sarcasm radar. "Wow. What an odd place for a séance."

"Thank God the lights have come back on," Coco said.

"Didn't you get the memo I sent out?" Brooklyn asked. She slapped her hands, and the lights went off.

Coco squeaked.

Brooklyn slapped her hands again, and they came back

on. "To conserve electricity, I installed a Clapper." She clapped three times, and the overhead fan turned on. "Twice for the lights, three times for the fan. Clever, huh?"

"I'm going to kill you, and in a very ecologically-friendly manner, compost your body," Babylon said.

The ominous tone in Babylon's voice was clear enough to pierce even Brooklyn's dense skull. Her smile disappeared.

Coco pointed at a new recycle bin next to the sink. "What is my hairspray doing in there?"

Brooklyn wagged a finger at her. "Why Coco, hairspray is a major no-no. Very damaging to the environment."

Coco marched over to retrieve the can. She picked it up, shook it, and her eyes grew wide. "What happened to the hairspray?"

Coco's harsh tone caused Brooklyn to take a defensive step backwards. "Well, you can't recycle an aerosol can unless you empty it first."

Coco lowered her voice and spoke very slowly. "Miss Brooklyn *Go Green* Green. If you don't buy me another can of this exact brand of hairspray today, and put it back here on the shelf where you found it, I'm going to do something to you that's a whole hell of a lot worse than what Babylon just threatened to do."

Brooklyn slapped her hands twice and made a hasty escape under the cover of darkness.

Molly braved the scratchy recycled toilet paper, bricks in the toilet, and lack of paper towels in the ladies room, then stopped to check her mail on the way to her office. There was a package of BioBags stuck in her inbox, courtesy of Brooklyn. The attached note said the biodegradable bags were for Talisman's poo, to reduce her carbon pawprint.

Paula Parry was checking her mail as well. She shook Brooklyn's new *Green Guide* memo. "She actually wants us to change the fonts we use on all our printers from Arial to Century Gothic. She says it would use 30% less ink, but since Century Gothic letters are larger we would apparently need to print all our documents double-sided to make up for the increased paper usage. Personally, I think this entire green movement is a conspiracy to undermine the democratic way of life."

Molly resisted the urge to point out that Paula thought everything was a conspiracy.

A soft chirping sound from Paula's keychain caught Molly's attention. It was coming from an odd-looking black and yellow gizmo that she couldn't identify.

Paula noticed Molly's interest. "It's a personal radiation meter, monitor, and alarm called a NukAlert. My clients can rest assured that if a dirty bomb is detonated nearby, I'll be able to let them know right away."

"So, is it chirping because we're radioactive?"

"No, sometimes it just gets cold and chirps."

Molly wasn't sure how to respond, so she opted for politeness. "What an interesting accessory."

"It's a great marketing strategy. This and my concealed carry permit, of course. My clients know they're safe with me." She patted her pocket where Molly knew her pearl-handled Derringer resided.

Molly wondered what kind of clientele she attracted. Paranoid Paula ferrying around a carload of panicky purchasers was a scary concept. However, the NukAlert did give her an idea for a closing gift for Liberty.

Molly continued to rifle through her mailbox, and at the very bottom was an envelope addressed to her in what appeared to be a child's scrawl. She used her fingernail to slit open the top and then removed the letter. In big, bold red letters it simply said, *You're going to die, bitch.*

When Molly gasped, Paula looked over her shoulder and read the letter. "It could be a terrorist threat. It's a dangerous world, Molly. You really should take some lessons in self-defense from me."

*   *   *

Detective Mendoza's desk was a mess. There were several half-eaten doughnuts lying about on napkins, two paper cups and one ceramic mug of coffee—all of which he took turns sipping from—crime scene photos, piles of unopened mail, and—most surprising to Molly since the man appeared to be utterly humorless—there was a Magic 8-Ball. Most notably, however, at least twenty case files were stacked in his in-basket. Molly wondered how there could be that much crime in Blackstone. Then she realized that probably a lot of his workload was related to her. Trouble knew her name.

The death threat she received was in the plastic evidence bag he held. "So, tell me about your enemies."

Molly took a deep breath. "My former sister, Rita, sent me a warning that the gangsters Miguel screwed over might come after me for revenge. And Miguel himself is really mad at me for getting the restraining order against him. There are Val's murderers and their friends. Lily Dalton hates me. The Ahmed family thinks I'm a bigot. Let's not forget the meth heads I turned in. Oh, and my ex-boyfriend's ten-year-old little boy would like to see me dead." She was shaking and couldn't make it stop. "I've got a smorgasbord of enemies. Take your pick."

Mendoza stared at her for a while. "Why are the feds asking about you?"

Molly shrugged. "I'm sure it's about the discrimination case brought by the Ahmeds."

"Well, yes, the Attorney General's office has been

making inquiries but so has Homeland Security."

"Why?"

"That's what I'm asking you."

"I have no clue." She fought back insistent tears. Could her life get any worse?

His fingers tapped the plastic bag. "We'll run this for prints. In the meantime, let us know if you see anything suspicious. Your home is isolated. Be careful. Stay alert."

Molly's panic surged. "Is that all? What about my daughter? I don't want to put her at risk."

"Perhaps you should send her away to stay with relatives."

"There aren't any relatives." She shook her head. "Can't I have police protection?"

"Not until there's an attempt on your life. I'm sorry. That's just the way the system works."

She didn't sense his regret, only his suspicion. Normal, upstanding citizens didn't usually have so many enemies.

Molly stood and gathered her things. "I see."

"You need to be straight with me. What are you involved in, Ms. O'Malley?"

"I'm just trying to live my life, be a good mother, do my job the best I can. I've done nothing wrong, Detective Mendoza. If I had, for the sake of my daughter, I would tell you."

He seemed unmoved. "Well, if you think of anything you've forgotten to tell me, you know where I am."

*   *   *

"What can I do?" Robin sat at his desk across from hers.

Molly had been trying unsuccessfully to focus on paperwork related to Liberty's upcoming closing, but her emotions were chaotic. "Could Angel stay with your

sister until this blows over? She's crazy about Rowan. I'd
send her to Rose's, but Angel is too much for Rose to
handle in all but very small doses."

Robin studied her for a long time before responding,
which made Molly feel like a fool for having asked in the
first place. Finally, he said, "The boarding house at Pagan
Place has some odd tenants. Harmless, but dotty. When
Angel visits us, we shield her from them, but if she were
living there full-on it would be a bit tough. Michael has
been practicing invisibility and walks around naked,
convinced no one can see him. Crimson sleeps in a
coffin. There's a lot of chanting around there at midnight.
Sybil—"

Molly held up a hand to silence him. "I get it. Sorry, I
was foolish to ask."

"You've a guest room. How's about I come round and
stay? I've that special gift I got from my mum. It might
come in handy."

Molly found the offer tempting but utterly ridiculous.

"I know it seems utterly ridiculous, but admit that it's
tempting."

Molly caught her breath. He knew exactly what she
was thinking.

"It's a gift. Let me use it to help you."

Molly's head reeled. "If you really have this gift, can't
you just tell me who wants me dead?"

"I wish I could, but I'm not getting a hit on that.
However, I do believe I'd be an effective alarm system."

Molly had never been able to count on a man. What
made her think that would change now?

"Let me help. You *can* count on me, even though I am
a man."

Molly struggled with all the possible repercussions.
"Angel must never know we're in danger."

"Rowan's been promising a fix-up of my flat, and I'll
need to leave while the work's done. We'll tell Angel

that's why I'm visiting."

"You would be in danger too."

"I'm a knight at heart—we're all about facing danger for the sake of the ladies."

Molly closed her eyes and wrestled with whether to accept his offer. She listened for Marina Night's now-familiar warning cries—she had come to rely on them as a barometer of danger. Instead, she heard a new voice, one she instinctively associated with her recent spiritual awakening. It suggested she consider having faith in someone other than herself.

*   *   *

Late in the afternoon, Jake appeared in Molly's office doorway. "Detective Mendoza called me," he said.

Molly looked up at him. "And?"

"He has serious concerns about what you're about."

She chuckled. "I got that impression."

Robin stood and grabbed his coat. "Right. Well, I'll leave you two to chat. I'll go home, pack, and be at your place in a couple hours."

Molly forced a smile. She really wished he hadn't said that in front of Jake but was sure it wasn't accidental. Another round in their alpha-dog pissing contest.

Jake refused to budge out of the doorway as Robin pushed past him.

After Robin was out of earshot, Jake asked, "Pack? Your place?"

"He's moving into my guest room. A bodyguard of sorts."

"Yeah, I just bet he's going to be guarding your body."

She sighed. "About Mendoza?"

Jake tugged on his beard. "You hardly know the guy."

"Mendoza?"

"Robin."

"I trust Robin, and it's really none of your business."

Jake tapped the heel of his boot against the door jamb. "I thought maybe since you and Steve broke up, you and I might reconnect."

Molly had been afraid of this and really didn't know how to respond. After a few moments of consideration, she opted for the truth. "My entire life I've just wanted to love a man and be loved back. It seems really simple to me, but for some reason it's never quite worked out. First Miguel, then you, now Steve. I need some time alone to try and figure out why. The pain, the loss, it doesn't just affect me, but Angel too."

He nodded. "Okay. You do what you need to do, but I'll be waiting."

Molly redirected the conversation. "Mendoza?"

"You're a mystery to him. He can't comprehend why so much trouble has found you."

"And?"

"Luis is a friend of mine and trusts my judgment. I've assured him that you're just a bad luck magnet."

Molly had to laugh. "Yeah, that sure does describe me, doesn't it?"

Coco appeared in the hall outside Molly's door. "I was just headed to see you, Jake. I need to ask why you've suddenly gone all ecological on us."

He shrugged. "When Brooklyn suggested it, I thought it was a good idea. Good PR really. She's the first broker in town to get that Eco-Broker certification. Gives us something to send out a press release about. A reporter from the paper is coming by to do a story, and it seemed prudent to have the office reflect a commitment to the theme."

Coco opened her mouth to say something but stopped herself.

"Desperate times call for desperate measures, Coco,"

he said.

Coco used her huge body to nudge him into the room, then closed the door behind them. "Is the company in trouble, Jake?"

"In as much trouble as any real estate company right now, I suppose. But with power agents like you on board, and crazy creative ideas like Brooklyn's, we have a better chance than many at staying on the horse."

"I've heard rumors that you're carrying some of the agents who can't pay their bills," Coco said.

"I'll do the best I can for as long as I can. Our industry's taken quite a hit lately."

She threw her hand to her hip in classic Coco fashion. "Well, we may stay on the horse, but this ride's getting mighty rough." Then she smiled at him. "Despite the fact that you're an irreverent, sinning cowboy, I'm sure glad you're our cowboy. I'm proud to work for you, Jake Dalton."

Molly was stunned. She had never heard Coco offer anyone such a genuine compliment.

Jake seemed equally surprised and only managed to stammer out a polite, "Thank you."

"However, you tell Miss Brooklyn *Go Green* Green that if I don't get my 3-ply toilet paper back, there's going to be some serious defecation hitting the rotary blades."

"Yes, ma'am. Right on it."

Coco grunted, opened the door, and left Jake and Molly alone.

"That woman scares the hell out of me," Jake said.

"Me too." Molly thought about it. "But Lily scares me more."

Jake's smile disappeared. "Me too."

"A lot of things scare me right now."

"I know," he said.

"Val once told me that courage is a choice."

"John Wayne said, 'Courage is being scared to death and saddling up anyway.'"

*   *   *

By the time Molly finally made it home, Robin was already there. He had sent babysitter Percy home and taken over the care and feeding of Angelina. A frozen organic cheese pizza was in the oven, and the coffee table in the living room was set with three place settings. Plush pillows were on the floor next to the table, and the DVD player was set up for the evening entertainment.

"Chance's person sent me a recording of his big win at Crufts," Angelina explained. "Tali's sad tonight and really wants to watch it."

Talisman was settled on the couch awaiting the appearance of her one true love.

Robin greeted Molly with a glass of wine. "Get yourself changed, and we'll settle in for an emotional evening of canine angst."

Molly had never before seen Robin dressed down, and was dismayed to find herself appreciating the way he wore his tight jeans and tee-shirt. Switching their formal work relationship to one more casual was going to present some unexpected challenges. She reminded herself that it was for Angelina.

Molly accepted the wine, kicked off her shoes, and went up to her bedroom. She changed into the baggiest sweats she could find. There was no need to tempt fate.

Then they all sat cross-legged on the floor around the coffee table and ate pizza. Talisman had refused to eat her own dinner, but did nibble on the occasional piece of pizza crust while Angelina told everyone about a letter she had received from Chance's person.

"Nancy told me that the Chance-man has what is called 'heart.' It means that a dog will go the extra mile or hundred miles for you. She said that after he won Crufts he greeted over five hundred people, and never once did he turn away from anyone. He greeted every single person with a butt wag and a hello. He did it for her, he did it because he had heart, and it touched her heart so much that she cried."

"Tali has good taste in men," Robin said.

They all looked at Talisman, who was sitting on the couch watching the blank TV screen expectantly.

"How in the world does she know that a DVD of Chance is queued and ready to start?" Molly asked.

"I'm guilty," Robin said. "I told her, and now she's just all beside herself with anticipation."

Molly laughed. "Well, start it already. The anticipation is killing me too."

Angelina hit the play button, and the gorgeous hunk of Australian Shepherd that was Chance appeared on the screen. Yes, Molly decided, Talisman certainly did have good taste in men.

The doorbell rang, and Molly jumped. She hadn't been expecting anyone. She glanced at Robin.

"I'll have a peek," he said.

He went to the foyer, looked out the peephole, and returned to the table. Keeping his voice low so as not to disturb the children, he said, "It's Steve."

That surprised Molly. Was it possible that Amber had died? She didn't want to disturb Angelina's happy mood and so waved Robin back to his seat. "Please stay with the girls," she whispered.

Molly went to the door and opened it. When she saw Steve, her heart jumped to her throat. God, how she had missed him.

"I'm sorry I didn't call first, but I wasn't sure I'd have the courage to do this until I actually got here," he said.

Trembling, she stepped aside to allow him entry.

Angelina's excited voice began to chatter about

Chance's hunkiness, Talisman yapped, and Robin laughed.

Steve seemed taken aback. "I guess I should have called first after all." He glanced around the corner of the foyer into the living room, then shot her a dark look and managed a mirthless laugh. "Here I've been all tore up about what I've got to tell you, and I see now it's not going to matter to you at all. You've already moved on."

"It's not what it seems."

He snorted. "Right. Look, I just came by to tell you that I'm marrying Amber. I want to do that for her and Kyle before she dies, and I didn't want you to hear about it from someone else."

Molly was speechless. What was she supposed to say? *Congratulations* didn't seem quite right. *I hope you'll be happy* was all wrong. *How can you do that to me?* was selfish. *What a compassionate thing for you to do* was too hard to admit.

Steve gave her a cool look. "So, now you know."

Before she could recover enough to reply, he opened the door and walked out, and this time Molly knew in her soul that it was forever.

After a few minutes, she was composed enough to return to the living room.

Angelina glanced up at her and said, "Chance and Tali would have made *such* a cute couple. Lost love is such a tragedy, isn't it?"

"Yes," Molly managed to reply. "It most certainly is."

CHAPTER ELEVEN

Helping Liberty True move into her new home became a community event. Students, friends, and fellow resisters gathered to celebrate her dream. Molly, Angelina, Talisman, and Robin were among them.

On Saturday, the day after the closing, a caravan of cars and pickup trucks moved all of Liberty's belongings from her small rental near the university to her new five acre spread in the foothills. Then everyone pitched in to help her make repairs, clean, unpack, and settle in.

Her friends gave her a flagpole as a housewarming present and erected it in front of her home. Reverently, Liberty raised the American flag and led her twenty-five guests in the Pledge of Allegiance. Molly and Angelina put their hands on their hearts and recited it with the group. Robin stood respectfully and watched.

Then, much to Molly's surprise, they lowered the flag, turned it upside down and raised it again.

"The flag flown upside down is a sign of distress," Liberty explained to her. "Our country is in dire trouble, and we must acknowledge that fact if anything is going to change."

"Isn't it illegal to fly it upside down?" Molly asked.

"Nope. Read Section 8 of the U.S. Flag Code. I love my country too much to ignore the extreme emergency it's in. God save America."

"Have you always believed in God?" Angelina asked. God was one of her favorite topics lately.

"Ever since AC. BC, I didn't."

Angelina shook her head. "What?"

Liberty gestured for them to follow her to the back yard. "Let's take a break, and I'll tell you all about it."

Liberty's students had bought her a picnic table as a housewarming present, and it was covered with containers of food for the moving party. Another gift, a fancy barbeque grill, was already fired up and meats were sizzling. Liberty dug around in the ice chest, pulled out chilled bottles of water, and handed them to Molly, Robin, and Angelina. Then they all found a sunny spot near the river and sat down together.

"AC and BC: After-Cornfield and Before-Cornfield." Liberty grinned. "I haven't told you about my cornfield epiphany?"

Angelina shook her head.

"Well, after my brother was killed in Afghanistan—"

"Your brother?" Angelina asked.

"My brother, Good, was a Marine. He died in the first Gulf war."

"Oh, I'm sorry. I didn't know," Molly said.

Liberty's eyes clouded. "I lived out in farm country then, and for weeks after I got the news I would walk by the hour in the fields and cry and curse. My parents were dead, my aunt was dead, I was debating leaving my husband…I was as low as I'd ever been. I came upon a bale of hay, broken and alone in the middle of a cornfield, and I thought to myself, *I am that bale of hay*. Then I shouted for help and asked if anyone was listening? Finally, clear as anything, a voice said to me, 'Well, you're in a corn field. There are ears everywhere.' Just like that. I figured either I had totally lost my mind or there was a God. I preferred the latter choice. Everything changed for me in that moment. Now my life is clearly defined by BC and AC."

Angelina grinned. "That is so cool."

"I didn't know you had been married," Molly said.

Liberty sighed. "The rift happened when I discovered that the cybersecurity program Dan developed was slated to be used by the government for what I deemed unethical purposes. He swore up and down its application was critical for national defense, however I saw it as enabling the surveillance state and a direct threat to personal freedoms and rights. I just couldn't stay with a man whose ethics were diametrically opposed to mine." Liberty's shoulders sagged. "Especially AC, I just couldn't stay with him."

"Do you miss him?" Angelina asked.

"Every single day of my life. I loved him. Still do. Always will. Leaving him was the most difficult choice I've ever had to make."

"You are a woman of great integrity," Robin said.

"Oh, Knight, if you have integrity, nothing else matters. Then again, if you don't have integrity, nothing else matters."

Molly glanced at the sweatshirt Liberty wore. It said WHEN INJUSTICE BECOMES LAW, RESISTANCE BECOMES DUTY. Molly also noticed that Liberty was wearing the NukAlert she had given her as a closing gift on a long chain around her neck. She was going to point out that it was designed to be attached to key chains but knew it would be pointless. Liberty had her own, unique style.

Liberty noticed her attention. "Thanks so much for this, O'Malley. I've always wanted one."

"Really?"

"Well, sure. It's used nationwide by federal, state and local first responders, law enforcement, and the Department of Defense. They know what's critical to survival."

Emily, one of Liberty's students, walked over to where they sat and deposited a big box of framed photographs and news clippings in front of Liberty.

"We've been unpacking your stuff and putting it away but didn't know what to with these."

"Oh, these are my most precious things." Liberty dug around in the box and withdrew one picture after another, passing them around the circle. "This is Good, and this is Dan. Here's my Aunt Elizabeth. And these were my parents."

The men were handsome and the women beautiful. Molly enjoyed the peek into Liberty's history. "Do you regret that you haven't had children?" she asked.

Liberty grasped Emily's hand. "But I do have children, O'Malley. I've had so many wonderful kids like McGee here."

Emily smiled. "And we love her too."

Liberty grabbed her box. "I'm going to go find a place of honor for these." She stood and headed off to the house.

"We really do love her." Emily smiled. "So much to admire. The other day in class she said, 'When they silence our voices, they steal our power. Education is our weapon, and our right to speak, to question, and to challenge is non-negotiable. So, we fight. We speak. We stand together.' I mean, those words are pure magic. She doesn't just teach—she lights souls on fire."

"You're lucky to have a teacher like that," Angelina said. "When I go to college, I want her as mine."

"Liberty will turn your world around—she's on a holy mission." Emily's smile vanished. "But she's got some powerful enemies, and the government has been disappearing dissidents from universities all over the country. It scares me and others who love her." Emily took in a deep, shaky breath. "Well, I'm off to help finish unpacking. Got to find her shortwave radio and put it in the microwave."

"Why?" Molly asked.

"Liberty believes that a microwave oven scrambles

food into unnatural molecules, therefore the only thing it's good for is a Faraday cage. So if an EMP blast from a nuclear bomb detonated high in the atmosphere fries all the circuit boards, the oven will protect her hand-cranked shortwave. That way she can still get news from the outside world." She shook her head. "Liberty is one of a kind."

After Emily left, Molly turned to Robin. "What do you think of Liberty?"

"She's remarkable."

Talisman lay between Molly and Robin, and Angelina sat on Robin's other side. They watched the river flow by and enjoyed the view of the woods on the other shore. The spring air was fresh and the smell of barbequing food, comforting.

"You didn't need to come today, Robin," Molly said. "Housewarming parties aren't part of the job description."

"I enjoy spending time with you and Angel. Besides, I was hoping maybe to see some deer."

"Oh, do you think we will?" Angelina asked. "I did a wildlife project about deer for school. Mom helped me. She said we'd go look for some, but we've never done it. I learned that deer don't often come out of hiding in the middle of the day, so do you really think we could see some today?"

"You never know what might happen," he said. "The world is an enchanted place where anything is possible."

"What made you decide to move to America?" Molly asked, eager to change the subject. She had forgotten about her promise to help Angelina find those deer.

"Missed Rowan. Besides, the voices told me I had a special quest waiting for me over here."

"Voices?" Angelina asked.

"There are always voices that whisper, Angel. We just need to learn to listen."

Molly loved Robin's smile. She had once told him he was cute, but that word didn't do him justice. Comparing him to all the other men who had been in her life she realized he was dashing like Val, sexy like Jake, good-looking like Steve, and intense like Miguel. However, it was his charming smile that made her think cute. It was devastating.

Robin laid one hand on Talisman's back, the other on Angelina's, and whispered, "Don't move girls, and don't say a word. Just look straight ahead."

A doe and two yearlings had appeared on the opposite shore and were at the water's edge, drinking. They wore dark winter coats with patches of white on their rumps. Their large ears indicated they were mule deer. The doe's belly was heavy—her new fawns would be born in late spring.

Angelina gasped and Talisman trembled.

Robin patted both in an effort to calm them down. However, within moments, Angelina was giggling and Talisman was whining.

The doe looked up at them, her big ears moving back and forth independently of each other. It was comical the way one would move forward at the same time the other moved back which, of course, made Angelina giggle more.

Talisman just couldn't contain herself any longer. She jumped to her feet and barked.

Startled, the deer turned, and in a series of stiff-legged jumps with all four feet hitting the ground together, ran back into the woods.

Giggles completely out of control, Angelina collapsed into Robin's lap, which set Talisman to howling. Molly, overcome by the joy of the moment, found herself laughing and leaning into Robin. He threw his arm around her and pulled her close.

"It…was…awesome!" Angelina managed to say.

"Magical," Molly said.

"Well, I do my best to please."

Molly wondered if he could possibly have summoned the deer. "Something you learned from your mum?"

Robin smiled his devastating smile.

*   *   *

Despite all the chaos going on around him, Ross fell asleep in front of the wood stove, snored like a New Year's Eve drunk, and didn't budge. For hours. And hours. Talisman kept nudging him but elicited no response. Finally, she plopped down next to him and whined.

Angelina said to Liberty, "Ross seems very lazy."

"Oh, my little flag isn't lazy. He just likes to conserve energy for the important stuff."

"What's the important stuff?" Angelina asked.

"Eating's very important to Ross."

"Tali can high-five me. Does Ross do any tricks?"

"He drools a lot. He sucks on his ears once in a while. His bodily noises are quite musical. He meditates like a Zen master. He wears a flag well."

Angelina shook her head. "I think Aussies are way more interesting."

"I respect Ross for his independence. It's something I can relate to. Besides, Bassets are all-American—George Washington had one."

Finally, Ross defied his vertically-challenged position, raised his head, and yawned. He stuck his tongue out all the way—filling the air around him with a decidedly bad smell—then slowly stood and waddled toward the open door.

Talisman leapt with joy at Ross's sign of life. She ran circles around him as he ambled along. She nipped at his leg to urge him forward. She butt-slammed him with glee.

He mumbled something incoherent and trudged ahead.

"Tali isn't used to being ignored," Angelina said. "It's making her crazy."

Curious as to how this would play out, Molly, Robin, and Angelina followed them outside.

Ross went just a short way from the house, relieved himself, turned around, and headed back in.

Talisman leapt in front of him and posed in a perfectly stacked show dog stance: she stood square and still, watching him with alert eyes.

He grunted and stopped.

She issued a happy yap.

He emitted a mournful howl.

Seemingly encouraged, she scanned the ground. There, near the barbeque, she saw a fresh rib bone. She raced to it, picked it up, and returned to lay it at his feet.

He sniffed the bone with mild curiosity.

She picked it up, tossed it in the air, then crouched in a play bow and waited for him to do something. Anything.

He uttered a sort of a moo, lay down, stretched out on his side, and closed his eyes.

"Poor Tali," Angelina said.

Talisman pounced on the bone, picked it up in her teeth, and proceeded to dig a hole right in front of his nose.

"Omigod, I've never seen her dig a hole before," Molly said. "That's something far too pedestrian for her."

Robin laughed. "I think she's trying to convey the impression that she's, well, a dog. I'm sensing she hopes it will charm him."

"Poor, poor Tali," Angelina said. "Her love life is so very challenging."

Ross started to snore.

Talisman stormed off in a huff and took a position on the back porch from where she could give him the evil eye.

Angelina sat down next to her to offer comfort. "Did you hear that Tali's a hero?" Angelina asked Liberty.

"I did. You must be so proud of her." Liberty took a seat on one of the porch steps.

"She's my hero now. I'm going to start a Facebook fan page for her."

"No!" Liberty shouted. "The entire WWW is a worldwide wiretap."

"Oh." Angelina's disappointment was evident.

"Speaking of which, did you notice the telephone company truck that's been parked out front for the past few hours?" Eric asked. He was one of Liberty's students.

That news attracted everyone's attention, and people started to gather around the back porch.

Liberty shook her head. "Probably the feds setting up surveillance. I'm sure my phones have been tapped wherever I've lived. I do tend to stir up controversy, you know."

A man named Seth—whom Eric had introduced as his new roommate—spoke up. "Well, I think we should go out there and confront them. I've got my gun, I'm sure you've got yours. Let's just go and let them know they can't fu—"

"There's a child here," Robin said, cutting off the vulgarity.

Molly didn't like the hostile tone in Seth's voice. His stance and attitude reminded her of the gang-bangers from the *barrio*. She moved to Angelina's side and tried to urge her into the house, but she wouldn't budge. Molly sat down and slipped a protective arm around her.

"No," Liberty said. "No guns. No confrontations."

"Eric told me you had balls," Seth said.

"I have brains," Liberty said, her voice steady. "I do not condone violence."

Seth grunted. "Well, Eric and I disagree with you, don't we bro?"

Eric's nod was half-hearted.

"We're planning something big, and you're so gonna wish you were part of it," Seth said. "There's gonna be blood in the headlines, and our voices will finally be heard."

Liberty looked at Eric and her expression revealed a sense of betrayal. "Tell me it's not so, Dunst. I thought I knew you better than that."

Eric looked at Seth, then her. He assumed a defiant expression. "Yeah, well I thought I knew you better too."

"You're stupid, stupid men," Liberty said. "Get off my property and don't ever come back."

Seth clenched his fists and took several steps toward Liberty, but Robin headed him off. Emily moved to stand by Robin's side.

Liberty stood and pushed through her two guardians to face Seth. "I won't let you hurt anyone."

"You turn us in and you are so dead," Seth said.

"Better me than someone else."

A humorless grin crossed Seth's face. "You have guns, so you obviously believe in violence."

"I have guns for hunting and protection," Liberty said.

"Yeah, you're gonna need protection if you stick your nose into our business." Seth stormed off.

Eric hung back for a moment. "Don't be a fool, Liberty."

After the men left, Liberty's guests crowded around, asking what she intended to do. The blood was pounding so hard in Molly's head that she only caught a part of Liberty's response—enough to know Liberty was going to report the men. She looked into the faces of the people there and saw expressions ranging from fear to outrage. Then there was a tall man standing on the outer edge of the group wearing a bright orange Denver Bronco's cap and a smirk. The expression was so out of place that Molly's streetwise radar kicked in.

When he noticed her attention and their eyes met, Molly's blood ran cold.

*   *   *

Before they left, Liberty gave Angelina a new scarf for Talisman that said SEMPER FIDO. Then she presented Molly with the gift of an American flag. "You raise this with pride at your home and know that when it's blowing it's not the wind, but the last breath of every soldier and true patriot keeping it aloft. Remember their sacrifices with respect and honor, and vow to uphold what they gave their lives for, O'Malley. Freedom isn't free."

CHAPTER TWELVE

When Molly pulled up to the office on Monday morning, she was surprised to see the outdoor marquee that was normally used to advertise new house listings had been changed to read OUR BACHELOR BROKERS ARE A BUNCH OF STUDS!

Robin pulled up next to her. They got out of their cars and regarded the sign with mutual wonder.

"I don't even need Mum's gift to tell me that somehow Brooklyn's involved in this," Robin said.

Talisman had ridden with Robin. He helped her out of the car, adjusted her new SEMPER FIDO scarf, and they entered the lobby where they were met by a chaotic crowd of brokers amid the forest of ecologically-friendly greenery. Jake stood in the middle of the group tugging on his beard. Brooklyn was at his side.

"It is infernal," Lois said. "Take it down this instant."

Coco threw her hand to her hip. "In all my years in this industry, I've never seen anything more unprofessional."

Paula pointed at Brooklyn. "Is this her doing? I swear that she's an undercover agent from another brokerage firm out to entrap us in some sort of vice sting in order to ruin our company's reputation."

"What does the sign mean?" Mrs. Rosen asked.

"It means that some of us are very studly," Ted said. "It's nice to finally be acknowledged for all our many talents."

"You're an ass," Babylon told him.

"Okay, everyone settle down," Jake said. "See folks, here's the thing. Brooklyn...well, Brooklyn, do you want to tell them?"

Brooklyn hopped up on a chair and flashed everyone her perky smile. "In these tough economic times, companies like ours need to think outside the box in order to attract clients. I don't know if any of you know this, but my mother's the editor of the New York-based magazine *Women at Play.*"

Surprise rippled through the room. *Women at Play* was one of the most popular women's magazines for the chic and sophisticated. Its content included articles about the world's most eligible bachelors, hot vacation spots, top fashion trends, and the best in women's entertainment.

Brooklyn's smile broadened. "Mom's going to do a feature called 'The Bachelors of Broker's Best.' Jake, Ted, and Robin are going to be showcased."

Molly gave Robin a startled look.

He shrugged and shook his head.

Molly glanced at Jake. He didn't appear to be surprised. Actually, he had an expression she had never before seen him wear—he looked all puffed up like a proud peacock.

"To boldly go where no Broker's Best stud has gone before," Ted said.

Coco shook her head. "Lord have mercy."

"*Women at Play* sent out a press release about them coming to town for the photo shoot," Brooklyn said. "*The Blackstone Daily News* is running a story about it in this morning's paper. We'll get lots of great press that can only benefit us all."

"You're not going to participate in this, are you?" Molly asked Robin.

His smile was sheepish. "Well, it is a bit flattering,

don't you think?"

Molly rolled her eyes. Men and their easily stroked egos. It was pitiful.

The crowded lobby erupted in chaos once again.

Brilliant Bouncing Brooklyn jumped up and down and waved her arms to regain everyone's attention. "Oh, and I'd like to take this opportunity to make an announcement of my own. Also featured in the 'Broker's Best Bachelor' edition of *Women at Play* will be an article about my first novel that's coming out this spring. It's called *Blue* and is an eco-erotic tale about the green movement."

A cacophony filled the lobby once again.

Jessie's shrill voice overrode the chaos. "The phone's ringing; will you all please shut up!"

Somewhere behind the green wall of foliage that shrouded the reception desk, Jessie's phones were ringing like crazy. She could be heard struggling to handle the flood.

Molly pushed her way through people and plants to answer one of the phones. "Broker's Best. May I help you?"

A somewhat breathless woman's voice on the other end said, "I've been trying to decide what company to list my house with and, well—" she giggled, "—I saw the morning paper and, well, I'd like to have one your bachelor brokers come out and do it."

Molly rolled her eyes again and took down the information. When she hung up, she raised the note and said, "This lead is for one of our bunch of studs."

Ted quickly made his way through the room to grab it from her hand. Paraphrasing one of his favorite Trekisms, he held it aloft and said, "Let history never forget the name, Broker's Best."

*   *   *

The Wackers had decided to represent themselves in the discrimination lawsuit. Molly was surprised they agreed to cooperate with the proceedings at all until her attorney, Liz, mentioned that she had written a helpful letter informing them they could face jail time for contempt of court if they didn't show up.

Molly, Leah, and Charles were all scheduled to be deposed the same day, back to back to back. Liz told Molly that she could and should be present for the Wackers' depositions. Since Molly's co-defendants were such wild cards, it would be enormously helpful to know where they were headed in their defense. She also added, "A man who represents himself has a fool for a client and a fool for a lawyer."

Molly met Liz at nine o'clock Friday morning at the offices of the Amheds' attorney, William Cowan. They were escorted into a large conference room where a court reporter was set up in the corner and poised to record the session. The Wackers were already seated and poised to do God knows what. Much to Molly's surprise, Mr. and Mrs. Ahmed were sitting with their attorney across the table from the Wackers. Molly and Liz took seats together at the head of the table.

Molly, Mr. Ahmed, and the attorneys were all dressed in business suits, Mrs. Ahmed was in a blue *burka,* and the Wackers were in matching bell bottoms and tie-dyed shirts.

Molly leaned into Liz and whispered, "Is Lily going to be here too?" She didn't think she could withstand the woman's withering glare and remain composed.

Liz shook her head. "Only actual parties to the civil lawsuit are allowed. Lily's just a witness in this case."

Relief flooded her. What was she going to do when it actually came to trial? And when the Real Estate Commission hearing was held? Not to mention the federal case, if and when they decided to charge her.

Even anticipating all that loomed ahead made Molly crave more Xanax and Jolly Juice.

Molly smiled politely at everyone in the room, but no one seemed pleased to see her. She got the distinct impression that they all blamed her for the situation, but then she hoped it was just her imagination working overtime.

William Cowan chose Leah to be deposed first. The court reporter swore her in. She was asked preliminary questions establishing her identity, given basic protocol instructions, and then the questioning began in earnest.

"Did you refuse to sell your house at 121 Wildflower Lane to Mr. and Mrs. Ahmed because they are Muslims?" Mr. Cowan asked.

"Of course not," Leah said.

"Why 'of course not?' What would make anyone think otherwise? Their offer was better than the one you accepted. What other reason would there be?"

Leah fiddled with her peace sign necklace. "There were several reasons. For each contract we received, I added the numbers of the buyers' names to the dates of their respective contracts and the amount of money they were offering. I chose the other offer because their number was a four and the Ahmed's number was a six."

Mr. Cowan blinked.

Leah sighed. "Four is a more auspicious number for a home sale. It's solid. Six is unsteady. A four contract is more likely to close and not experience delays or problems. Don't you know your numerology?"

Mr. Cowan shook his head. "Seriously? You're being serious here?"

"Of *course* I am."

Mr. Cowan shook his head again. "But you would have made significantly more money with the Ahmed's contract. It's irrational that you wouldn't have accepted it."

"My wife is as rational as they come," Charles said. "She's a psychologist."

Liz leaned forward. "Mr. Wacker, I realize I'm not your attorney, but I should advise you that you're not permitted to interrupt another's deposition."

Charles glared at her. "You're right, you're *not* my attorney."

Properly chastised, Liz sat back in her seat.

"And what did your real estate broker, Molly O'Malley, advise you in this situation?"

"She told me to trust my judgment."

Mr. Cowan looked at Molly. "Seriously? She told you to base your decision on numerology?"

Molly started to speak up in her own defense, but Liz placed a hand on her arm.

Leah sneered. "She didn't say to base my decision on numerology. I don't think *she* knows what it is either. How you two can presume to advise people on contracts without understanding the basics of numerology, I'll just never know. It's scandalous."

"When she presented the offers to you, did Ms. O'Malley advise you not to discriminate against the Ahmeds?" Mr. Cowan asked Leah.

"When we listed the house she told us we couldn't discriminate. She didn't need to tell us again. We're not idiots."

Mr. Cowan's expression did not appear to agree with that assessment. "Did Ms. O'Malley suggest you take the other offer because those buyers were also her clients and she would make more money in that scenario?"

"No."

"Mrs. Wacker, you said earlier there were *several* reasons you didn't sell the house to the Ahmeds," Mr. Cowan said. "Would you please elaborate?"

"Well, I did use my pendulum over each contract. The pendulum gave me a 'no' signal over the one the Ahmeds submitted. The Hoyts' offer received an enthusiastic 'yes.'"

Mr. Cowan smirked. "Your pendulum?"

"Yes, it's a very nice one made of rose quartz crystal. His name is Rock Hudson. He's never steered me wrong."

Mr. Cowan snorted. "Your pendulum is named Rock Hudson?"

"Yes. He's quite handsome, but I do think he's gay so I always have to take that into account when he responds to my questions."

Mr. Cowan emitted a sharp chuckle, which quickly morphed into a giant belly laugh that shook the conference table. Finally, when he could catch his breath, he said, "You're going for an insanity defense here, aren't you?"

"How *dare* you, sir," Leah said. "I'm a psychologist."

Charles glared at Liz. "Aren't you going to tell him to be more respectful to my wife?"

Liz shrugged. "I'm not your attorney in this matter, Mr. Wacker."

Mr. Cowan collected himself, took a drink of water, and managed to continue. "I see, well. So, back to the day that the Ahmeds looked at your home. You made a comment to Mrs. Ahmed about how her *burka* didn't allow her *chi* to flow. Would you please explain that?"

"*Burkas* are so bulky and all-encompassing," Leah said. "The *chi*, a person's lifeforce, is restricted by such garments. It's not healthy. I was just trying to be helpful."

"And how do you presume to know this, Mrs. Wacker?" Mr. Cowan asked.

"Well, I was an Arab woman in a past life and wore *burkas*. I remember what it felt like. Most unhealthy."

Mr. Cowan leaned forward. "Excuse me?"

"In one of my past lives, I was an Arab woman named Yasmin. I lived in Persia—what is now called Iran. I was married to a man named Omar. We had three sons and two daughters. We were a happy family, but I wasn't very healthy at all. I died young. I think it was because I wore a *burka* all my life."

Mr. and Mrs. Ahmed looked at her with alarm. Mr. Ahmed scrunched down in his seat and tapped his temple.

Mr. Cowan had no response and everyone sat in uncomfortable silence for a long time.

Finally, Mr. Cowan asked, "Because of your *past life* as a Persian are you prejudiced against people of Arab descent or the Islamic faith?"

"Of *course* not. I just told you I was very happy as Yasmin. The Ahmeds here could even be my direct descendants."

Mrs. Ahmed squeaked.

"Is there any class of people for whom you do hold a negative bias?"

"Republicans. Would never have sold my house to a Republican."

Despite herself, Molly grinned. Republicans were not a federally protected class. Yes, there really was a God after all.

*   *   *

That afternoon, following the depositions, Jake did something he had never before done. He invited Molly to go to lunch with him. Even during their romantic relationship, he had never taken her out—he didn't want people to know he was dating one of his brokers.

What Molly found even more surprising than the invitation, was that he didn't invite her to some remote café tucked away in the foothills. He invited her to accompany him to Fort Blackstone Grill, the popular bar and steak house located right next door to the Broker's Best office. Molly wasn't sure what to make of his out-of-character behavior.

Familiar faces from the office were seated at tables scattered throughout the restaurant, and their expressions of surprise mirrored Molly's own internal state. Jake was such a loner that it was unlikely anyone had ever before seen him with a lunch companion, female or otherwise.

"You feel okay?" she asked him as they settled into the plush leather booth.

"Sure. Why?"

"Just wondering." She didn't need to look at the menu. The chili and cornbread plate was her favorite.

Midday news blared from the TV at the bar, and a rowdy crowd of people sat at the bar drinking their lunch. Molly took note of the fact that the booth she and Jake were seated in was the same one where she, Val, Ben, and Summer had shared a meal their first day on the job as new rookies. Was that only seven months ago?

"How are the newest rookies doing?" Molly asked after the waitress had taken their orders.

Jake grinned. "Babylon is a force a nature. An extremely tall, solid, humorless, *purple* force of nature. She's already doing deals. However, I'm not sure if it's because of savvy marketing skills, or due to the fact she scares the hell out of everyone she encounters."

Molly laughed. "That'd be my theory."

"Brooklyn would have made a better real estate assistant than broker. She's just too much of a cheerleader and not enough of a quarterback. And Ruby? Well, this is a tough business, and I'm not sure she's got the *chutzpa* to survive it."

"I wasn't very confident when I started either." Molly knew that was a major understatement.

Jake smiled. "Yeah, but I never doubted you for a second."

His eyes penetrated her and she felt the intense connection. The electricity between them had always consisted of serious voltage.

Molly was determined to ramp down the amperage. "The depositions today were interesting. My attorney told me that she thinks the Ahmeds may drop their case."

"Don't get too hopeful. Lily can be very persuasive, and she's determined to get your license revoked."

Molly's hope wilted. "I had to pay my attorney more money today. There went most of what I made from Liberty True's closing. I've just got two more deals lined up: my soon-to-be-wed couple and the closing on Val's house. Chief Waters' estate is my only listing, and the showings we've had have all been people interested in the gore factor. These really are tough times." Molly's anxiety level was high.

Jake took a swig of his beer. "How are Angel and Tali?"

His question took Molly by surprise. Normally, Jake had no interest in her family, which had been a major point of contention during their romantic involvement. Jake was a man who liked women and horses, not children and dogs.

"Angel hates me and Tali's depressed."

"Dogs." He chuckled. "Did Jessie ever tell you about the Border Collie she used to have?"

Molly shook her head.

"Cody was completely OCD. A total neurotic obsessive-compulsive. He had this little coyote toy he took everywhere with him. When squeezed, it would yip and howl just like a coyote. Cody thought this was hilarious and drove us all nuts with it. One day this coyote started howling and wouldn't stop—the thing inside got stuck and we couldn't turn it off. Made us totally crazy and made the dog go bonkers. So, I had to take him outside and shoot him."

"Cody?"

Jake laughed. "No, silly. The coyote toy. Cody got

real depressed after that, and I don't think he ever forgave me."

Jake rarely laughed or told tales on himself, and in a million years Molly would never have imagined he would affectionately refer to her as silly. The only endearment he had ever used for her was wildcat. What was happening?

Their food was served and they dug in with gusto. After a few minutes of concentrated eating, he asked, "So, how's it going living with Robin?"

A light bulb went on inside Molly. This was all an attempt to court her because Robin had him worried. She knew there had to be a rational explanation for his irrational behavior. "Robin's presence in our lives right now is an incredible blessing."

He didn't respond. She could sense he was waiting to hear more, but there was nothing more to say.

"So, how is Jessie's pursuit of Preacher Levi?" Molly asked.

"He's hard to catch. We Daltons always seem to have trouble catching the ones we want." He set down his fork and cleared his throat. "Something I should have said a long time ago is how sorry I am that I hurt you. I have no excuses and hope you can find a way to forgive me."

He had apologized the day she walked in on him and Lily, but he had never asked for forgiveness. She thought back to what he said when he followed her out to her car that day. *What you and I had was about wild, mutual passion. It was never about love.*

She took a deep breath. "You still loved Lily, and you didn't love me. I didn't completely understand that until I found you two together."

"Actually, my brief reconciliation with Lily helped me finally get over her."

"I'm glad you were able to find resolution," she said honestly.

He was about to say something else when all hell broke loose at the bar.

"Turn the TV up!" someone shouted.

"Can you believe that?" the bartender said. "I guess you can only get away with being a radical left lunatic for so long before justice catches up to you."

Raucous laughter filled the air as Molly dropped her spoon full of chili, leapt to her feet, and ran over to the television. She couldn't hear the reporter's words over the uproar but saw a photo of Liberty that had been taken at the recent rally. The chyron at the bottom of the screen read: *Professor Liberty True has been fired from Blackstone University for alleged un-American activity.*

* * *

The atmosphere at Liberty's home was grim. Liberty sat on the floor in front of the cold wood stove holding Ross's head in her lap. Her face reflected utter despair, and Molly could tell she was struggling to hold back tears.

Liberty's friends sat around the living room in various states of distress.

Emily wept, another of Liberty's students named Ryan kept punching a pillow on the sofa, and Vince, a fellow resister, paced.

"They called me un-American," Liberty said. "How could anyone do that? How can they even suggest such a thing? Un-American?"

Molly sat down on the floor and slipped her arm around Liberty. Tough, unflappable Liberty had been leveled, and Molly had no idea how to help.

Angelina sat on Liberty's other side and patted her back. Talisman sniffed and licked Liberty's face before lying down a respectful distance away. Robin started building a fire in the stove.

"You're a fighter, Liberty. *A freedom fighter,*" Emily said. "You need to fight this. We'll all help you. We'll rally support, we'll raise money for your legal fees, we'll—"

"Anyone who stands with me will be targeted too. It's the way it works."

"I'll take that chance," Vince said.

Ryan punched a pillow. "Me too."

"We mustn't let them win," Emily said.

Angelina squeezed Liberty's hand. "We won't let them hurt you. Will we, Mom?"

Molly didn't know what could be done. It was a case of David and Goliath.

"So, what do you think happened here, exactly?" Molly asked.

Liberty shrugged. "I've had enemies within the school for a long time—officials overly concerned about the university's image. And some of the more conservative kids have complained about me, but because I have tenure my job was secure. However, Warner said that serious charges against me had come to light, and I was considered a clear and present danger to the institution and students."

Molly remembered the smirking man from Liberty's housewarming party. "Whatever happened about Eric and Seth?"

"I contacted the Homeland Security hotline and told them what I knew," Liberty said.

Vince stopped pacing and turned to her. "Didn't you hear? Wednesday night the feds raided their house and found explosives. They were arrested."

Liberty's face paled. "Well, at least they were stopped before they did something awful."

"Maybe they figured out you turned them in and implicated you," Ryan said.

"At your party there was a tall man wearing a

Bronco's hat. Who was he?" Molly asked.

Liberty thought about it for a few moments. "His name was Masterson."

"He's Laura's new boyfriend," Emily added. "Why?"

"There was something not right about him," Molly said. "I have good internal radar."

"So, Eric Dunst has a new roommate who incites him to violence, and Laura Williams has a new boyfriend who sets off your radar," Liberty said. "Government plants? I'm not important enough to warrant that kind of operation."

Emily's laugh was mirthless. "Seriously? You underestimate yourself, Liberty."

"Well, there is the presumption of innocence in this country," Molly said. "Surely, this can all be straightened out."

Vince shook his head. "Not when the accusation involves terrorism. Once that word's attached to your name, it's game over. The government can detain without charges, limit access to an attorney, and classify evidence so it can't be challenged. They can search your home, seize your assets, and wiretap everyone you've ever known without even showing probable cause."

"How is that even legal?" Molly asked.

"It shouldn't be," Liberty said. "But after 9/11, the Patriot Act gave the federal government sweeping powers in the name of national security. A few things were rolled back in 2015, but not nearly enough. And now? The new regime has brought back the worst of it—and then some." Liberty angrily swiped away a tear rolling down her cheek. "Benjamin Franklin once said, 'They that can give up essential liberty to obtain a little temporary safety deserve neither liberty nor safety.' And here we are."

Molly's head reeled. However, the thought did cross her mind that in the case of David and Goliath, David won. Liberty had righteousness on her side. Now if they could only figure out how to master the proper slingshot, there might be hope.

CHAPTER THIRTEEN

Coco's weekly *Real Help* charity project was scheduled late Sunday afternoon, after the offices of Broker's Best had closed for the day. A group of volunteer brokers gathered in the conference room to advise the hapless and soon-to-be-homeless.

The conference tables were well-stocked with laptops and office supplies. The breakfast bar had a spread of coffee and Danishes, and Angelina had thoughtfully provided bowls of dog and cat treats in case anyone brought their pets. The restful sounds of whale song floated from overhead speakers; even without Robin's mum's gift, Molly was certain it was Brooklyn's inspiration. Of course, ecologically-friendly plants abounded.

This was the first time Molly had participated in *Real Help*, and she only came because Angelina insisted on moving forward with her program to help find foster homes for people's pets. Robin was supposed to attend, but he took Talisman to an emergency visit with the canine massage therapist—she had pulled a muscle that morning while performing her rousing celebratory tribal dance of success.

Coco, Babylon, Mrs. Ruby Rosen, Brooklyn and her dog Sami were in attendance. An awards banquet had claimed the rest of the Broker's Best agents. One of Coco's assistants was accepting an award on her boss's behalf, which given the size of Coco's ego, Molly found surprising. Coco's commitment to her charitable cause was impressive.

Coco's preferred lender, Karen Phelps, arrived, as did a *Blackstone Daily News* reporter named Anne Hutchins. Molly decided that it must have been her presence that drew the unexpected appearance of Lily Dalton. Molly wondered if Lily had heard there would be press coverage and didn't want her own company to be without representation at the philanthropic event. Lily brought along her assistant, Maria Madrid—also known as Natasha Fatale.

Lily timed her arrival after everyone else, and she made a grand entrance. Tall, lithe, and stunning, Lily always made Molly feel as if she were a mere peasant. Of French and Chinese ancestry, Lily had mastered the art of sultry, and her style was elegant. The most expensive designer clothing and jewelry, perfectly coiffed hair and nails, and an attitude that reeked of superiority intimidated most everyone Lily encountered. Molly thought Lily and Jake were the most unlikely couple she had ever known. Actually, she found the pairing utterly fascinating.

Lily strolled into the room, stiletto heels clicking loudly on the flagstone floor, and Maria trotted in behind her. They took seats at the head of the table, where Lily settled in and then removed an iPad from her briefcase. She refused to make eye contact with Molly, which suited her just fine. Molly condemned the other woman's apparent motives for being there, and then a quiet inner voice questioned Molly's own motives.

Molly wasn't entirely sure about this new relationship she was developing with God. It seemed as if He wasn't going to let her get away with much.

Maria glanced furtively at Molly, who was sorry the woman hadn't yet managed to escape Lily. She tried to offer a placating smile, but Maria wisely refused to acknowledge it.

"Now that I'm here, we may begin," Lily said.

Coco threw her hand to her hip. "Say what?"

Lily gave her a withering stare.

Molly was surprised to see Coco flinch. She had not thought anyone could ever intimidate Coco.

Coco picked up the *Real Help* sandwich sign. "Now that *you're* here, Lily, I'll set this outside on the sidewalk to let people know we're open for business."

Molly smiled at the sarcasm in Coco's voice. She glanced over at Anne Hutchins and saw she was taking notes. Lily's expression was cool.

Coco moved to step from the conference room into the lobby when a man blocked her path and backed her into the room. A woman followed him and slammed the door shut behind them. Molly saw it happen, but it took several moments before her mind registered the handguns that both strangers held. When the man spoke, Molly's stomach flipped over and burning bile rose to her throat.

"We're looking for Miss Molly O'Malley of Broker's Best, located at 1601 Main Street in the heart of Blackstone."

Molly's eyes flew from the guns to the faces, and she recognized Ronnie and Gina Jackson, the meth heads she had reported. Out of the corner of her eye, Molly saw that Angelina was standing next to the breakfast bar, a Danish in her hand, her eyes wide with alarm.

Please, God, protect Angel. To help God along, Molly stood up and stepped forward. "If it's me you want, just get it over with…whatever you plan to do."

Gina's eyes narrowed. "It's because of you that my little girl was taken away from me." She marched up to Molly, and placed the gun to her left temple.

Angelina screamed, "Mom!"

All different kinds of panic flooded Molly, but she fought to rein it in.

Gina tilted her head to one side and looked at Angelina. "Is that your daughter, Miss Molly O'Malley? Maybe I'll show you what it's like to lose a little girl."

Terror filled Molly as she realized that her worst fear had come true. By reporting the meth house to the police, she had put her daughter's life at risk. Havana's warning flashed through her mind. *Dere be crazy peoples and angry guns.*

"Are you blind as well as stupid?" Lily said, her voice smooth and condescending. "Does the child look like cheap Irish trash? Angelina is my assistant's daughter." Lily sat at the head of the table, her arms crossed in a casual gesture, her attitude imperious.

"*Sí.*" Maria didn't miss a beat. She jumped to her feet and gathered Angelina into her arms. "Hush *chica, mamá* is here."

Molly had never been more grateful for Miguel's strong genetic imprint on their daughter.

Angelina didn't fight the ruse, but she didn't take her terrified eyes off Molly either.

Gina exhaled heavily into Molly's face, who resisted gagging from the sickly stench. "Well, that makes you a lucky little mother now doesn't it because I'd just love to shoot your baby right in front of you so you can feel the pain I feel right now."

"What do you want?" Molly asked.

"What do you think we want, bitch? We want our little girl back. They took Lisa away from us, and if we don't get her back tonight, you're gonna die."

Ronnie pointed his gun high overhead and fired a shot. Plaster fell and screams echoed the blast. "You're all going to die," he said.

Maria wrapped her arms more tightly around Angelina, and Sami jumped up onto Brooklyn's lap. Ronnie pointed his gun at Sami. "What's that dog wearing?"

Sami was all decked out in bling. Brooklyn responded without her usual perky little smile. "Her pink leopard velvet collar is studded with black Swarovski crystals in sterling silver settings and is matched by a crystal ankle bracelet. Isn't she adorable?"

Ronnie waved his gun around like a wild man. "Get rid of it. The shadow people will use the crystals to direct their radio frequencies into our heads. Get rid of it all *now*!"

Brooklyn jumped. With trembling hands she stripped Sami of her bling and held it up to Ronnie. "What do you want me to do with it?"

Ronnie's frantic eyes scanned the room. He pointed the gun at one of the larger potted plants. "Bury it. Bury it fast."

Brooklyn pushed Sami from her lap and scurried over to the big, potted Ficus. Using her fingers, she dug a hole, dropped the items in, then buried everything. Her hand swiped away tears from her cheeks as she retrieved Sami, sat back down, and clutched the dog. Dirt smeared her face and caked Sami's snow-white fur. They looked very earthy.

Ronnie picked up a black, plastic trash can. "Everyone sit down at this big table *right now*. I'm gonna walk around, and you're gonna put your cell phones, computers, and all your other demonic devices in here."

Everyone moved to comply with Ronnie's directive.

He stopped next to where Babylon sat and blinked. "What are you?"

Babylon gave him a cool look. "What the hell do you think I am?"

Gingerly, he touched the dog collar she wore and the long leash attached to it that hung by her side. Then he gazed with wonder at her hair. "A really, really tall purple dog?"

"Damn, but you're a smart guy."

He held up the trash can, and she deposited her phone.

Karen sat next to her, scribbling furiously on a notepad.

Ronnie kicked her chair. "Are you passing notes to the shadow people?"

"I...I'm writing a letter to my parents. I've been mad at them lately, and I don't want to die without them knowing how much I love them."

His eyes narrowed and he glanced down to read her letter. "Dear Mommy and Daddy? That's pitiful. How old are you anyways?"

"Twenty-five."

He read some more, then shrugged. "Yeah, okay, write. But give me your phone."

Trembling, Karen dropped her phone in with the rest.

Molly stood still as a statue, Gina's gun still pressed into her temple.

Through clenched teeth, Gina said, "Turn yours over too."

Molly reached into the pocket of her suit jacket and withdrew her cell phone. Gina snatched it from her hand and tossed it into the trash can as Ronnie walked by.

Ronnie pointed at Anne's camera. "What's that for?"

"I'm a reporter from *The Blackstone Daily News* and am here for a story. Looks like I've got a good one too. Would very much like to take some photos, if I may?"

Ronnie shook his head. "No way."

"Yes, she can," Gina said. "A reporter can tell the world how we so unjustly lost Lisa. A reporter is good, Ronnie."

The wild look in Ronnie's eyes was replaced by one more pensive. He waved his gun at Anne. "Yeah. Okay. Report."

Anne picked up the camera and took a photo of him. He flinched at the flash and seemed uncertain.

"Report. Okay," Gina said.

"Yeah. Report." Ronnie finished collecting the rest of the hostages' hardware.

"It's almost six o'clock," Coco said. "I ran an ad. People are coming at six."

"We turned out the lights and locked the outside doors," Ronnie told her.

Gina tapped Molly's temple with the barrel of the gun. "Now, you're going to that phone over there and you're going to call the cops. You're going to tell them that we want our daughter turned over to us tonight and then safe escape outta here. We're gonna kill one of you every half hour until it happens. Do you understand me?"

Molly's voice was a whisper. "I understand perfectly." She walked to the telephone on the wall and dialed 911.

The operator answered, "Nine one one, what is your emergency?"

"This is Molly O'Malley. I'm a broker at Broker's Best on Main Street—"

"1601 Main Street in the heart of Blackstone," Ronnie said.

"1601 Main Street, in the heart of Blackstone," Molly repeated. "A couple named Gina and Ronnie Jackson are here, with guns, demanding the return of their daughter Lisa, who was recently taken by Child Protective Services. If Lisa is not delivered to their custody immediately and they are not all allowed to leave, they will begin killing hostages…one every half hour. There are ten hostages being held, including a child."

Gina poked her in the ribs with the gun. "Tell them who we got here."

"Besides the child, the hostages include five Broker's Best agents, Lily Dalton of Blackstone Realty and her assistant Maria, Karen Phelps of First National Bank of Blackstone, and a reporter from *The Blackstone Daily News* named Anne Hutchins. Shots have been fired. This is bad."

"And the dogs," Ronnie said. "We got two dogs, and we'll shoot them too."

Brooklyn squealed while Babylon rolled her eyes.

"There are also…dogs," Molly said. Her head was swimming, and she had no idea how she was managing to stand, let alone speak.

Before the police operator could respond, Gina snatched the phone from Molly. "We're gonna kill them all, one-by-one. No negotiation, nothin' to talk about. You get us our daughter and let us all walk outta here. You got a half hour before we start killing. Call us back at exactly 6:30 with news you got it all arranged, or we start taking them out." She shot the wall next to the phone, then slammed the receiver back onto the hook.

Everyone jumped.

In the silence that followed, the whale song seemed particularly loud.

"What the hell is that noise?" Ronnie asked.

"It's supposed to be restful," Brooklyn said, pointing to the speaker on the wall.

"That's shadow people talking, if I ever heard them." Ronnie shot the speaker.

Three down, Molly thought. Both Ronnie and Gina had .38s. Each held six bullets—she had learned a lot about guns during her years spent in the ghetto. However, as much as she hated them, she thought with longing of paranoid Paula Parry, her concealed carry permit, and her ever-handy Derringer.

Mrs. Ruby Rosen screamed and then broke out with robust, earth-shattering wailing.

Ruby's hysterics appeared to further fray Ronnie's sanity, and he stalked over and yanked her from her chair. "You shut up *right now.*" He pushed the barrel of his gun into the side of her nose.

Ruby was shocked into convulsive gasping. Then a flood of urine poured down her legs and splattered on the floor.

Ronnie jumped back and regarded the sight with horror. "You're going to be the first to die, lady." He cocked the gun and pointed it at her. "I think I'll put you out of your misery right now, before you make a worse mess...if you know what I mean."

Everyone held their breath.

"Before you go killing anyone, why don't you take a few minutes to tell me your story so I can write my article?" Anne said, her voice calm and professional.

Ronnie's free hand picked at sores on his face.

"So, why did CPS take Lisa?" Anne asked.

Gina shoved Molly into the middle of the room. "This bitch here called the cops and told them lies about us."

Anne scribbled in her notebook. "What did she tell the police?"

Gina slammed a fist into Molly's back. "Yeah, why don't you tell what you told."

Molly noticed that Angelina had stood up, retrieved some dishtowels from the breakfast bar, and was headed down the table toward Ruby. Angelina had too much compassion for her own good.

Molly was quick to start talking, desperate to capture Ronnie's attention. "I showed the Jackson's home, and their daughter appeared cold and malnourished. I was concerned."

Gina struck Molly again, harder than before. "Tell her the rest."

Molly ignored the pain. "In real estate school they teach us to look for signs of meth labs, and I saw those signs at the Jackson home."

Anne scribbled. "I see. So, Mr. and Mrs. Jackson, how is it that if you had a meth lab in your home, you aren't in jail?"

Ronnie turned toward Anne, uncocked his gun, and threw his arms apart in an exaggerated shrug. "'Cause there weren't no meth lab."

Detective Mendoza had told Molly that when the police arrived, the Jacksons had already disposed of all the evidence that could have implicated them in a meth lab operation.

"But they took Lisa anyway?" Anne asked.

Gina sniffed. "Well, we were so damn busy getting ready for the damn real estate showing that we forgot to feed Lisa that day and, yeah, it was a little cold in the house but nothing she wasn't used to."

Anne nodded. "Well, it seems to me that you got a raw deal."

Lily said, "Miss Molly O'Malley does tend to venture where she doesn't belong and stick herself into other people's business. She even had an affair with my husband."

Molly resisted the urge to point out that he was her ex-husband at the time but knew that the more the Jacksons focused on her, the safer everyone else would be.

Angelina looked up from her job of helping Ruby clean her mess. It appeared as if she might defend Molly on her own, so Molly blurted out, "That's true."

Lily leaned forward, a slight smile playing at her lips. "But I heard your precious Steve left you for another woman. Payback's a bitch, isn't it?"

"Yes," Molly said. "It is."

"But you didn't mourn that loss very long because I hear you're already living with another man," Lily said.

Once again, Molly wanted to defend herself, but was grateful to deflect attention. "I'm shameless."

Lily shrugged and looked at Anne. "There you have it. What do you expect from a busybody slut without morals? Seems to me the Jacksons here got a raw deal. I think we should help them get Lisa back. I'm richer than God, and of course the most important woman in Blackstone. I'd be more than happy to pay for their attorney. I can hire the best, and after they get their daughter back, I think the Jacksons should sue Miss Molly O'Malley for slander."

Anne nodded and gave Molly a dirty look. "I definitely think she should pay for her crimes."

Gina slugged Molly's back again. "Yeah!"

"Getting even is good," Ronnie said.

Despite the battering she was taking, Molly was starting to breathe again. Perhaps they had achieved killus interruptus.

However, when Brooklyn's perky smile reappeared, Molly experienced a sinking feeling.

"My mom owns the internationally famous magazine *Women at Play*, and I bet she'd help spread the word about how awful Molly is and how she messed up your lives."

Ronnie's face went blank. "Women what?"

"Wow," Gina said. *"Women at Play?* Loved the Johnny Depp article. Do you know Johnny Depp? He is *so* sexy."

"Johnny who?" Ronnie asked.

Brooklyn's smile faded a bit. "Well, no, I don't know Mr. Depp, but—"

"Johnny who?" Ronnie asked again.

"You know, Johnny Depp," Gina said. "He's so dark and handsome, and his eyes are sexy sad. I'm just crazy about him."

Ronnie aimed his gun at Gina. "You screwing around on me?"

"The actor, you moron. He played Captain Jack Sparrow."

"The pirate guy from the movies?"

"Yeah." Gina aimed her gun at Ronnie. "You wanna make something of it? If you can have your fantasies— Mr. I Just Want a Piece of Angelina Jolie—then I can have mine."

Molly held her breath. Yes, please just shoot each other.

"Now, we mustn't be negative here," Brilliant Bouncing Brooklyn interjected. "In The Secret Power of Intention and Visualization in the Now school of thought we believe that fantasy is a healthy part of one's sexuality."

Molly—and most everyone else in the room—exhaled as their hopes deflated.

Both Gina and Ronnie turned their guns toward Brooklyn.

"What?" Ronnie asked.

"What?" Brooklyn asked.

"So, let's get this straight," Gina said. "Supposedly, your mom owns this big magazine, and yet you say you don't know Johnny Depp. That just don't make no sense."

Brooklyn paled. "I bet my mom knows him. Maybe she could ask him to be a character witness for you in court."

"What?" Ronnie asked again. His shaking fingers found the sores on his face again.

Gina's eyes narrowed to slits. "Wait a minute here. I think we're being played for fools, Ronnie. This just don't make no sense. They're trying to pull one over on us."

"Damn, I don't feel so good. I need some ice," Ronnie said.

"I bet there's some ice in the kitchen," Brooklyn said.

Babylon shook her head. "That's not the kind of ice they need, you ditz." She raised a tube of glue. "I've been sitting here sniffing this, and I sure feel better."

Ronnie moved to snatch it from her hand. "A good high?"

"A super one," Babylon said.

He opened the tube and sniffed.

"But it's made me have to pee," Babylon said. "I gotta pee bad or I'm going to lose my bladder like Mrs. Rosen did." She looked at Molly and raised a pierced eyebrow.

"Me too," Molly said.

Gina chuckled. "You ain't going nowhere."

Babylon stood. "Just take us to the goddamn toilet. You can stand over us with your precious gun and *clap* for us as our piss successfully hits the pot."

Molly wasn't sure what exact plan Babylon had, but it was clear that she had something in mind.

Anne's camera flashed as she took a photo of Gina. "Don't you want me to say in my article that you treated your prisoners humanely?"

Gina blinked. "Yeah, okay, humane."

"It's getting pretty close to six-thirty," Babylon said. "I'd bet we're in for the long haul. Lily, why don't you kick off your killer heels and get comfy. Coco, I think you need to put all your weight into prayer. And Butthead Babbling Brooklyn, I think you should cuddle up with one of your prickly cacti and get all affectionate because that's just so all eco-erotic and totally you. Anne, while we're gone, why don't you use that camera to get a shot of those Broker's Best FOR SALE signs over there— they'll be great for your story. Maybe Karen could hold one up for you, but have her be careful of the sharp, spiked legs. Maria, you need to take care of that precious little girl of yours 'cause, well, you just never know what's going to happen next."

Ronnie looked only momentarily confused by Babylon's comments before his attention was recaptured by glue.

Molly's head was perfectly clear. She understood the messages Babylon had just imparted to their fellow prisoners and sensed that they did too. There was a sudden, shared clarity in the face of death—something that went beyond the ordinary. It felt like a shift in time and space. It was tangible.

Gina opened the door and used the gun to wave the two women out ahead of her. "Let's hurry. They're gonna call us in less than ten minutes."

As they left the room, Molly glanced back at Angelina who was sitting by Ruby, holding the woman's hand. She watched as Maria moved around the table to sit with them.

Yes, protect my little girl, Maria. And may God protect them all.

When they stepped into the dark lobby, Molly could see through the front windows that the police had arrived. Blue and red lights flashed, floodlights glared, and uniformed officials swarmed. Gina quickly closed the door behind them and shoved the women toward the ladies room. The door was marked with a glowing cowgirl nightlight.

As Babylon pushed through the door first she clapped her hands twice and the lights came on. Molly glanced at Gina, who was anxiously looking back over her shoulder and didn't seem to notice the Clapper action.

Once inside, Gina leaned back against the door with the gun leveled at them. "Go on, then. Get it done."

Molly and Babylon entered adjacent stalls and closed the doors. A minute later, Babylon's hand reached underneath and held out a Bic lighter for Molly. "You grew up in the *barrio*, didn't you?" Babylon whispered.

Molly took the lighter. "Yes."

"Bet you learned a thing or two from those girl gangsters."

"Some."

"Gotta love those girls and their hairspray, huh?"

Yes, Molly knew exactly what the Latina girl gangsters did with their hairspray. She palmed the lighter.

"What are you two doing in there? Hurry it up. This ain't no social hour."

Molly flushed the toilet and stepped out to the sink where she washed her hands. She took a moment to look at herself in the mirror, grimaced, and fluffed her hair. "God, if I'm going to die, I want to look better than this." She grabbed the can of Coco's hairspray sitting on the shelf, and as she did so, Babylon clapped the lights off.

Gina shrieked. "What the hell?"

A gunshot exploded in the darkness, the muzzle flash flaring like lightning. Molly heard something clatter across the tiles—maybe keys—then Gina fired blindly toward the sound.

Molly dropped to the floor. Her trembling fingers clutching the hairspray, she aimed toward where she'd seen the flash, then flicked the Bic. A burst of flame whooshed through the air like a mini blowtorch, catching Gina's blouse and setting it ablaze.

Gina screamed and fired wildly again, the shot shattering a mirror.

Babylon lunged from behind and looped her dog leash around Gina's body, yanking it tight. Gina shrieked again, flailing, managing to get off two more shots.

The sound triggered the Clapper. The lights blazed on.

Babylon yanked the flaming blouse off Gina and slammed her head against the floor. She went limp.

Molly scrambled to grab the gun, even though she had already counted the shots and knew it was empty.

"Give me your scarf," Babylon said. Molly untied the soft fabric from around her neck, handed it over, and Babylon stuffed the scarf into Gina's mouth. "We've got to hurry—Ronnie must've heard the shots."

They raced back toward the conference room. Babylon reached it first, flung the door open, and charged inside with Molly close behind.

"Ronnie," Babylon said, her voice breathless and tone urgent. "The shadow people surprised us."

Ronnie stood swaying in the center of the room, eyes

glazed, panic etched across his face. He waved the gun in wild arcs. "Gina?"

"She's holding them off, but they're trying to get past her," Babylon told him.

"Hide Angel!" Molly shouted.

Maria shoved Angelina underneath the conference table, then shielded Ruby—frozen in terror—with her own body.

Ronnie's panic grew. "Shadow people? Angels? What's happening?"

"Now!" Babylon cried.

The women surged forward. Babylon grabbed Ronnie's arm, forcing it up as the gun discharged into the ceiling, showering them with plaster.

Lily charged in wielding a stiletto heel and struck him in the head, while Brooklyn shoved a thorny cactus into his face.

He screamed and squeezed off another wild shot.

Karen barreled into fray with a FOR SALE sign and jabbed the sharp metal base into his back.

The gun flew from Ronnie's hand, and Molly caught it midair.

Anne yanked his legs out from under him, and Coco followed with a two-hundred-pound body slam to the chest.

Molly, Babylon, Brooklyn, and Lily pinned his limbs while Karen sprinted to unlock the door for the police.

Sami barked excitedly at the pile of people on the floor, and Anne snapped a photo for the front page of the morning paper.

*   *   *

Angelina rushed into Molly's arms. All through the crisis, Angelina had never shed a single tear, but now that the police had arrived and the danger was over, she was in hysterics. After giving full vent to her tears, she managed to say, "I thought she was going to kill you. I'm so sorry I've been mad at you. I just don't know what I'd do without you."

Molly held her in a fierce hug. "It's okay now." She glanced up to see Lily watching them. "Thank you for saving Angel."

Lily tossed her head. "I did it for her, not you."

Molly nodded. "I know."

Lily turned to Anne. "Be sure to report that I saved the child's life." She smiled at Babylon. "I like you. You should come work for me." To Ruby, she said, "Mrs. Ruby Slipper Rosen…you're just not in Kansas anymore, are you?" Finally, she regarded Brooklyn with disdain. "You're an utterly inane twit and are on my radar now, so watch yourself."

For a moment, Molly felt an overwhelming sense of relief. Perhaps Lily had found a new victim to torment and would leave her alone. However, that brief moment passed when Lily's final words were directed at her. "And Miss Molly O'Malley of Broker's Best in the heart of Blackstone…I'm not done with you yet."

*   *   *

On Monday morning, the marquee outside of the Broker's Best offices was changed to read OUR BROKER BABES ARE RED HOT!

CHAPTER FOURTEEN

Robin spent the following week pampering Molly, Angelina, and Talisman, who had decided to take the week off and stay at home. Molly asked Jake to cover her business, and the four of them hunkered down, cut off from all contact with the outside world.

Robin immediately forwarded Molly's cell phone directly to Jake, and then made a new recording for the home phone voicemail: "All callers may be assured Molly and Angelina are fine after their frightening ordeal, but they do not wish to be disturbed. They are busy designing a new line of Red Hot Broker Babes Action Dolls. If you love Molly and Angelina, you'll respect their need for undisturbed rest and recreation. If you don't love them, then they don't want to talk to you anyway. Please do not leave a message as they won't listen to it."

Angelina tugged on his sleeve. "Talisman too," she whispered.

Robin nodded. "Oh, and Miss Talisman would like you to know that despite all the recent canine angst she has endured, she is recovering nicely and is hard at work designing her new Speed Dating for Dogs program. Please do not leave her any messages either, but prospective suitors may leave their biographical information and photos on her new Facebook page. Thank you, and cheerio!"

Molly and Angelina gave Robin a rousing round of

applause, and Talisman got so excited by the excitement that she gave him a spontaneous high-five.

Molly wasn't used to rest and recreation. "I have no idea what to do with myself."

"Why don't you start the decadent self-indulgence fest by taking a bubble bath?" He handed her a vial of pink oil wrapped in ribbon. "Rowan sent this over for you. She made it herself from rose petals and white lilacs."

Molly removed the stopper and sniffed. "Heaven."

"In the meantime, Angel and I will unpack my car. I stopped by the Fort Blackstone Grill and stocked up on their famous chili, cornbread, barbequed ribs, potato salad, and six kinds of homemade fruit and cream pies. We're going to feast and not worry about how unhealthy or fattening anything is. We're simply going to celebrate the fact that you two are still alive to eat."

Talisman issued a happy yap.

"There will be bones," Angelina interpreted.

Molly bounced up the stairs to draw her bath.

One of the advantages of old plumbing was the oversized, deep, and comfortable clawfoot tub. Usually Molly was in too much of a hurry to enjoy it, but today she filled it with hot water and bubbles, then settled in to soak. She stuck a rolled-up towel behind her neck, leaned back, and closed her eyes. The delicate aroma of Rowan's bath oil blend was soothing, and the sound of Angelina's giggles from downstairs was more enjoyable than any music she could have played. The meth heads were only one danger they had been facing, and Molly wasn't entirely sure that she and Angelina were truly safe now, but for today she chose to believe they were.

Molly was lulled into such a deep state of relaxation that she wasn't prepared for Talisman's sudden appearance. Somehow, she had opened the bathroom door, and with a running leap, jumped into the tub right on top of her. The forty-five pound dog stole her breath, so Molly wasn't even able to utter any sound of alarm. She gasped and opened her eyes to see Talisman's happy smile.

When Molly could finally speak, she said, "Tali, this isn't about you."

Talisman blinked—it was obviously not a concept she grasped.

"You're a very weird dog."

As if to prove Molly's point, Talisman dipped her nose into the water and blew bubbles.

Molly laughed and kissed her forehead. She had come to truly love this crazy dog who had become like a second child to her. "Thank you Val for the gift of your precious little girl," she whispered. "She has changed our lives in so many delightful ways."

Molly struggled to rearrange the two of them in the tub so they could both luxuriate. At that moment, she didn't care about dog-hair-meets-old-plumbing or the flood of water that had spilled over onto the bathroom floor. For just a moment, she was truly happy.

*   *   *

After Molly and Talisman were clean and dry, they all ate lunch and then went for a walk. Molly had bought the home in the middle of winter, and this was their first spring in it. None of them had ventured much beyond the small yard and picket fence that surround the house. Most of the property's five acres were still largely unexplored, and it seemed a perfect time to change that.

"There's just a split-rail fence enclosing the acreage, so we don't let Tali run loose back here," Molly said. "I don't want her to escape."

Robin laughed. "Escape from what? She'd be a fool to run off, and our Tali's no fool."

Talisman ran ahead of them, then circled back behind

as if trying to herd her family along. She certainly was devoted to her new little pack, but Molly preferred to play it safe. The alternative would be horrible.

It was a warm March day, the snow had melted, and the smell of smoke from nearby farmers burning their weeds tinged the air. Late winter, early spring flowers bloomed; tiny snowdrop flowers and clumps of dwarf irises painted the ground with white and shades of blue and purple.

Over the half century that Rose and Gilbert owned this property they had planted an abundance of trees on the land. Towering oak, pine, and maple trees thrived and were home to a variety of birds and squirrels. Those creatures, unaccustomed to human interlopers, filled the air with a cacophony of hoots, chirps, chatter, and excited birdsong. Squirrels dropped from one tree and raced for another, and Talisman gave chase. The determined rapping of a woodpecker stopped as they passed and began again with renewed gusto after they moved on.

Molly, city born and raised, was delighted. "There's just so much…nature."

"When you listed it for Rose last year, didn't you investigate back here?" Robin asked.

Molly shook her head. "I know that makes me a bad real estate agent, but I was new and more than a bit overwhelmed. There was a lot I did wrong."

"Look, there's a path," Angelina said. She headed down it, and everyone else followed.

The flagstone pathway led through the trees to a clearing where they discovered a large, freestanding gazebo. It was square with railings around the sides, and had a sloped cedar-shingled roof. It rested on top of a gorgeous flagstone patio that acted as its floor.

"Wow!" Angelina shouted as she and Talisman raced ahead to check it out.

"Did you know this was here?" Robin asked.

"Rose never told me."

Inside the gazebo were a picnic table and a stone barbeque.

"This is just so cool." Angelina said.

"Very cool," Molly agreed, delighted. They had their very own private park. It was heady stuff for two inner-city girls. While Angelina and Talisman explored the area, she sat down at the table and Robin took a seat across from her. The two of them watched the children frolic.

"Angel is at times so young, and at other times so adult," Robin said. "Some of the things she says are way beyond her years."

Molly nodded. "She was raised in a war zone. Living in the trenches forces one to grow up way too fast."

"Like you?"

That wasn't really a subject Molly wanted to revisit, but the contrast of the then and now in her life had stirred up emotions, and she felt an impulsive need to share. She waited until Angelina was well out of earshot. "My mother was an alcoholic; I never knew my father. They were bikers. When I was eleven, the day after my mother's new boyfriend raped me, they abandoned me at the place we'd been living—a rental in a bad neighborhood of Denver. After about a week, my neighbors—the Sanchez family—took me in. They just took me in and kept me. I wasn't adopted, no official was ever notified, no one ever came back to claim me. I grew up there. I spent my life living in books and dreaming of making a better life for myself. Then Angel came along, and I had to better myself. I've tried so hard to do everything right, but somehow things just keep going wrong."

Robin's jaw clenched, and his eyes reflected compassion. "You once mentioned an ex-sister?"

"Rita Sanchez was like an older sister. We were close

until I was disrespectful to her last year."

"What did you do?"

Shame rose in Molly. "Lily came to the house unexpectedly, and I implied that Rita was Angel's nanny—Lily intimidated me and I foolishly tried to impress her. Rita cut me off. The Sanchez family disowned me."

"What about Angel's father?"

"Miguel and I never married. He loved drugs more than us. He's in prison now." Molly marveled that she could so succinctly and matter-of-factly sum up her life. In a way, it was as if she was talking about someone else. She had never before told her entire story to anyone.

Robin stared at her in silence for a long time. Finally, he took her hand and said, "Thanks for trusting me enough to share."

Strangely, Molly felt a sense of release. All her secrets were finally laid bare, and she had nothing left to hide. She felt free.

After leaving the gazebo, they walked in the open fields that bordered the back side of the property. Despite the barrenness of the land, Rose and Gilbert had left their touches: a comfortable bench to rest on, a large statue of the Virgin Mary next to an old stone well, a small windmill, and a beautifully complex butterfly garden.

Robin studied the garden for a few minutes. "This is brilliant." He pointed out the various components of the colorful oasis, beginning with the large flat border stones painted red, yellow, orange, pink, and purple. "Those are for the butterflies to sun themselves on, painted the colors they most fancy. The wall of lilac bushes is on the north side to provide a wind block. There are butterfly houses, or hibernating boxes, so they can survive the winter. The log piles are where the little buggers like to hide." He squatted down and examined the perennials. "And look at this. All these flowers bloom at different times of the year, for a constant supply of nectar." He pointed to a shallow bird bath bowl that was sunk into the ground and filled with coarse, wet sand. "This is for puddling, where they can gather to drink." He stood and spun around to face the windmill. For the first time they all noticed that a pipe led from the windmill to the garden. A trickle of water poured out the end. "The windmill brings water up from the well to irrigate the garden. Bloody brilliant."

Robin's enthusiasm was contagious, and Molly became so overjoyed at the discovery of this magical treasure on her very own land that she began to laugh. Then Angelina laughed, which inspired Talisman to run in circles around the perimeter of the garden.

All the activity captured the interest of a huge yellow swallowtail who came out of hiding, flew up high into the sky, and then swooped down toward Talisman. Right as it approached, Talisman veered away from the garden, laid back her ears, and raced across the length of the field. The swallowtail followed and flew the entire way a few inches above her. When Talisman turned around and raced back toward the garden, the butterfly rose high in the sky, then dropped down, landed between her shoulder blades, and rode her all the way.

"Wow," Angelina said.

Talisman skidded to a stop a few feet from them, panting and looking deliriously happy. The swallowtail circled her for a few moments before landing on her nose.

Talisman stopped panting and stared at the creature that was staring at her.

"It's Val," Robin whispered.

Molly caught her breath. At Val's memorial service, Toby said in his eulogy, *Just when the caterpillar thought the world was over, it became a butterfly.* Then hundreds of butterflies were released in the auditorium. It seemed a fitting symbol of Val's transition from life to death, then and now.

Talisman and her butterfly both remained still as statues.

Finally, Talisman seemed unable to contain herself any longer. She kicked up her back heels and emitted a happy yap.

The swallowtail flew up high into the sky, and as they all watched, simply disappeared.

On the walk back to the house, Molly felt as if she were floating. Her heart and step were light. She wasn't convinced the butterfly had really been Val, but it had been a miraculous event nevertheless.

Talisman stopped on the path ahead of them, sat down, and barked. Curious, they all investigated what had captured her attention.

A cluster of dark blue irises appeared to be dancing. The petite flowers were swaying in a non-existent wind, and the petals were opening and closing rhythmically.

As they all huddled around to watch, Talisman whined and tipped her head to one side.

"The spirit of the plant is waving," Robin said.

Angelina giggled. "Plants don't have spirits."

"Of course they do," Robin said. "Even science has proven that each individual plant has its own unique DNA, just like people and animals."

Molly found that hard to believe. "Seriously?"

Robin nodded, his expression very serious.

"Don't tell Brooklyn," Molly said, "or she might require we begin naming and baptizing each individual member of her jungle."

"What's really happening?" Angelina asked.

Molly knew Robin had unusual gifts—she'd experienced them. "Are you making the flowers do this?"

His eyes twinkled.

"Who are you, Robin?" Molly asked. "What are you?"

"I'm someone who's here to show you both that it really is an enchanted world where all things are possible."

*   *   *

When they returned to the house, Angelina asked Robin to help them raise Liberty's flag. "She gave it to us at her party, but we can't figure out how to get it attached to the pole."

He examined the flag and the twenty foot high aluminum pole that stood in front of the house. "Well, you're missing some parts. It looks like no one's used the pole for a long time. What do you have in the way of tools and hardware?"

Molly pointed to the nearby tool shed. "Rose left all of her husband's stuff for us. I'm not sure what's there."

Robin disappeared into the shed for a time and returned with what he needed. It took only a few minutes to make the repairs and attach the flag.

"Go ahead and raise it," Angelina said.

He shook his head. "Don't you think Liberty would be horrified to think an Englishman raised her American flag?"

"We'll never tell her," Molly said.

"Right. Okay, stand at attention, put your hands over your hearts, and prepare to pledge your allegiance."

Slowly, Robin raised the flag to the top, then stepped aside while Molly and Angelina performed their recitation. Afterward they all stared at the flag, which was now dancing proudly in the wind.

"I feel so bad for Liberty," Molly said. "Teaching is her life."

"She chose the path of a warrior, and that path is never

easy," Robin said. "It's lonely, frightening, and involves risk. But it's a noble path, and it's hers."

Molly couldn't imagine choosing the path of a warrior. Rita had done it, Liberty had done it, and both had suffered so much. Her mind was just not able to wrap itself around the concept.

*   *   *

Robin went to work in the kitchen fixing them all dinner, so Molly, Angelina, and Talisman primped. They sat at the dining room table and Molly braided Angelina's hair, while Angelina braided Talisman's. Then they traded places and Angelina braided Molly's hair, while Molly painted Angelina's toenails blue. Afterwards, Angelina painted Molly's toenails red, and Molly painted Talisman's toenails pink. As they shared their mother/daughter/dog bonding ritual, they listened to music by the cast of the TV show *Glee*. When the song "Say A Little Prayer" came on, Talisman whined. It was one of Val's favorite songs.

"Miss Tali wants to dance," Robin said from the doorway into the kitchen.

Molly hadn't realized he had been watching them.

It had been too long since Molly had performed the rousing celebratory tribal dance of success, and she jumped to her feet and turned up the music. Angelina and Talisman ran to the living room where they shook, shimmied, pranced, and shared play bows.

Molly took Robin's hand and drew him toward the dance floor. "It may have been Tali's idea, but you translated, so you're a part of it now."

He surprised Molly by pulling her into his arms. His eyes captured hers, and he moved her around the room while their hips rocked to the beat. She had little experience in touch dancing, but under his command she

instinctively knew just what to do. With their eyes
locked, she merged first with him and then with the
music. When the rhythm slowed, their bodies came
together in sensual swaying, and when it sped up he
swung and twirled her until she was dizzy with
excitement. The friction of bodies, the merging of
energies, and the trust she put in him stirred her blood
and brought her fully into the moment. Her lungs filled
with his scent—the pine and musk she always found so
invigorating. Above all, she was overcome by Robin's
wild sexuality, something she had always before done her
best to try to ignore. Now she welcomed it, and when the
song faded and he pulled her close, she wanted him to
kiss her. Time stood still, and it seemed as if the universe
contained just the two of them. Shaken by the magic of
the moment, Molly caught her breath and held it. She
sensed Robin's desire for her too, so was startled when he
released her and stepped away.

Angelina laughed and bounced around. She ran up to
Robin and threw her arms around him. "You've done the
ritual. You're a member of the family now."

He grinned. "Fancy that."

*   *   *

Molly, Angelina, and Robin sat down together for a
sumptuous meal of barbequed ribs, potato salad, and corn
bread, then retired to the living room to eat coconut
cream pie and check Talisman's Facebook page. Despite
Liberty's warnings, the family had decided that it was
unlikely the feds would have a reason to spy on
Talisman.

Molly set up her laptop on the coffee table. Angelina
and Talisman sat on the floor in front of it, while Molly
and Robin settled in on the couch behind them.
Talisman's scarf of the day said LOOKING FOR LOVE.

Angelina set her pie down on the table and logged into Facebook.

"Tali is so eager to hear the posts that she's totally ignoring the pie," Robin said. "That's a girl on a mission."

Angelina nodded. "She's looking for love."

That morning, Robin had helped Talisman post a request for romantic personal ads.

"Here's a very handsome Border Collie named Doc," Angelina said. "His message says, 'Seeking pastures, sheep, and love. Send photos of sheep and pastures.'"

"Based on Tali's recent experience with sheep and pastures, I'd say that wouldn't be a good match," Molly said.

"Nope," Angelina said.

Talisman grunted.

Robin patted her head. "She agrees."

"Here's an Australian Shepherd named Bailey. He competes in agility. His post says, 'Single Blue Male seeking agile partner for bar-hopping fun. I'm athletic and handsome with blue eyes that will put you in a trance. Don't worry, my bark is worse than my bite.'" Angelina sighed. "He's a blue merle just like Chance, so we'll have to reject him too. I'm sorry, Tali."

Talisman appeared stricken.

"There's more," Angelina assured her. "Romeo, a Greyhound, says, 'I'm a dashing hunk who loves heavy petting. Will share food. My bad boy reputation is unwarranted as I have absolutely no idea how playdog.com or dogsgonewild.com got in the web browser history.'"

Molly burst out laughing. "Oh, dear. Not for our Tali."

Talisman didn't say anything, but her expression seemed irritated.

"She's not so sure about that," Robin said.

Molly shrugged. "Well, women do tend to go for the

bad boys."

"Really? Do you?" Robin asked.

Molly considered her choices. "I used to. I'm trying to do better now."

"There's a Black Russian Terrier named Igor. His post says, 'SBM seeks affectionate woman to minister to my needs. Seeks casual K9 for long walks and candlelight kibble. I have a live-in girlfriend, but we have an open relationship.'"

Molly choked on her pie. Perhaps she should have vetted these first.

"Another bad boy," Robin said. "Next?"

"This Red Setter named Fergus wrote, 'Rugged Irish outdoorsman looking for hunting companion who is athletic and earthy. Wants a no muss/no fuss kind of gal who doesn't whine.'"

Talisman whined.

"Most definitely not a match," Robin said.

"Tali is a very special girl and deserves a special boy," Angelina said.

"Only the best for our Tali," Molly agreed.

"A Labradoodle named Bocker says, 'I have movie star good looks and a compassionate heart. As I live in New York, we would have to have a long-distance relationship, but my person has Zoom.'" Angelina tilted the laptop so Talisman could get a good look at the big blond with soulful brown eyes. "What do you think, Tali?"

Talisman sniffed the screen with interest.

"A long-distance romance wouldn't be a lot of fun," Molly told her.

Robin leaned forward and took a closer look at Bocker. "Hmmm. My gift tells me that they just might have a chance to meet someday."

"Can you wait, Tali?" Angelina asked.

Talisman walked away and plopped down by the

fireplace to think about it.

*   *   *

Robin started a roaring fire in the fireplace while Molly turned down the lights so they could better enjoy it. She curled up on one end of the couch, while the others made themselves comfortable on big floor pillows.

"Now all we need are ghost stories," Angelina said.

Given his special gifts, Molly thought that was something Robin could certainly do well. "Robin?"

"Well, I do know a few, but they're perhaps a bit too intense to be fun."

Angelina nudged him with her foot. "Come on."

"I've got a better idea," he said. "How about if Tali tells a story? I'll translate."

"Awesome," Angelina said, her eyes lighting up with excitement.

Robin scooted closer to Talisman and communed with her in silence for a few minutes before telling her tale.

"Tali knows a Border Collie named Bibbidi Bobbidi Boo. Boo's person is a medium, so there are always stray ghosts hanging around after séances whom Boo generally chases off by giving them the famous Border Collie eye. However, there was one that was more powerful even than the eye, and it attached itself to Boo and followed her everywhere, including to one of the dog shows where she and Tali competed."

Angelina was breathless. "Wow."

"So, there's this strange, invisible bloke that only the dogs can see, and it's making them all wonky. They're standing pretty for the judges, and then they growl at the ghost, only the judges think they're growling at them, and, well, everything gets all mucked up.

"The dogs have a powwow and decide they need to chat up the ghost and find out what he wants so they can get rid of him. Well, they elect Tali to do it, since she's so psychic."

"Wicked," Angelina said, her eyes widening with wonder.

"So, now there's this show going on within the show that the dogs themselves refer to as *The Twilight Bone.* They give Tali their own championship title, The Wizard of Pawz. Overall, there's a lot of high-stakes drama going on."

Molly's smile was so wide her mouth hurt.

"Our Miss Tali does her ritualistic dance of success to summon up all her courage, then confronts the ghost. She demands he tell her what he wants." Robin paused.

"And?" Angelina asked.

"And?" Molly asked.

Robin lowered his voice. "He's trying to locate his dog, a Golden Retriever named Belle, who died before he did. He refuses to move on until he finds her."

"Awww," Angelina said.

Talisman, who had been watching Robin intently, made a guttural sound.

Robin continued. "Tali tells all the other dogs at the show what she's found out, and they decide to do a spirit calling. They pass the word among themselves. It moves all through the arena, and at an appointed time *all* the dogs start howling. All of them together. They're calling for Belle. The humans go bonkers, but the dogs keep it up for a full minute. The eerie sound of their long, plaintive wails fill the air, echoing back from the high ceiling and far walls. It's haunting and primal, and it summons Belle from the distant reaches of the universe. She suddenly appears, runs up to her person, and leaps into his arms. All the dogs in the arena stand at silent attention to witness the glory of the reunion. Then a brilliant white light that only the dogs can see fills the air, and when it fades, the ghosts are gone."

Angelina gasped. "What happened after? Did Tali ever have to do that kind of thing again?"

Robin communed with Talisman for few minutes before replying. "Well, she says no, but sometimes after Val and Peter had been watching scary movies, she'd mess with their head by howling at absolutely nothing."

They all laughed at her revelation.

"Tali, you're just a wild child," Molly said.

Talisman rolled over, jumped to her feet, and issued a happy yap.

"You're so wonderful," Angelina said to Robin.

Molly was surprised to hear the passion in her daughter's voice and see the adoration in her eyes. She was even more surprised to realize that she was beginning to feel the same way about him.

*   *   *

The Valentino DeMitri Gay Epiphany Fan Club closed the purchase of Val's home on Friday. Molly had never before missed one of her own closings, but Jake had insisted she take the full week off, so he went in her place. Although Jake was one tough cowboy—or perhaps because of that—she simply couldn't imagine how he would cope in a business situation with a room full of flaming gays and drag queens. At one point she considered calling her closer and asking for the entire thing to be surreptitiously streamed live to her computer, but Robin talked her out of it. He said she would be better off not knowing the gory details.

So, when Molly, Robin, Angelina, and Talisman showed up at the house Friday night for the housewarming party, she was surprised to see Jake's truck parked out front.

"Do you think they coerced him into coming?" Robin asked. "Perhaps the Carol Channings threatened him with rose-filled love serenades at the office."

Molly shook her head. "No one could coerce Jake into doing anything. He's…well, he's Jake." Her instinct told her that he was there because he knew she was going to be.

They all got out of Robin's car and stood for a few moments on the sidewalk, looking at the house. It was the first time Molly, Angelina, or Talisman had been here since the private gathering of Val's friends and family immediately following his death. Molly was worried about how the little ones would handle it but hoped it would be okay. Their week had been so perfect that she didn't want it to end on a bad note. Talisman's scarf of the day said I'M VAL'S BIGGEST FAN. The rest of them were decked out in their most elegant clothing; Molly had long ago learned that when Val's friends said an event was "a gussy-up affair," they meant it.

She took a deep breath and led her pack up the lantern-lined pathway, past the large statue of St. Francis and the lighted two-tiered fountain, to the gorgeous, rose-colored stucco house. A new bronze plaque attached to the front door said FALCON LAIR. Molly opened it, and they stepped inside.

The first thing that hit her was the sound of Val's voice—his famous real estate DVD played on the big screen TV. He and a chorus line of drag queens had filmed the production for his use in self-promotion. A rush of love filled Molly when she saw him all decked out in his tuxedo and top hat, singing and tap dancing his way through the song "Big Spender."

Molly noticed Angelina and Talisman were also instantly mesmerized by it. Talisman cocked her head from side-to-side, so Robin squatted down and conducted one of his silent conversations with her. After a moment he stood up and said, "I've explained it to her. She'll be okay."

Molly liked to believe Robin's gift was real. At that moment she really *needed* to believe it was real.

Inside, the house was exactly as Val had left it—all of his personal possessions, photographs, and the memorabilia of a life lived with passion and panache remained intact.

Toby greeted them at the door decked out as Liza Minnelli: his curly red hair tucked up into a short, black Liza Minnelli wig, his eyes Liza Minnelli large, and his gown Liza Minnelli slink. "Kiss kiss." He grabbed Molly and kissed her on both cheeks. Then he did the same to Angelina and Talisman, but when he reached for Robin he was intercepted by Robin's bottle of champagne. Toby grasped it with a petulant expression. "I'd really rather have a kiss."

"If I were gay, I'd be so into you," Robin said.

That seemed to appease him.

"How did the closing go?" Molly asked.

"It was simply spectacular. Your cowboy handled the reins just fine."

Molly gestured to his outfit. "Did you go as Liza?"

"But of course. Life is a cabaret, you know."

"Who else was there?" Molly asked.

"Barbara Streisand, Bette Midler, Tina Turner, and Val's mother."

Molly's eyes scanned the room looking for her. "How's Margo doing?"

"Sober and sexy," Toby said. "Back to being her gorgeous self. She was all over your cowboy."

Molly smiled at the thought. Margo's interest in Jake had always made him extremely uncomfortable. "I hope you took pictures."

"Oh, a boatload. I'll email them to you, babe."

Molly noticed Jake leaning against a nearby wall, watching them. He wore his fancy jeans, dress boots and cowboy hat, and although he looked out of place in the midst of the glitz and glam, he was terribly sexy. As Molly had once described his unique brand of charisma, he simmered. "Guess we better see how he survived the experience."

Molly and her group wove through the crowd. She greeted Jake with a chipper smile, while Robin and he shook hands.

"So, how'd the closing go?" Molly asked him.

"Harrowing."

"I heard you handled the reins quite handily."

"That's what I do best." A slight smile played at his lips, and his eyes looked at her with fire in them.

Despite her growing attraction to Robin, Jake's intensity still filled Molly with heat. She had come to accept that the connection would always be there. Looking away, she glanced at Robin and knew he could feel it too. A person didn't need a special gift to see sparks fly.

"It was nice of you to attend the party," Molly said to Jake.

"I wanted to make sure you were okay, and since you weren't accepting phone calls this week, this seemed an ideal occasion."

She nodded. "We're doing fine."

Jake gave them a frank look of appraisal. "I see that. I think you're all glowing."

"We had a fantabulous week," Angelina said. "We had barbeques at the gazebo, and ran with butterflies, and danced with the irises, and Robin taught me how to talk to the birds, and he helped me power through my homework so I could stay out of school all week, and he even summoned deer again for us to see."

"Robin did all that, huh?" Jake said. "Seems like your mom has found the ideal assistant."

"Oh, he's more than an assistant," Angelina said.

Jake grunted and took a swig of his beer.

Someone from across the room called Talisman. "Tali, come see us! We miss you."

Talisman trotted off to commune with old friends, while Angelina wandered away to the buffet table.

"Champagne?" Robin asked Molly.

She nodded. "Thank you."

Robin headed toward the kitchen.

Jake gestured around the room with his beer bottle. "What do they plan to do with the house?"

"It's going to be a shrine of sorts, to keep Val's memory alive. They'll have parties here. Maybe AA meetings for those in the program. Rehearse their shows and have cast parties following their productions. So many people loved Val."

"I'm sorry you lost him."

"Me, too. I think—"

He reached out and grasped her hand. "I want you back, Molly. I was holding onto the past when we first came together. Now that I've let that go, I want a future with you. I'm in love with you."

Molly caught her breath. He had never before told her he loved her, and it wasn't in his character to say something like that unless he meant it. She was so stunned that she couldn't respond.

Robin returned with two glasses of champagne. Awkwardly, Molly released Jake's hand and accepted one of them.

Jake set his bottle down and grabbed his leather jacket off the floor. "I'll be going now." He looked at Molly with soft eyes. "See you Monday." Challenging eyes seized Robin's. "Take care of her." With that, he walked away.

Molly's hand trembled as she took a sip of champagne.

"Everything okay?" Robin asked.

She thought about it. "No."

"Anything I can do?"

Her mind and heart wrestled with each other. "Maya Angelou once said to believe people the first time."

"With all respect to the esteemed Ms. Angelou, people have been known to change."

"How do you know if they have?"

"You watch. You listen. You wait."

Molly sighed as she realized that her life had just gotten a whole lot more complicated.

"Oh, no." Margo ran up to them. "Where did the sexy cowboy go?"

"He left," Molly said.

"Well, damn. I wanted to tell you both the big news."

"What news?" Molly asked.

"Val's father just signed on to star in a new movie and they're looking for a location to shoot. The scout checked out Chief Waters' estate, and they want to lease it for the summer. You could make some serious money for negotiating it, and the positive notoriety would help you eventually sell it."

"Val's father?" Robin asked.

Molly nodded. "His father is actor Sean Clooney." Their secret relationship had been revealed at Val's memorial service.

Robin grinned. "Smashing."

"Wouldn't making a movie where Val died be upsetting to you and Sean?" Molly asked Margo.

She flashed a sad smile. "Oh, kitten, I think it would be a way to honor him. There's even a possibility that the movie will be dedicated to Val. Sean is lobbying for it."

Toby joined them. "Did you tell them? Did you tell them that they're going to use local actors too? We're all in line to audition. Margo's going to coordinate."

Angelina appeared with a heavily-laden plate of munchies. "They're going to make a movie here? Do they need a dog? Tali has movie star potential."

"They're bringing in a canine actor from New York with movie experience. He's even worked with Steven Spielberg. His name is Bocker the Labradoodle."

Molly choked on her champagne while Angelina began to scream.

"O.M.G!" Angelina managed to say between shrill shrieks.

At the sound of Angelina's hysterics, Talisman charged over, sat down, and howled.

"Tali, don't go and freak us all out again," Toby said, shaking his head. "Did Val ever tell you about the time she got hundreds of dogs howling in unison at that AKC show down in Texas? It was beyond spooky."

Molly and Angelina stared at Robin in mute disbelief.

Robin's eyes twinkled.

The night was a fabulous mix of nostalgia, tribute, and entertainment. At one point, Robin even joined Liza in a snazzy duet of the song "Cabaret." Robin, it seemed, was a man of many talents.

When the time came to leave, they couldn't find Talisman. Fighting a growing panic, Molly finally noticed the door to Val's once secret room slightly ajar. It hadn't occurred to her to look in there because during Val's life it had always been locked. Following his death, they discovered that it was a private chapel Val built for himself after he had been forbidden to practice his beloved Catholic faith. Val, it turned out, was a closet Catholic. Molly couldn't comprehend how a church could reject a person for being gay.

Molly pushed the door wide and peeked in. Talisman was lying on the floor next to the single pew, so she went in and sat down next to her. "Did you used to sit with him while he prayed, Tali?"

The altar was candle-strewn, and the air still held a

faint smell of basilica incense. A magnificent crucifix sat in the center of the altar, while piles of books about the Catholic mystical tradition lay scattered about.

Talisman's chin rested on her paws, and she stared at the altar.

Robin came in, sat down next to Molly, and took her hand.

She wrapped her fingers around his and hung on for dear life. Her emotions were an intense mix of swirling colors. They sat in silence until Angelina appeared and sat down on the other side of Robin.

"Recently, I've come to accept that there may indeed be a God," Molly said. "However, if there is a loving God, why do such bad things happen? Why did Val have to die? He was one of the good guys."

Robin squeezed her hand. "Death isn't an outrage. It seems like it to those left behind, but the soul survives. It just changes form. I know that for a fact."

"But the world needs all the good guys it can get," Angelina said.

Robin's foot nudged a book that lay on the floor in front of the pew. It was a biography of a Catholic saint named Maximilian Kolbe. "I've read about this Saint of Auschwitz bloke. He died in the camp. Lots of miracles surrounding that. But what I remember most about him is that he said helping others while alive was like working with one hand tied behind his back. In death, he expected to have both hands free. You don't know what Val's up to."

"I don't have that kind of faith," Molly said.

"Well, your faith's young. Besides, faith isn't a feeling—it's an act of will. A commitment. Give it time."

Angelina leaned over and snuggled into Robin. "We love you so much."

After a moment Robin said, "And I love you ladies too. So much."

Molly released his hand, laid her head on his shoulder, and he slipped his arm around her.

Above the altar was a mural of a glorious rainbow, and Molly studied the words that were inscribed in the design. *It doesn't matter how much you're loved in life. What really matters is how much you love.*

CHAPTER FIFTEEN

Mrs. Ruby Rosen decided that being a real estate broker was much more excitement than she could stand, so she clicked her heels together and went home.

Besides that, nothing much had changed in the week Molly was gone.

The first item of new business for Molly was the closing scheduled for her Be-in-Harmony couple. A camera crew was scheduled to film the closing and then the wedding, which was to occur immediately afterwards. Shannon and Brian were one of Be-In-Harmony's many success stories, and the company planned to feature the couple in a series of television commercials. The fee the newlyweds were set to receive for allowing the film crew to tag along was enough for the down payment on their new love nest.

To accommodate the camera crew and equipment, the closing was held in the large conference room at Broker's Best. The happy couple arrived already decked out in wedding gown and tux. Shannon was all shiny teeth and flowing lace as she flitted about, giddy with excitement. Brian's smile was forced as he tried to maneuver in a tuxedo that was far too small for him.

Molly stood right inside the door of the conference room, waiting for everyone to arrive.

"Hi, gorgeous. I'm Dirk, the movie director."

The man who introduced himself to Molly appeared to be a teenager. He wore jeans and a tee-shirt with the famous silhouette of Alfred Hitchcock on it. His black movie crew hat was embroidered with the word DIRECTOR. Pimples peeked out from behind heavy pancake face makeup.

Molly smiled and extended her hand to shake. "Molly O'Malley, the buyers' agent."

He grabbed her hand and planted a wet kiss on it. "Ever consider a career in show biz? You've got serious oomph appeal."

It wasn't the first time a director had used that line on her. She wondered if they taught it in director's school.

One of the members of the film crew bumped into them as he carried a tall, gold folding chair into the room. When he unfolded it, the black canvas back said DIRECTOR.

Dirk winked at Molly. "You just relax and flash that million dollar smile, and I'll make you a star." He swaggered over to his chair where the script girl handed him a megaphone.

"God help us," Molly mumbled.

Jake came up behind her. "How's it going?"

"I've got serious oomph appeal, and Director Dirk is going to make me a star."

Jake chuckled. "Well, at least the kid recognizes serious talent when he sees it." He gave her shoulder a gentle squeeze and walked away.

Much to her dismay, he took her breath with him.

Ted walked in and handed Molly one of his business cards. "Give it to the director and ask him to call me. I want to talk to him about filming my *Star Trek* convention."

"I have a feeling he's no Steven Spielberg."

Ted shrugged and rubbed his shaved head. "Sometimes a case can be made for style over substance. Not that I'd personally know anything about that, of course."

Molly bit her tongue and tucked his card into her suit pocket.

Finally, the closer, the listing agent, and the sellers showed up. Eager to get the entire thing over with, Molly ushered everyone in and got them seated around the big central conference table.

Molly was pleased that the listing agent had chosen her own preferred closer, Jackie, to handle the deal. Jackie was good at rolling with the punches.

Jackie laid all the paperwork out and had just begun to go over it with the buyers and sellers when Dirk's voice boomed out at them through the megaphone. *"I didn't say action!"*

Jackie looked up and gave him a withering glare. "Okay, well move your ass, Mr. Hollywood, because I've got another closing in an hour and we need to barrel though this one."

Dirk raised his megaphone and said, *"Quiet on the set!"*

Molly flinched.

Dirk gave a signal to the script girl who slapped the clapperboard, and he announced, *"Action!"*

Jackie picked up right where she left off.

"Cut!"

Jackie slammed the pen down on the table. "Now what?"

"Take it from the top!"

"What?"

Dirk's sigh whooshed out through the megaphone. *"Start at the beginning!"*

"Oh, for crissakes." Jackie rolled her eyes and took a deep breath.

Dirk signaled again for the clapperboard. *"Action!"*

Jackie began the closing at the beginning.

Ten minutes into it Dirk boomed, *"Cut!"*

Jackie glanced at her watch. "Now what?"

"The groom is sweating!"

"Grooms sweat. That's what they do," Jackie said.

The makeup girl scurried over with her kit and did her best to repair the beleaguered groom.

"This suit is just a little snug. Having trouble breathing," Brian said.

Shannon's smile disappeared.

The flood mopped up, the makeup girl scurried away.

"Quiet on the set!" Dirk signaled the clapperboard, *"Action!"*

"I ain't taking it from the top," Jackie said through clenched teeth.

"Just pick it up where you left off!"

Molly was getting a headache. She forced a million dollar smile.

Another ten minutes into the closing, Jackie presented Brian with the official name affidavit. "This document lists all the variations of your name that our search associated with your social security number," she explained. "Brian Doyle, Brian A. Doyle, and Brian Aloysius Doyle. Please sign at the bottom acknowledging these are all you."

Huffing and puffing, Brian managed to sign the document and push it back across the table to Jackie.

Jackie presented Shannon with hers. "And this is yours. Shannon Flanagan, Shannon P. Flanagan, Shannon Penelope Flanagan, Shannon Flanagan-Henriksen, Shannon P. Flanagan-Henriksen, Shannon Penelope Flanagan-Henricksen, Shannon Flanagan-Arriola, Shannon P. Flanagan-Arriola, Shannon Penelope Flanagan-Arriola, Shannon Flanagan-Kaminski—"

Brian snatched the document out of Jackie's hand. "What's this? You've been married before? *Three* times? You said I was your first. You said I was your first *everything*. You lied to me."

Shannon grabbed the document from his hand. "And

you posted a Photoshopped picture of yourself on Be-In-Harmony that showed you to be three times smaller than you really are. That's not exactly honest, is it?"

Brian stood up. He was really sweating now. "We need to go outside and talk about this." He shook his fist at Dirk. "And don't you dare follow us out with that damn camera, either."

Shannon jumped to her feet and got tangled in her long train. "Fine." She struggled with the dress but managed to storm out of the room on Brian's heels.

"*Cut!*" Dirk said.

Jackie shook her head. "The last time this happened at one of my closings, it was a lesbian couple and it turned out one had previously been married to a man. They went outside to discuss it and never returned."

Molly's stomach turned over. She had worked so hard on this deal and desperately needed the income. Her bills were staggering: an eighteen-hundred-dollar-a-month office fee paid to Jake, enormous advertising costs, E&O insurance, professional membership fees, the BMW payment, and Robin's salary. Not to mention all the money she was paying her lawyer. And then, of course, her home mortgage and living expenses. No closing, no paycheck.

Jackie looked at her watch. "Well, I'm going to slip out back and have a smoke. If they don't return by the time I'm done, I've gotta leave for my next closing."

The sellers looked shell-shocked. "We'll get to keep the earnest money, right?" one of them asked.

Molly nodded.

The listing agent stood. "Let's walk over to Starbucks. I'll treat."

Everyone left the room, except for Molly and the film crew.

Molly laid her head down on the table and moaned.

"I bet with your va-va-voomness Be-In-Harmony

would give you a free membership," Dirk said. "And then when you find your fairytale ending, we could do a commercial about you."

She sat up and shook her head. "I'm not the kind of woman who is destined to live happily ever after."

"The really gorgeous women in history rarely do. Ironic, isn't it?"

Jackie reappeared. "Well, I didn't even get my cigarette lit when I saw our happy couple tearing out of here, down the back alley. Gotta get moving." She patted Molly on the back. "Tough break, kid."

"That's a wrap!" Director Dirk's megaphone announced.

*   *   *

By the time Molly dealt with the necessary paperwork and cleared everyone out of the conference room, it was late afternoon. She stopped by the coffee pot and filled a cup, then headed for her office.

Robin had already picked up Angelina from school, and they were waiting for Molly's return. From the expression on Robin's face, she knew that he had already heard her bad news.

Molly hugged Angelina. "How was your first day back at school?"

"Good. How was your first day back at work?"

Molly was tempted to lie, but Angelina seemed to like her again, and she didn't want to risk losing that. "It was a difficult day. I'm glad it's over."

"Molly O'Malley?" a man's voice asked from the doorway.

She turned to see two men in black suits. "How did you get past the receptionist?" Jessie had been extra vigilant lately about screening her visitors.

They flashed government badges. "My name is

Shelton. This is Brown. We're agents with a Homeland Security task force and have some questions for you." They both stepped inside and closed the door behind them.

Their bold intrusion filled Molly with trepidation. "Robin, take Angel home. I'll be there soon."

"No, Mr. Knight and Angelina should stay," Brown said.

Molly moved to stand protectively in front of her daughter. "What do you want?"

"Information about Liberty True's whereabouts."

Molly shrugged. "At her home, I suppose."

"Dr. True no longer has a home. The property she bought—with a suspicious amount of gold I might add—was seized today by the government."

Molly, Robin, and Angelina gasped as one.

"Why?" Molly managed to ask.

"Dr. True has been deemed a terrorist, and all of her assets have been seized. She wasn't home at the time. We don't know where she is and thought you might, as our sources tell us you're more than just business associates."

Their sources? Molly shook her head. "Liberty is *not* a terrorist. Liberty is in love with this country. Deeply, passionately in love."

Angelina peeked around Molly. "Where's Ross?"

"Who's Ross?" Shelton asked.

"Her dog," Angelina said.

Shelton seemed confused and looked at Brown.

Brown nodded. "The dog was taken to the pound. That's where it'll remain too. We hope she'll come claim it. It'll make our job a lot easier."

Molly was horrified.

"What are you going to do if you find Liberty?" Angelina asked.

Brown walked to Molly's desk and began rifling through her papers. "She'll be arrested on charges of terrorism against this country."

"Leave my stuff alone," Molly said.

Not only did Brown ignore her, but Shelton started examining items on her bookshelf.

"We'll search your things if we choose to, Miss O'Malley," Brown said. "You were all seen at a gathering at Dr. True's home where a terrorist bombing was being planned."

Molly shook her head. "It was a housewarming party, and when the subject of violence came up Liberty ordered the people who suggested it to leave her home."

Shelton looked at her. "Really? Did you report this incident to authorities. And if not, why not?"

"Liberty did."

Brown opened a desk drawer and peeked inside. "I've heard from local police that you're not known for stepping forward, that you prefer to leave that to others."

Molly's face reddened. "Your information is outdated."

"You just told us that you left the reporting to Dr. True."

"I didn't know who those men were. She did."

Brown slammed her desk drawer shut with such force that both Molly and Angelina jumped.

"I can't believe you took Ross," Angelina said. "You're very bad men."

"You'd be wise to keep your daughter quiet, Miss O'Malley."

"No," Molly said. "This is America, and as Americans we have the right of free speech."

Shelton and Brown shared meaningful looks. One of them placed a business card on Molly's desk, while the other put his on Robin's desk.

"If you hear from Dr. True let us know immediately. If you don't, or if you assist her in any manner, you'll be considered accomplices to her terrorist activities, and the consequences will be dire."

With that, they left the building.

Molly stumbled to her desk chair, sat down, and struggled with her emotions as the full impact of Liberty's tragedy sank in. "Oh, poor Liberty." Her home, her dog, all the dreams of a lifetime, gone in an instant. How would she survive?

Angelina knelt on Talisman's bed and hugged her.

Robin sat at his own desk and grew pensive. "If Liberty doesn't claim Ross by the end of the week, the shelter will put him down."

Angelina shrieked. "No!"

Babylon stepped into the office and shut the door behind her. "I don't know what you're involved in, Molly, but the men in black just planted a tracking device on your car."

Molly grew dizzy. "Are you sure?"

"Molly, I live on the dark side."

"Thank you for letting me know."

"If you need me to do anything...."

Molly nodded. "Very kind."

Babylon gave her a Goth hand signal. "Hey, we're not Red Hot Broker Babe Action Dolls—we're the real deal, you and me." She winked at Molly and left.

"Well, that's a bit of a sticky wicket," Robin said. He scribbled a note, stood, and handed it to her. It said, *If they've done that to your car, assume they've also bugged your computer, phone, home, and office.*

All of Liberty's paranoid ramblings tumbled through Molly's mind. Who would have believed what she said was real? Not in her wildest drunken dreams had Molly believed that the United States could do this to someone without due process. What should she do? Robin had said that faith was a decision, an act of will rather than a feeling. Val had said courage was a choice. Could she rise above her fear to help Liberty?

Molly and Robin stared at each other for a long time, each lost in their own thoughts. Finally, he picked up a pad from her desk and wrote another note. This message said, *Do you want to help her, given the risk?*

Molly looked at Angelina. What she did would affect her daughter. Should she allow a nine-year-old child a say in her own destiny? "Come here, Angel."

Angelina heaved herself off the floor, shuffled over to Molly, and climbed onto her lap.

Molly hugged her tight and whispered, "I want you to listen very carefully. The bad men have electronic ears everywhere, just like Liberty told us. I have to make the decision right now if I'm going to help her. If I do, it'll put us both at risk. I've spent my life protecting you, but I need to know your feelings about this. It's okay if you're scared and want to play it safe." She tapped her own ear to indicate she wanted Angelina to whisper.

Angelina didn't hesitate. She leaned into Molly and repeated the words written on the wall in Val's private chapel. "What really matters is how much you love."

Molly was so moved that she struggled to hold back a flood of tears. She picked up a pen and wrote a note for Robin. Paraphrasing one of Liberty's favorite slogans, she said, *All tyranny needs to gain a foothold is for women of good conscience to remain silent.*

*   *   *

Robin came home late that night after Angelina was already in bed. Molly was dozing on a pile of pillows in front of the fireplace, and she woke to find him sitting next to her.

"You're incredibly beautiful, Molly." His voice was tender.

She smiled. "And you really are the shock and awe of cute."

He placed a note in her hands. *Have plan to rescue Ross. Meeting set up with doggy jail escape team tomorrow noon at Pagan Place. Since our walls may have ears, we're having lunch with my sis.*

Molly sat up and put the note in the fire. "So, how was your evening?"

"Good. Rowan misses me and invited us both round for lunch tomorrow."

"I'd like that. Angel says she's a great cook."

"I did mention you were beautiful, right?"

She smiled. "Unless I was dreaming."

He leaned forward and brushed her lips with his, then pressed his forehead to hers and closed his eyes. "You have no idea how much I want you." After a moment, he stood and went upstairs to his room.

Molly wasn't sure if his words were meant for her or the walls, and she had no clue what her response should be.

*   *   *

The next day when they arrived at Pagan Place, Robin led Molly down to the basement apartment where Michael lived. "If he's naked, just pretend you don't see him. He's been experimenting with invisibility, combining ancient magical techniques with virtual computer technology. But mostly, well, he's just naked."

Molly nodded as if she completely understood.

Thankfully, everyone inside the apartment was fully clothed.

Besides Michael and Rowan, there was the young woman named Crimson whom Robin had once mentioned slept in a coffin, and Sybil, who made her living as a fortune-teller.

"We've swept the place for bugs and demons, and cleared it of both," Michael said in greeting.

"That's very reassuring," Molly said.

"You did leave your phone in the car, right?" Michael asked.

Molly nodded.

"Good, because not only can they use cell technology to track you and listen to calls, but they can turn it on at will and hear what you're saying."

Liberty had once told Molly the same thing. She didn't believe her then, but she believed her now.

Michael's apartment was a strange blend of Gothic and sci-fi. Molly counted at least four computers and a huge assortment of techno-gadgets amid the décor heavy in dragons and gargoyles, black roses and skulls, spaceships and aliens.

"I made sandwiches and there's iced tea," Rowan said. "Can't have you stopping for fast food on the way back to the office. They might be following you."

That was a distinct possibility.

Molly and Robin sat next to each other on the couch and helped themselves to the refreshments served on the coffee table.

"I've volunteered at the animal shelter for five years," Sybil said. "I go three times a week and walk the dogs. I'm scheduled this afternoon. I'll get Ross outside, then Michael is going to snatch him from me. The shelter will never suspect I'm involved."

Molly wasn't so sure. "The feds could find out you live here and make the Robin connection."

"I'm willing to take that risk."

Molly studied the middle-aged woman. She wore a brightly-colored gypsy skirt and blouse, and her dark, curly hair was captured in a gold bandana. Large crystal moons and stars dangled from her ears. "Has Robin explained just how big a risk you're taking?"

Sybil's eyes narrowed and her chin jutted out. "I'm not afraid of men in suits. They know nothing about true power."

Molly looked at Michael. He wore ragged jeans, an old *Star Wars* tee-shirt, and was barefoot. For obvious reasons, clothes didn't appear to be important to him. "Yours is the bigger risk," she said.

He shrugged. "I'll be invisible. No one will see me."

Molly's eyes flew to Robin. She hated to ask an insane man to do something he might not fully comprehend.

Robin gave her a reassuring nod, as if he understood her concerns. "Michael's a genius. He gets it."

"After you snatch Ross, what then?" Molly asked.

Crimson said, "Michael will put Ross in his car and drive him to where I'll be waiting in mine. I'll take Ross to a safe place until we can get him back to Dr. True."

Molly wondered where a girl who slept in coffins considered safe. Crimson sported a *Buffy the Vampire Slayer* sweatshirt and wore a vial of blood around her neck.

"Crimson is going to ferry Ross to a special circle of our friends," Rowan said. "Our oath is mutual trust. He'll be safe."

"Then, of course, we need to find Liberty," Robin said.

Molly had an idea about that. "I think I know how we can find her."

"I can do a divination, so we can be certain," Sybil offered.

One thing the kaleidoscope of recent events had taught Molly was that anything was possible. "Okay, and once we confirm it we need to make a battle plan."

Robin grinned. "Are you going to be the rebel leader?"

Molly only took a moment to think about it. "If I need to be."

Sybil raised her hand in the sign of V for victory. "Welcome to the revolution!"

*   *   *

It was late afternoon when Babylon ducked her purple head into Molly's office. "Come quick, both of you."

Molly and Robin dropped what they were doing and followed her to the break room where the TV was on. The local access channel from the university was airing the news, and a group of brokers were standing around watching it.

The anchorwoman was saying, "...and to learn more about the bizarre incident that happened today at The Blackstone Animal Shelter is our man in the field, Jason Vaughan."

The camera cut to a young man standing in front of the shelter. "I am standing with Sybil Moonhawk, a longtime volunteer here at Blackstone's animal shelter. Can you tell us about what happened to you today?" He thrust his microphone in Sybil's face.

"Well, I was walking one of the dogs and this naked man ran up to us, picked the dog up, and ran off with him." Sybil's trembling hand swiped at her tear-stained cheek. "I feel horrible, but the man was stark raving *naked.* I didn't dare chase them down because who knows what a naked man with his ding dong flapping in the wind who stole a dog is capable of doing. I mean, it was just flapping back and forth like a rattlesnake looking for something to bite and—"

"Thank you very much, Miss Moonhawk. A terrible experience, I'm sure." The camera zoomed in on Jason Vaughan's frowny face. "Authorities say that witnesses who saw the theft of the Bassett Hound today were too flustered to remember details of the vehicle the naked man escaped in. A deeply troubling situation here today at The Blackstone Animal Shelter."

It took every bit of self-control in Molly's personal

arsenal to keep from bursting out in hysterical laughter. She gave Robin a sidelong glance and could tell he was also having a mighty struggle.

"How evil!" Lois said.

Babylon's expression was deadpan. "I don't know. Snakes have always fascinated me."

"Lord have mercy," Coco said.

Jake looked at Molly. "A Bassett Hound, huh?"

"What is Blackstone coming to?" Molly asked.

Robin shrugged. "Probably just a college prank."

Jake grunted.

Molly avoided Jake's eyes, reached into the pocket of her jacket, pulled out an envelope, and handed it to Babylon. "By the way, here are those tickets you wanted. The show was already sold out, so Margo comped these to you. She's got a soft place in her heart for Broker's Best rookies." The envelope actually contained a letter requesting help, and Molly was winging it.

Even though Babylon had no idea what Molly was babbling about, she didn't miss a beat. "Epic."

"You going to be home tonight, Jake?" Molly asked.

He nodded. "Plan to. Why?"

"I've got to go up and check on Chief Waters' place. There are some papers I'll have that I need you to sign and hoped I could just bop by."

Jake gave her a slow, sexy smile. "You're welcome to just bop by my house anytime and stay just as long as you like. Forever even."

Lois and Coco gasped in unison.

"Epic," Babylon said.

*   *   *

On the drive up the hill, Molly performed an emotional inventory. She was both terrified and exhilarated by the path she had chosen. Courage was a heady drug. She hoped the high would be enough to sustain her.

Thinking about what she was about to do, she had to shove the crowning head of guilt back inside. Who would ever have imagined she would play the role of Mata Hari? If Jake didn't love her, this wouldn't work. Was it right to play that card? What would the price be if she did? What price if she didn't?

Molly glanced in her rearview mirror as she drove up Thundermountain Road and saw a car tailing her. She rolled down her window, took in a deep breath of the fresh, cool air, and tried to think happy thoughts.

When Margo had once tried to lure her into show business, Molly had told her that she couldn't act, sing, or dance. Margo replied that she had so much oomph appeal she didn't need talent in order to be successful. Molly sure hoped that Margo was right.

She turned the radio volume high so electronic ears couldn't hear her recite the mantra Val had always used before a performance. Despite the wall of noise, Molly only whispered the words. "It's showtime."

The sun was low in the sky when she pulled up to the front gate of Chief Waters' estate. She made a big production of checking the lock on the gate to make sure it was secure and filling the literature box with new flyers. Then she headed toward Jake's.

Liberty's house stood like a tomb, and Molly slowed as she approached it. Noticing that the flag had been removed from the pole, she slammed on the brakes, skidded to the side of the road, shifted into park, and got out.

The sedan that had been tailing her pulled over. Out of the corner of her eye, she could see another black car sitting in the driveway.

With great flourish, Molly opened her trunk and removed a small American flag from a box, then marched into the front yard and to the obscenely naked flagpole.

Molly heard car doors open and close and the crunch of heavy feet as they walked toward her. "What are you doing, Miss O'Malley?" Shelton asked. "You're trespassing."

"You bastards took down Liberty's flag. I'm putting up a new one." She worked as quickly as possible to hook the flag onto the rope.

"You are trespassing on government property," Brown said.

"Well, since it's United States government property, it should at least have a flag." She pulled on the rope and the flag started up the pole.

"The one Dr. True had was upside down," Shelton said. "It was disrespectful."

Molly shook her head. "An upside down flag is a sign of distress, a sign the country is in trouble."

"That's a load of crap," Shelton said.

"What are you really doing here?" Brown asked.

Molly was shaking. "I'm doing the right thing. What about you, Agent Brown?"

"You always carry American flags with you, just for special emergencies like this?" Shelton asked.

"I give flags to my clients," Molly said. "I keep a box of them in my trunk."

Shelton moved to her car to investigate.

Molly tied off the flag and regarded her handiwork with pride. The small American flag danced proudly in the wind. She slapped her hand over her heart. "This is for you, Liberty True." With great passion, she recited the Pledge of Allegiance.

Shelton and Brown regarded each other uneasily. Arresting her for raising a right-side-up American flag and saying the Pledge of Allegiance was probably a stretch, even for them. At least she hoped so.

While the men continued to silently debate their

course of action, Molly stomped back to her car, slammed the trunk closed, and jumped into the driver's seat. She threw the car into gear, released the brake, and floored the gas, kicking up a bucketload of gravel that she hoped hit someone in its wake.

In her rearview mirror she could see Shelton race to his car. She smiled and slowed down so he could catch up.

When Molly pulled into Jake's driveway, she did it with as much tire squealing as she could manage, hoping it would bring him outside. However, when he appeared, she felt her resolve weaken and wondered if Mata Hari would have remained resolute in her espionage mission if she had known a passion like theirs?

Molly tried not to think about the fact that Mata ended up being shot by a firing squad.

Molly stepped out of her car and froze. She had wanted to kiss him again for so long and now it was her sacred mission as leader of the rebellion. The prospect was both thrilling and terrifying. Jake took a few steps toward her and stopped as if he sensed her storm clouds. She knew his emotions were also a tempest because lightning crossed the expanse between them, jumping from cloud to cloud, and the strike practically knocked her to the ground. She used the car to steady herself as rolling thunder rocked her world.

Their eyes locked, and she was lost.

He came to her slowly, intently. His fingers drew her hand to his mouth and his soft breath sighed into her palm. He bent to bury his face in her hair, and she closed her eyes, inhaling his familiar scent of leather and pipe tobacco. Every cell in her body seemed to respond to the memory, long-buried embers exploding in flame.

He looked at her, and his fingers traced the contours of her face.

"I can't breathe," she managed to say.

"I'll be your breath," he whispered.

He leaned into her, the length of his body pressing her back against the car. His expression was tender as their lips came together and their tongues, former dance partners, remembered familiar steps.

He breathed life back into her once again, as he had with that first kiss so long ago. Their connection drew forces from the center of the earth, and she felt incredibly alive.

When he withdrew, she grasped fistfuls of his shirt and held on while desperately trying to regain her senses. "I'm a bad, bad *femme fatale*," she said.

"What?"

"*Femme fatale*, a woman of great seductive charm who leads men into compromising or dangerous situations."

"I know the definition." He sighed and hung his head. "Oh, Molly, what's this really about?"

"I needed the feds to see us kiss as a cover for my coming here, but once I got here all I wanted to do was really kiss you, and Mata Hari would never have had this problem, so—"

He silenced her with another electrifying kiss. Afterward, he looked into her eyes for a long time before his slow, sexy smile made a welcome appearance. "Come on, Mata." Throwing his arm around her, he guided her to his house. "So the guy in the black car parked across the road was our audience, huh? I hope he took pictures."

She nodded. "Think we could get copies?"

Jake's house was a luxurious stone and glass A-frame that resembled a rustic ski lodge. Molly hadn't been inside since they broke up, but it appeared to her that little had changed.

He grabbed two bottles of beer from the fridge, and they settled down together on the cushy couch in the den. Jasmine the Siamese cat was draped over the back of a nearby chair. She opened startled blue eyes, assessed the situation, then stretched and went back to sleep.

"So what's your secret mission?" Jake asked.

She took a long swig of beer to bolster her courage. "I need you to have an Easter party. A really big, chaotic, outdoor Easter party here at the ranch. Invite the brokers from our office, your rancher friends, lots of kids, and lots of dogs. I know it's short notice, but this is the only way our plan is going to work."

"*Our* plan?"

"The plan of the Resistance."

"This is about Liberty?"

"Yes."

He groaned. "Oh, you shouldn't be involved in this."

"I'm the rebel leader."

"You?" He burst out laughing. "Where did all this reckless courage suddenly come from?"

She struggled to find the words to express her feelings. "I made the choice to not live in fear anymore."

His laughter dissolved in an instant. "Well, now."

Molly removed an envelope from her pocket and handed it to him. "Please give this to Jessie. If she's willing, I need her to borrow Maddie from Preacher Levi for the day and bring her to the party. This letter has all the details. Ask her to please let me know if she'll do it. This morning Robin found a listening device in our office, so tell her to be discreet."

Jake raised an eyebrow. "Whoa. The feds are playing hardball."

"Any of you who help are also taking a risk."

He made a sound of exasperation. "Why are you doing this? Why are you risking *everything*, and putting others in danger, just to help one eccentric nutcase of a woman?"

How could she explain it? "The real reason they've charged Liberty as a terrorist is because she dared to say what she believes and her words were having an influence on others. Agree with her or not, she has a right as an American to do that. I don't want my daughter growing up in a country where rights can be so easily violated. You have to stand for something in life, and this is where I make my stand."

Jake stared at her for so long that Molly was certain he was going to say no. She hadn't even considered the possibility and had no Plan B. Her mind raced to construct one.

Finally, he asked, "Besides the party, what else can I do to help?"

Relief flooded her, and she pulled two small American flags from the pockets of her jacket. "Please raise these high on your property, perhaps one here and one at Jessie's cabin."

He accepted them. "And what about us, Molly? You and me."

Her stomach wrenched. "I want to be with you again so badly it hurts, but not now. In my entire life I've only made love to three men, and I'm not very good at sorting out the emotions that go along with that. Miguel was my first love and the father of my child. You brought me back to life and helped me discover my strength. Steve made me feel safe and loved. But none of those relationships worked. I'm so tired of being hurt, of misreading, of seeing what I want to see and not what is. I need time before trying again."

He wrapped her in his arms. She felt his need and sensed his struggle. Finally, he said, "You're worth waiting for."

CHAPTER SIXTEEN

Thursday morning Jake stepped inside Molly's office and closed the door. His grim expression scared her.

"What's wrong?" she asked.

Jake glanced at Robin. "Maybe we should talk alone."

Molly shook her head. "It's okay."

"The Ahmeds have decided to drop the discrimination lawsuit, so Lily's building a different case against you to file with the Colorado Real Estate Commission. She's given me the heads-up that they're going to attack you on the issue of agency, claiming that you didn't remain neutral in the transaction as you should have—that you acted on behalf of your own buyers so you could double-dip."

Molly was stunned. "Do the Ahmeds want to file this case, or is it Lily's doing?"

"It's Lily. She's good at making people bend to her will."

Molly's heart sank. She had hoped the hostage situation might have softened the woman's resolve to destroy her. "How bad is it?"

"Bad. The Ahmeds are claiming financial loss to the tune of tens of thousands, which you would have to make restitution for. And you would likely lose your license. Agency is a hot-button issue with CREC; they take it very seriously."

Molly was horrified. How would she survive this? "And you?"

"They'll come after me for not doing a better supervisory job. Yeah, it's very bad."

Molly looked at Robin, then back at Jake. She felt she had let them both down. "I'm so sorry."

"There's nothing you can do to help her?" Robin asked.

"I'll stand by her," Jake said. "Otherwise it's out of my control."

A rap on the door interrupted them.

Jake opened the door to Babylon.

"Hey, boss. Thanks for the invite to your very special party Sunday," she said. "I'm not known for having fun during daylight hours, but I'll show up. Bringing my niece Sophie and her dogs."

"Glad you'll make it," Jake said.

"Didn't mean to interrupt you but wanted to tell Molly that Sophie's about Angel's age, and I thought it'd be cool to connect them there."

Molly was incredibly relieved that Babylon had accepted her request for help. "Angel will love that. Since we've moved to the country, she doesn't have a lot of playmates."

"Just a word of warning: Sophie wants to be just like her Aunt Babylon and dye her hair purple for the occasion. I'm trying to convince her mom that purple is Easter-eggish. Hopefully, we won't corrupt Angel."

Jessie stuck her head in the room. "Hey, Jake, can my friend Maddie come to the party?"

He sighed. "The more the merrier."

Molly gave them a thumbs-up.

Babylon winked at Molly.

Jessie tipped her pink Stetson.

Jake tugged on his beard.

Robin blew Jessie and Babylon a kiss.

Jessie caught the kiss, and Babylon flashed a Goth hand signal.

The secret sign language of Molly's new band of rebel patriots.

*   *   *

Friday morning Liberty's student, Emily McGee, arrived unexpectedly at Molly's office. Dressed in jeans and a sweater, she carried a book bag slung over her shoulder and wore a haggard expression. Molly urged Emily to take a seat across the desk from her.

"Would you like a cup of coffee?" Molly asked. The girl looked as if she could use it.

Emily shook her head. "I'm sorry to just show up like this, but I'm beside myself about Liberty and hoped maybe you had heard from her."

"No, honey, I wish I had. But no, not a word." While Molly spoke she scribbled a note and pushed it across the desk. *Office bugged. Be careful what you say.*

Emily read the note. "Well, a bunch of us who love her got together and raised some money. We want to figure out how to get it to her." She opened her bag and pulled out a zippered pouch which she put on Molly's desk.

"I have no idea," Molly said as she scribbled another note. *Have plan. I'll try.*

Emily's eyes lit up. "We stayed up all last night and sewed an American flag too. Everyone contributed a star or stripe. It was a big old effort of love." She pulled out the flag and laid it on Molly's desk.

Molly took the money and flag and tucked it into her briefcase. "Well, I wish I could help you, but you need to keep all this in case she contacts you. You're much closer to her than I am. You forget that I've only known her a short time."

Tears filled Emily's eyes. "It's awful what they've done to her. I'm so ashamed to be an American right now."

"Oh no, don't go there." Molly leaned across the desk and grasped her hands. "If Liberty heard you say that, it would hurt her more than what they've done to her. Continue to stand up for what's right, defy what's wrong, be a good American. Love this country as much as she does."

Emily's tears flowed harder, so Molly set out the Kleenex box and gave her space to vent. Finally, the girl recovered, stood up, and slung the bag back over her shoulder. "Okay, I'll hold onto this stuff in case she does get in touch. But promise me that if you hear from her you'll tell her how much we love her...how *much* she's loved and respected by so many."

Molly stood. "If I hear from her, I promise to pass on the message."

Emily came around the desk and grabbed her in a tight bear hug.

"You're my new hero," she whispered. "May God keep you safe."

*   *   *

On Saturday Molly, Robin, Angelina, and Talisman held a solemn ceremony and reversed the flag that flew above their house. A dozen of Liberty's pithy political slogans floated through Molly's mind, but all she said in closing was, "God save America."

It was Easter weekend, so Molly had not planned any work. She was going to tend to her last minute preparations for the party and hoped to spend some quality time with Angelina in case things went horribly wrong.

"Take a walk with me out to the gazebo?" Robin asked Molly.

"Sounds good."

"Okay," Angelina said.

"Just your mum and me. We need to talk."

"Okay," Angelina said. "Tali and I will go check out the latest posts on her Facebook page." She and Talisman disappeared into the house while Molly and Robin headed toward the gazebo.

The day was one of Colorado's finest. Molly was grateful that the weather appeared to be cooperating with the weekend plans. They walked slowly, enjoying the fresh air and brilliant sunshine.

"There's really not a reason for me to stay living here anymore, is there?" Robin asked.

Molly shook her head. "No more threats, so I guess we can presume they were from the meth heads. I mean, there's still the worrisome issue of the gangs that Rita warned me about, and Val's murder trial is still pending, but danger is my middle name and I have to figure out a way to live without a bodyguard." She shrugged. "Hey, if I lose my job, you'll lose yours too, and the house will go next. So, yep, you should go home now."

He reached out and stopped her. "Molly."

When she turned, she was shocked to see his pained expression. "What's wrong?"

His eyes met hers and he started to say something but stopped.

"Robin?" Panic flickered at her edges.

He took a deep breath. "I've struck a deal with Lily. I'm going to work for her in exchange for her not filing the case with the Real Estate Commission against you. She's agreed to stop all future harassment as well."

Molly didn't understand. "But why would stealing my assistant count for so much to her?"

"She believes we're lovers."

The full impact of what he was saying finally pierced her fog. "She doesn't let her employees socialize with anyone else in the industry."

"That's one of the rules. Yes."

She began to tremble. "No, Robin, we love you."

He gathered her into his arms. "Good. Love is good."

Molly's tears exploded. Losing yet someone else she loved was too much to bear.

He pulled her closer, and she held on as tightly as she could.

"It's the only way I know how to protect you right now," he said.

"She'll never let you go."

"Maybe I can help her find a bit of the enchanted universe and she'll reach a point where she's not so angry anymore."

Havana had predicted, *A knight who slays dragons.*

"I want to stay," he whispered.

She sobbed harder.

"I would be so much better for you and Angel than Jake. I want to win your heart. *Really* win your heart. But that's selfish. Right now I need to walk in the darkness so you two can walk in the light."

Her inner storm raged. "No. We need you. Please don't go."

He wiped away her tears. "Since we met, you've gone from fearful to courageous. Angel's gone from angry to loving. You've both got the stirrings of faith. You've finally discovered what you stand for. You don't need me."

"When?"

"I start Monday morning. I arranged it so I could be there tomorrow."

"Angel's going to be heartbroken." Anger flared and Molly socked him in the chest. "You're going to break her heart."

"She's got those angel wings now. We need to be honest with her, and she'll be okay."

Havana's voice came back to her again. *An angel who*

sprouts wings.

"Don't forget me," he said.

In desperation, she grabbed and kissed him. The pain was awful, and she wanted him to make it better. He always made everything better.

He tried to resist but then uttered a soft moan and pulled her into him. A wave of golden warmth spread from their lips to her heart, and for a time, the pain disappeared.

*   *   *

Right before dawn, Molly dreamed. She and Val stood together on the edge of a cliff high above a deep canyon. Val looked dapper in his tuxedo and top hat, and his smile was more dazzling than the overhead sun.

"I miss you so much," she said.

"I'm never far away."

"I'm scared."

"If you're not afraid, it's not courage."

Molly thought about everything she stood to lose. "Am I doing the right thing?"

"You can always try to play it safe, but that keeps you small and earthbound. Most people live that way. I want you to take wing and soar. I pray for that every single day."

She felt his hand on her back, and then he shoved her off the cliff.

Molly took wing and soared.

*   *   *

Molly and Angelina packed the car with everything they needed, dressed Talisman in her bright red scarf that said FREEDOM FIGHTER, then they all piled into the car and headed for Jake and Jessie's ranch. The familiar black car tailed them, the driver no longer even making an effort to be discreet.

Last night, before he moved out, Robin sat down with Angelina and Talisman and explained what he was going to do. Surprisingly, Angelina took it better than Molly had. And Talisman, used to losing special people, had also been brave. Molly was humbled by their strength.

"You doing okay this morning?" Molly asked Angelina.

"Yeah. I dreamt of Val last night. That helped."

"Really? So did I." Molly thought that was too strange to be a coincidence.

"Our life here in Blackstone has been so good," Angelina said. "We've met such awesome people. No matter what the future holds, life has been good."

Molly needed to hear that. "I love you more than life itself, Angel."

"I love you too, Mom."

Molly couldn't remember the last time Angelina had told her that, and she was grateful. There was so much she wanted to say but was concerned about who might be listening.

As they approached The Double J, Molly was startled to see how many black cars were parked in surveillance positions. It was a veritable army of federal agents. Had they figured it out, or were they merely acting from an abundance of caution? However, why would they even presume that Jake and Jessie were planning something requiring their attention? She clutched the steering wheel and tried to hold back a panic attack.

When they reached the crest of the hill that overlooked the ranch, Molly slowed and drank in the majesty of the place. It had been in the Dalton family for generations. If Jake and Jessie were implicated in Molly's plan, they stood to lose it all. They could also lose their business and, possibly, their very freedom.

Then there was the risk all the others involved were facing. And what about Angelina? Molly's sole concern for nine years had been the security of her child, and now she was leading her into danger.

What had she been thinking to put them all in this position?

With a heavy heart, Molly pulled into the driveway and drove slowly through the mass of people and wandering dogs to Jessie's log cabin near the back of the property. She glanced at her watch. It was noon—everyone else involved in the plan should have already arrived.

Molly, Angelina, and Talisman got out of the car and headed into the cabin.

They were all there: Robin, Jake, Jessie, Babylon, Maddie, Ross, and a purple-haired little girl whom Molly presumed was Sophie. Molly met Jake's eyes, and despite his cowboy cool, she could see his concern.

Molly shook her head. "I'm sure you've all seen what we're up against out there. There's still time to call this off."

Babylon chuckled. "Yeah, I noticed the gathering of the Sith Lords. Mega doom." She shrugged. "I live on the dark side. It's what I do."

Molly looked at Jake. "You have so much to lose. It's okay to bail."

Jake sighed. "I'm not doing this because I have feelings for you; I'm doing this because I'm an American. Besides, a man who doesn't keep his word isn't much of a man."

Molly's eyes slid to Jessie.

"Hell, I'm a cowgirl. I live by the cowboy code of 'Always fight for what's right, even when the odds are against you and you're greatly outnumbered, because sometimes there are things more important than victory.'"

Molly looked at her daughter. "Angel, do you still

want to do this?"

Angelina nodded. "I think there's good and bad in this world. I think the government has both good and bad in it. I think if people don't stand up for the good, the bad will win."

Would Molly be a better mother if she grabbed Angelina and ran to safety now, or if she helped her child stand up for what was right? Liberty's words flitted through her mind. *You have to stand for something in life. Figure it out, and help your daughter figure it out too.*

Molly opted for taking a stand. "Robin?"

"I'll *always* have your back, love."

Molly had never been more moved. She felt honored to know this amazing band of rebel souls.

Molly and Angelina had dressed in blue jeans, red shirts, and white sneakers. Molly wore a white scarf tied around her neck, and Angelina sported a white ball cap. Not only had they wanted to make a patriotic statement, they wanted to stand out.

With their purple hair, Babylon and Sophie had no problem standing out at all.

The four of them, the Australian Shepherd sisters, and Ross spent the next hour hanging out together and making themselves as visible as possible.

"I'm glad you were able to enlist the help of your niece," Molly said to Babylon. They were standing in front of Jake's house within sight of a black car parked across the road. Angelina and Sophie were sitting on the grass sharing a bag of potato chips.

"Sophie's not really my niece—that's just the cover story I used. I stole her to use for the mission. She seemed about the right size and shape for the part."

Startled, Molly was relieved when Babylon winked.

"And the handoff of Ross went down without a

hitch?" Molly asked her.

"We met at a dog park. I told them I would be the one with the dog collar on. It got a little confusing, but we figured it out."

Molly grinned. "I like you, Babylon."

Babylon tossed her purple head. "Don't get caught because I'd hate to lose you. It's never dull when you're around."

Molly figured that was Babylon's way of saying that she liked her too. "I presume Jessie managed to get Maddie dropped off to you in time for you to arrive here with her?"

"I unloaded both dogs from my car with tons of hoopla in full view of Darth Vader."

Jessie joined them and gave each a cold beer.

"Thanks for picking up and delivering Maddie for us," Molly said.

Jessie nodded. "I went to the Preacher's sunrise service. It was a very spiritual experience. Not to mention carnal. He sure gets me hot."

"How did you explain wanting Maddie for the day?" Molly asked.

"It was time for a Maddie and Tali play date, we were having a big barbeque here today, and I thought it would be good times."

The Aussie girls were having a great time. They had teamed up to herd nearby children. Molly watched in fascination as they got five of the little ones bunched in a circle and then sat down to guard them.

"Tali's recent experience at Heavenly Acres seems to have taught her a thing or two about herding technique," Molly said.

"When I have kids I'd like an Aussie to help me babysit," Jessie said. "I'll let the Preacher know that. It might plant the seed that I'm perfect wife material."

Molly saluted her with the beer bottle. "Good luck

with that."

Jessie reached into the back pocket of her jeans, pulled out a piece of paper, and handed it to Molly. "The preacher said God told him to send you this message."

Surprised, Molly unfolded it. The neatly written note said, *Don't tell God how big your storm is. Tell your storm how big your God is.* The words were so powerful, so timely, that Molly felt her spirit leap in response.

Babylon glanced at the note. "Epic."

Ted Borgman walked by and pointed to Babylon and Sophie. "Beware of the purple people eaters." He laughed hysterically and walked on.

"Ted's an ass," Babylon said.

Molly nodded. "The first time we met he told me I was a red hot property with lots of curb appeal, and I showed real well. He said I would be a great addition to his inventory."

"He's *such* an ass."

Molly looked at Ross, who was lying in a patch of sun, dead to the world. "Ross doesn't seem too traumatized."

"Oh, he's seriously bummed," Babylon said. "Sad eyes."

"That's normal for a Basset Hound," Molly said.

Robin walked up to them. "He is sad, actually. I need to have a talk with him." He handed Molly a book. "Michael and I put this together for Liberty. I know how much her pictures meant to her and they're all gone now, so Michael used his stealth technology to comb the internet for everything he could find in every archive out there. We printed out photos of her parents, brother, aunt, husband. We also found newspaper articles, wedding announcements, obituaries."

Molly set her bottle down on the porch railing and flipped through the leather photo album. "What an amazing thing for you to do." She looked at him.

"Everything you do is amazing."

Molly and Robin stared at each other for so long that everyone began to stare at them stare at each other.

Finally, he reached for the album. "I'll put this with the things you'll be taking."

Molly watched him walk away until he was out of sight. Her heart was in shreds, the pain much more complex than she first realized. The thought crossed her mind that her career, money, and home weren't worth losing Robin over.

When she reached for the beer bottle, Jake handed it to her. She hadn't realized he was there.

"What was that about?" he asked.

"Robin's going to begin working for Lily tomorrow. He made a deal with her. In exchange for his services, she's not going to file charges against me."

It was a few moments before Jake responded. "He must really love you."

"He does."

An awkward silence fell over the group.

Jessie said, "It's time."

Casually, they all made their way back to her cabin.

Robin was waiting for them inside. "While you were gone, I grabbed Brooklyn's dog and took her for a long walk on the backside of the ranch. Federal agents are surveilling there too."

"We're the best damn Resistance team in history," Babylon said. "We shall prevail." She grabbed Molly's arm and tugged her toward Jessie's bedroom. "I can't believe you decided on white tennis shoes. You are so going to owe me, bitch."

Molly, Babylon, Angelina, and Sophie gathered in Jessie's room to swap identities. Babylon and Sophie changed into blue jeans, red shirts, and white tennis shoes, while Molly and Angelina donned black. The corseted top that Molly put on barely contained her lush cleavage, and the pants were tight, but thankfully the boots were of the practical hiking variety. The women scrubbed their faces and each applied their own style of makeup to the other. Black lipstick and eye shadow decorated Molly's face, while shades of bronze and copper highlighted Babylon's beauty. Finally, each pulled on a wig: Molly's was purple, Babylon's red. Angelina put Sophie's purple wig on and gave the other girl her white ball cap to tuck her own hair up into. Molly put on the dog collar, and her white scarf was wrapped around Babylon's neck to hide a snake tattoo. They traded sunglasses.

When the transformations were complete, the ladies all gathered in front of the mirrored closet door to witness their artistic genius.

"Wow," Angelina said.

"See how Sophie is taller than Angel?" Babylon asked. "I did that because I'm taller than you. So, from a distance with Angel by your side, it's going to look like me with Sophie at my side."

"Very well thought out," Molly said.

"Hey, I'm not just another pretty face."

"No, you're certainly not." Actually, underneath the heavy Goth makeup, Babylon was much more beautiful than Molly had imagined.

Babylon gestured to Molly's image. "With your incredible bod you're every man's erotic fantasy. Use that to your advantage if you get caught."

"What's your plan?" Molly asked.

"Sophie, Maddie, and I are going back to Jake's. Hang out on the front porch. If anybody from Broker's Best heads our way, I'll duck inside the house. We'll wait for you to return."

Molly reached out and embraced her.

Babylon stiffened. "The Goth don't hug."

"That's okay. You don't have to hug back."

She gave Molly a tentative pat on the back.

"Thank you for everything, Babylon. You really are legend. May the Force be with us."

When the women came out of the bedroom, Jessie greeted them with a whistle. "Hot damn."

Jake grinned. "This moment almost makes the entire thing worth it."

Robin smiled. "You're both so beautiful."

Babylon snorted. "Freakin' lame white tennis shoes."

Molly noticed that Maddie was now wearing Talisman's FREEDOM FIGHTER scarf.

"I've explained to Ross that he needs to lead you to the cave," Robin said. "I think he understood, but he's a hard one to read. He's guarded."

Molly nodded. "I have a general idea where it is, from when Liberty tried to point it out to me the day we first looked at her house. She said it was due west from this cabin. Since she has spent every single Easter of her life there, that would mean Ross has too. Hopefully, he'll remember."

"I've told Tali to alert you if you're being followed," Robin said. "I'm sure she'll do her best."

"If you find you're being followed, just turn around and come back," Jake said. "They can't charge you if you didn't actually do anything."

Everyone in the room turned to look at him.

"Um, that's not exactly true," Angelina said. "Remember Liberty?"

"Good point. I stand corrected."

"I'd turn back anyway," Molly said. "I don't want to lead them to her."

Jessie helped Molly put on the black backpack that carried all of the special items they were bringing Liberty, then everyone stood for a few minutes looking at each other.

"My work is done," Robin said. "I'll say my goodbyes now." He knelt and hugged Angelina and Talisman. "I'll always love you two."

"We love you *so* much." Angelina hugged him fiercely, and Talisman licked his face.

Robin stood and took Molly's hand. He kissed it, then pressed her palm against his heart. Tears rimmed his eyes.

Molly could feel the pounding in his chest. "You have such a noble heart," she whispered.

He started to reply but stepped away and turned to Jake instead. His voice broke as he said, "Take care of her."

Jake nodded and extended his hand to shake. "You have my word."

Robin shook his hand, glanced back at Molly one last time, and walked out.

Molly, Angelina, Talisman, and Ross headed due west. They crossed acres of pasture and a bridge that ran across the river, then hiked up into the foothills. Ross trudged steadily forward with seeming intent, and Talisman kept running ahead and then circling behind to keep them moving. Neither Molly nor Angelina looked back—they didn't want to appear nervous. Molly trusted that Talisman would perform the mission she had been assigned.

Molly and Angelina walked most of the way in silence. Ever since they had become so cautious about what they said, both used words more sparingly.

"Liberty is like family now," Angelina said.

Molly thought about it. Liberty had taught her more than any woman ever had. She had been a strong mentor both to her and Angelina. They loved Liberty. They were risking everything for Liberty. "Yes. Yes, she is."

Molly remembered Havana's words, and now she understood.

Jour family, it grow bigger.

*   *   *

"Oh, my little flag!" Liberty's voice rang out from the mouth of a cave ahead of them. "My precious little flag!"

Ross, who had travelled the entire way at one steady pace, scurried ahead at what for him was supersonic speed. Liberty ran to meet him.

"It's like a scene from a movie about long lost lovers," Angelina said.

Molly laughed.

Liberty and Ross had a passionate reunion filled with kisses and slobber. Then she looked up and gave them the once-over. "Good God, look at you. When Liberty's away, the Goth will play."

"We're on an undercover mission," Angelina said.

Liberty opened her arms wide. "Come here, my dear girls."

Like Ross, Molly and Angelina scrambled into her arms.

"We're so relieved that you're safe," Molly said.

"I'm always prepared for any emergency." Liberty kissed them both. "Come, sit. You've had a long walk."

Molly was tired, and the backpack had been heavy. She was grateful for the opportunity to rest.

Liberty led them to a secluded spot on the west side of the cave where the afternoon sun warmed a small campground. A sleeping bag was thrown over a thick foam pad, and a coffee pot simmered on a tiny Sterno stove.

"Take the bed," Liberty said. "Get comfortable." She took a seat on a nearby rock. Ross stretched out at her feet and promptly fell asleep.

Molly shrugged off the backpack, sank down on the bed, and was joined by Angelina and Talisman.

"Have you been staying up here this whole time?" Molly asked.

Liberty shook her head. "Not the entire time. As soon as I saw the signal that Ross was okay, I headed up into the mountains to visit friends and make plans. I just came back last night."

"What signal?" Angelina asked.

"The clever little flags flying above my home and the houses next door. Saw those and knew my little flag was in good hands. Wasn't sure how you'd get him to me. I never figured you would remember about this place." She shook her head. "What the *hell* is with the crazy costumes?"

"Federal agents have been tailing me," Molly said. "I had to figure out a way to elude them. It's complicated."

"I'm impressed, O'Malley. Truly."

"A lot of people were involved in the operation. The most unlikely people risked everything to help you. And I mean *everything*."

"Uncommon heroes are the most inspiring kind," Liberty said. "Tell me about them."

Molly opened her backpack and turned over the money, the flag that Emily had delivered to her office, and the promised message about how much Liberty's students loved her. She gave Liberty the memory album that Robin and Michael had compiled. Then Molly told her about what her own friends and coworkers had done.

Liberty surprised her by crying. Tough, unflappable Liberty wept like a child. At last, when words came, she said, "I've always believed there's a spark of heroism in everyone. Sometimes it just needs the right moment to catch fire."

"I'm so sorry for what's happened to you," Molly

said. "I can't even imagine how much it hurts."

Liberty dug in her pockets for a tissue and blew her nose. "Oh, O'Malley, what's really important in life is so much more than careers, and money, and houses."

Molly caught her breath and thought of Robin.

"This has forced me to assess my values and revisit my faith," Liberty said. "I have come to the conclusion that everything happens for a reason. Just look at the good that has already come from this travesty. There are people whose spirits have grown because they took a stand for liberty and truth. Look at how this has changed you. And I've been offered an opportunity to do something I never would have been able to do if I hadn't lost my job. The friends I turned to when my home was seized are a rebel band of true patriots who live in the mountains. Their underground network has an online pirate radio station, and I'm going to have my own talk show."

"But the government will use it to track you down," Molly said.

Liberty shook her head. "Our techno-geeks are better than theirs. Well, actually, they used to be theirs."

"Oh, I want to hear the show," Angelina said.

"You will. A lot of people will. The station has millions of listeners. I'll get a message to you about how to find my program."

"*Liberty True Tells The Truth About Liberty?*" Molly said, tossing out a possible title.

"How about, *True Liberty?*" Angelina offered.

Liberty laughed. "Actually, I was thinking of *This Is Why We can't Have Nice Freedoms*."

Molly's laughter joined hers.

"We brought Easter dinner to share with you," Angelina said.

"Wonderful! Easter is a time of new beginnings."

Molly marveled at Liberty's capacity for joy, given the

circumstances. From her backpack she pulled a small tablecloth and spread it on the ground in front of the bed. She laid out ham and cheese sandwiches, potato salad, and a bottle of sparkling apple cider. Plastic cups and forks, paper plates and napkins completed the setting. Finally, she filled bowls with water and kibble for Talisman and Ross.

Liberty scooted to sit on the ground by the makeshift table and opened the bottle of cider. As she filled their cups, she said, "Always remember that your life is like a pebble thrown into a pond, sending out ripples into space and time. When you speak up for truth, when you defend life, when you fight for liberty, you can change the world forever." She raised her cup. "To truth."

Angelina lifted hers. "To life."

Liberty danced in Molly's thoughts: Liberty True, the principle of liberty, and the personal liberation she experienced upon claiming her own courage. Molly considered the future and the hopes she held for both Angelina and herself. She thought about the men in her life and the choices she had to make about them. The dangers that loomed ahead cast dark shadows and evoked grave concern. However, in that moment, in this secret place, her family had come together in the midst of tragedy to celebrate hope and resurrection. It was a wondrous thing.

Reverently, Molly held her cup high. "To liberty."

AUTHOR'S NOTE

The creative process is a mystery to me. When I sat down to write *Red Hot Liberty*, I intended it to be a funny little tale about single mom Molly O'Malley and the kooky people and animals in her life. I never expected it to become a modern fairy tale about knights, dragons, and heroes. I am filled with wonder at the final product, and eternally grateful to my magical Muses.

ABOUT THE AUTHOR

Devin weaves tales in a variety of genres, but at the heart of every story is a common thread: the emergence of uncommon heroes. From urban fantasy and paranormal thrillers to science fiction and humor, her fiction features characters who discover they are capable of far more than they ever imagined. Explore her body of work and discover a hero to inspire you!

www.DevinWrites.com

THE RED HOT NOVELS

If you enjoyed this novel, please check out the entire series, including the delightful *Show Dog Diaries* spinoff novellas told from Talisman's perspective:

Red Hot Property
In this seriocomic adventure, Molly O'Malley is a plucky rookie real estate agent learning to swim with the sharks at the town's most cutthroat agency. A former cocktail waitress, Molly uses her street savvy to avoid being eaten alive by vindictive office staff, neurotic colleagues, crazy clients, and an abundance of sexy men. A delightful tale of a woman trying to become more than she believes possible, and discovering herself in the process. "Sassy and simply hilarious!" -*Women Writers Worldwide*

Red Hot Liberty
Life, liberty, and laughter! Rookie real estate agent Molly O'Malley's latest client isn't just looking for a home—she's looking for a revolution. Liberty True, a firebrand history professor and unapologetic voice of the American Resistance, believes deeply in liberty and justice for all. When Homeland Security arrives on the scene, Molly finds herself at a dangerous crossroads. Rallying to her side? A Goth colleague who lives on the dark side, a charismatic cowboy preacher who lives on the light side, a sexy Englishman determined to be her white knight, and a dog with romantic problems. Filled with humor, heart, and unforgettable characters, *Red Hot Liberty* is a spirited tale about a woman who undertakes a quest to slay the dragon of fear—and become her own hero.

Red Hot Stars (coming soon)

A horror movie is being filmed at Molly O'Malley's haunted real estate listing on Thundermountain Road. But when self-proclaimed werewolves protest the casting of humans in werewolf roles, things take a wild turn and Molly's Australian Shepherd, Talisman, is accidentally kidnapped in the chaos. Now two alpha queens are on a collision course. Add to the madness a rival vampire gang, a crew of dangerous barrio gangsters, a heroic roller derby team, and a beloved ghost determined to set things right before he moves on—and Molly's life is about to get hotter than ever!

Show Dog Sings the Blues

In an unfortunate case of mistaken identity, pampered show dog Talisman is switched with a cowdog and has to work on a ranch for the day. By the time her harrowing adventure is over, she is in desperate need of a massage, a session with her Reiki Master, a consultation with the pet psychic, a full grooming, and a pedicure. However, along the way she learns powerful lessons—including the discovery that she's so much more than just another pretty face.

The Twilight Bone

In this witty tale of the paranormal, Talisman the Australian Shepherd is a feisty, young show dog with psychic gifts who is called upon to ghostbust at a prestigious dog show. Tali's colorful companions include her neurotic sisters, the spirit of Mae West, a hyper, freestyle-dancing Border Collie, and her heart person Valentino DeMitri—who has just found his own heart person. In the midst of chaos, Tali must deal with star-crossed love while facing down a terrifying ghost. Can she save the day? A delightful treat for humans of all ages!

THE BEST FRIENDS RAFFLES

Devin O'Branagan held two raffles to benefit the animal rescue organization Best Friends Animal Society, the nation's largest sanctuary for homeless, abused, and abandoned animals. The winners' pets were chosen to become characters in the *Red Hot Novels* All proceeds went to benefit Best Friends: **www.BestFriends.org**

The grand prize winner of the first raffle was a Basset Hound named Ross owned by Dr. Camille Hemlock. Ross was famous for winning costume contests. Using this fact, Devin found a clever way to incorporate him into *Red Hot Liberty*. He was a wonderful addition and will forever be immortalized as Liberty True's "Little Flag."

The grand prize winner of the second raffle was Bocker the Labradoodle, who really was a famous canine model and actor. His appearance in Steven Spielberg's *War of the Worlds* inspired the core plot of the upcoming novel *Red Hot Stars*, in which Bocker will also appear.

Devin chose six other individuals who entered the Best Friends Red Hot raffles and featured their pets in walk-on roles in *Red Hot Liberty*:

Marina Night's person is Angie Clark, Sami's person is Lori Pavlo, Rex's person is Donevon Murrell, Tyler's person is Jennifer Bussott, and Lump, when awake, acknowledges Amy Abern as her person.

Talisman's sister, Maddie, belonged to the Coakley family. Although the Coakleys did enter both Best Friends' raffles, there is another connection that led to Maddie's inclusion. Talisman is based on Devin's late Aussie, Kolbe, and Maddie was Kolbe's daughter. They were both awesome Aussies!

Devin learned all she could about these real cats and dogs and created the fictional characters accordingly.

To see photographs of these wonderful animals and read more about them, visit Devin's website at **www.DevinWrites.com** and click on "The Dogs and Cats page.

CHANCE

2006 Crufts Best In Show - BISS MBIS AKC/ASCA Ch Caitland Isle Take A Chance AX AXJ RS-E JS-E GS-E STDs TDI "Chance" was the first Australian Shepherd to win Best In Show at the prestigious international dog show, Crufts. His person, Nancy Resetar, graciously granted permission for him to make guest appearances in *Red Hot Liberty* and *The Twilight Bone*.

www.ChancesRAussies.com

ACKNOWLEDGEMENTS

Sue Campbell of Sue Campbell Graphic Design designed an amazing cover for this book. I am so grateful. And special thanks to Aeryn Havens for the second edition cover revisions.

For suggesting the title, credit goes to author, friend, and writing mentor, the late Ed Bryant.

For editing assistance, I would like to thank authors J.A. Campbell and Nicole Riviezzo.

My highly intelligent, wildly creative, and incredibly sexy writers' groups were amazing. The members of both my real world and online critique groups contributed so much to this project that I can't begin to express my gratitude. For generously offering brilliant ideas that found their way into these pages, I especially want to thank Tammy Crosby and Sue Campbell.

For help with research, I'd like to thank Detective John Tefft (Retired) San Diego Police Department and Cher impersonators Steven Andrade and Lisa Irion.

Then there are my oh-so-special Facebook friends whom I can turn to any time of the day or night to find a name for a character, help me with research, offer advice, and lend support. I couldn't do what I do without you guys!

www.ingramcontent.com/pod-product-compliance
Lightning Source LLC
Chambersburg PA
CBHW070305260626
47160CB00003B/721